THE
WELL OF
THE SOUL

A GRAHAM ELIOT NOVEL

THE
WELL OF
THE SOUL

DOUG POWELL

BRENTWOOD
PRESS

THE WELL OF THE SOUL

First Edition: 2021 White Fire Press
Second Edition: 2025 Brentwood Press, LLC
P.O. Box 132
Arrington, TN 37014
BrentwoodPress.net

ISBN: 979-889689-486-5 (print)
979-889689-490-2 (digital)

10 9 8 7 6 5 4 3 2 1

ONE

The old Graham Eliot would have allowed a smile at the irony on display in the conference room of the Dallas convention center: the Ancient Near East Society meeting in the modern Wild West. It wasn't that the incongruity was lost on him, just that it didn't amuse him like it would have in years past. He couldn't remember the last time he had authentically smiled at anything. Every attempt had been smothered by guilt or grief before it could take shape.

He had hoped being surrounded by other scholars—many of them friends and colleagues—would feel safe and bring some measure of comfort. Beginning in grad school, the meeting had been a pilgrimage he looked forward to throughout the year. Although it was held in a different place each time, the three-day-long data-dump of papers and reports on the latest research contributing to the understanding of biblical history was far more interesting to him than exploring whatever the host city was. Not that he had time to spare; his own presentations had made him a popular and respected speaker, and the balance of his time was devoted to networking.

But the familiar rhythm of the convention—an annual pulse—had been broken, and he was making his first appearance after a two-year absence. However, the continuity with the world he had once known and wanted to take refuge in now felt like a facsimile, as if he had entered an imperfect replica of his own life, similar enough to navigate, and yet not quite right. In truth, he knew that he was the stranger, not his environment.

It took all his effort to make a show of interest in research meant to verify the existence of the God he no longer believed in. He felt like a ghost in reverse, physically present but spiritually empty, haunting the sessions, merely existing. It didn't help that friendly looks of recognition quickly transformed into concern. More than once, he had seen the unasked question in the eyes of friends, wondering if he was wasting away from some disease. The toll of the last two years had left him a remnant of his former self. Stress had carved away forty pounds—almost one for each year of life—sharpening the features of his face almost unrecognizably, like a damaged object revealed in one of his digs.

That was another irony he acknowledged without a smile: He looked like he wore a gaunt mask of himself while he actually wore a mask of faith. And, of course, there was the physical mask, the one on the stage in front of him. It was the reason he was here.

Dr. Andrew Singer had just begun his presentation, a plenary session that had packed the room.

"If I asked you which of these masks was more valuable, which one would you choose?" An image of a gold mummy mask appeared on a large screen behind him, while at the same time he reached below the podium and held up a mask that looked like ornately painted cardboard. "Sure, the gold one is worth a lot of money. And, of course, it is an important historical artifact. But it holds no secrets. You can hear everything it has to say almost immediately."

Singer lifted the other mummy mask high again and looked at it with appreciation. "But this one holds many secrets. Why? Because of what it is made of: papyri. As many of you already know, the funerary attendants who made these masks used papyri coated in glue in order to make an ancient form of papier-mâché called cartonnage. But stop and think for a minute. Papyri was common, but not so common that new sheets were used for masks. The attendants used only what had been discarded. And what was that? Books, letters, business documents, inventories. It occurred to me that there was a chance that if I could find a mummy mask from the right time period and from the right place, some of the papyri used to make it might be discarded copies of writings of the Church Fathers, or even the books and letters that make up the New Testament.

"Over the past couple of years, I have been experimenting with different ways of deconstructing cartonnage to recover the individual scraps of papyri that made up its structure. Unfortunately, I destroyed several pieces in the process, as well as a couple of my wife's favorite saucepans." As Singer paused for laughs, Graham's left thumb folded into his palm to rub the wedding ring still on his finger. "But now I've found a way to remove the majority of the structure while preserving the mask at the same time. And I'll demonstrate that for you now."

Graham watched Singer spring from the podium with the same energy they'd had when they were at graduate school together twenty-five years earlier. Singer's prematurely white hair looked like it sat atop the wrong man, borrowed from his future self. It had been Singer who finally convinced Graham to attend the conference, promising his demonstration would be seen as a significant advance in the field. He even floated the idea of their working together on the projects that might result from it. Seeing his old friend usually evoked memories of Olivia, given that Singer had introduced them and had been a groomsman at their wedding. But Graham was so

9

intrigued by the presentation that for the first time in a year his mind was completely focused on something other than his wife or daughter.

As Singer disappeared behind the stage, the image on the screen cut to a stainless-steel industrial sink shot from a camera mounted directly above it. The electronic tick of a microphone turning on came from the speakers mounted in the room's ceiling, followed by several taps on the microphone, and then Singer's voice.

"We've set up a camera over the sink in the pantry so you can see the work in real time. I've developed a solution that I will immerse the mask in, which will dissolve the adhesive that holds the mask together." The white top of Singer's head saddled with a headset microphone appeared as he reached across the sink to turn on the water. He then emptied an unidentified liquid from a glass jar. "Also, I have applied a fixative to the front of the mask that will protect it from the solution. If all goes well, the mask will hold its shape even though I'm removing most of its structure from the back."

Bubbles began to form as the water rose in the sink, as if Singer were about to wash dishes.

"Before I get started, I'd like to remind everyone that no photography is allowed. Please put all phones away."

The mummy mask appeared faceup in Singer's hands. He held it in place for a moment, creating a dramatic pause as the audience took a final look.

"This mask was found in northeastern Egypt, and is probably from the late first or early second century AD. And now, let's see what secrets it literally took to the grave."

Singer lowered the mask slowly into the sink. He kept it submerged as his hands gently massaged the backside of the mask, working the surface pieces loose. The audience stared at the veil of bubbles obscuring the work for nearly a minute in growing anticipation before Singer extracted his hand. He held a tiny fragment about the size of a fingernail under the camera as he gave it a cursory look.

"It's so small, it's hard to tell, but it looks like Greek letters…possibly Coptic."

He placed it in an aluminum specimen tray lined with a paper towel to let it dry, then continued working the mask. Within a minute he had pulled out several more pieces, some so black that no letters could be seen on them.

"Ah, here's an interesting one." Singer lifted up one of the largest fragments, about three inches wide and four inches tall. "Greek characters, another Coptic writing. Appears to be a letter of some kind, maybe an official report. Not sure what century just by glancing."

He set it aside and picked through the other two with characters on them.

"Yes, we might find something really interesting here once we get a chance to dig into these. After they dry, I'll run these black pieces under ultraviolet light to see if anything can be recovered."

His hands disappeared again into the sink.

"Oh, my goodness. Feels like the back is melting away. Several pieces have come off."

He lifted the mask out of the water, revealing that the face had stayed intact.

"Excellent. Looks like the fixative on the front surface is working. I'm going to set this to the side, so it doesn't completely disintegrate. A number of pieces are loose in the sink."

Again his hands slipped into the bubbles, but this time they emerged holding a long strip of papyrus supported by both hands.

"This is amazing! I've never found a piece this large before. Looks like it's about eight inches tall by four inches wide. Greek characters. I can make out some words…"

Singer's voice drifted off as he became distracted by the

content, lost in thought as he studied it.

"Can't be right," he mumbled to himself. "I don't believe it."

Carefully, he flipped the fragment over, revealing more writing on the other side. He leaned over the find, apparently forgetting about the camera, inadvertently eclipsing most of the view. A low murmur broke the silence as the scholars stared at the back of Singer's head, wondering what he was seeing.

"Incredible…This is…"

The screen suddenly went black, leaving only the audio feed.

"I apologize." Singer's voice was suddenly urgent, running words together. "We'll have to continue this at another session. I'll report my findings then."

The sound of the headset being wrested loose scratched from the speakers along with Singer's final words, punctuated with a pop as the PA system cut off.

TWO

A gap of silence eroded into a murmur of confusion and speculation. Graham continued to stare at the screen, wondering if Singer had made a mistake during the presentation and cut the audio/video feed to avoid embarrassment.

"Looks like the mummy's curse is alive and well, eh?"

Graham turned toward the familiar English accent and found Nigel Horne sitting behind him. Although they had never worked together, he and Horne had become friendly through various conferences. Horne always asked about Graham's latest research with an intensity that would have been off-putting except for the genuine enthusiasm he had for the work. Singer had shared the same observation and added that the most interesting thing about Horne's work was that it wasn't interesting at all. It was workman-like scholarship, but derivative, corroborating the research of others without furthering the field in any substantial way.

"Nigel. Good to see you." Graham twisted around to shake Horne's hand, surprised by how much he meant the words.

Horne's round face was stamped with a permanent smile. Graham thought it looked vaguely frog-like, an effect enhanced by his moist eyes and stocky build as he hunched forward.

"I confess I wasn't quite sure if it was you or not." Horne seemed to catch himself, realizing how insensitive he might sound, and glanced away awkwardly before stammering an attempt to rescue himself. "I—mmm—must say, you've started to favor Peter O'Toole somewhat. Anyway—quite something, don't you think?" Horne said, changing the subject abruptly, motioning toward the blank screen. "I hear Singer may have found a fragment inside one of these masks from one of the Gospels that he dated to the first century."

"I heard the same thing," Graham said, cautiously lowering the emotional armor that went on alert reflexively after Horne's tactless small talk. He threw himself into the topic, distancing the awkward moment with words. "That would be an amazing discovery. But I worry about what it will do to the market. Some of these collectors ask outrageous prices once they realize what they have. And if they get what they ask for, then it makes every new find that much more expensive. If we're not careful with how we acquire new finds, we may not have enough resources to get these pieces into the hands of people who can properly conserve them."

Horne turned his palms up in a futile gesture. "Yes, it's not like the old days when Egypt and Palestine were practically giving this stuff away and happy to see it go." He paused as he put a palm across his heart, looking compassionate. "I am truly sorry to hear about your wife and daughter. Olivia was a lovely woman, so kind when I met her. I'm sure your Alyson was the same."

Graham's defenses had gone back up before Horne even said the words, but the sound of the names still stung, almost angering him. *How dare you be so casual with what was so precious.* He struggled to restrain himself, an effort Horne apparently interpreted as Graham still coming to terms with tragedy.

"We don't know why these things happen," Horne said,

shaking his head. "But God is good, and he is sovereign. And you are a man of faith. Without that, there would be no way to make sense of it. Of anything, really."

Suppressed rage strained Graham's self-control to its limit, making him appear more calm. *Even your words of comfort have no originality. I don't need platitudes, and I definitely don't need you to—*

"Remember the words of Paul," Horne said with a nod. "'All things work together for good for those who love God.'"

Graham tried to disguise his wince with a quick nod and a sad smile before staring blindly at the floor, making them both uncomfortable. The last thing he could find comfort in was quick-fix Bible quotes from people who had no clue how he felt. *The apostle Paul never lost a wife and daughter.*

Horne patted Graham's shoulder. "Please let me know if there is anything I can do for you, my friend. Any way I can help."

The sincerity in Horne's eyes instantly convicted Graham, muting his bitterness. "Thank you, Nigel. I appreciate that. I really do." He turned and glanced at the empty screen. "I'm going to go see what happened with Andrew. Talk to you later."

Graham tried to shed the conversation—the exact thing he had been hoping to avoid—as he picked through the crowd that remained. He walked around the side of the partition holding the screen and spotted the president of the Ancient Near East Society emerge from a service door, his face a mixture of confusion and concern. The man recognized Graham and motioned back to the room he had just exited.

"He's gone."

"Gone?" Graham brushed past without waiting for a response.

The door opened into a pantry used to hold meals for guests when the conference room hosted a banquet. A video camera was suspended above an industrial-sized stainless-steel sink, and a microphone headset lay on a countertop dotted with several small pools of water. He walked to the spot where Singer had stood a few minutes before and saw bubbles still floating on the surface of the solution in the sink. But Singer was gone, along with the mask and fragments.

An open door yawned from the wall on the far side of the pantry, leading to the network of corridors that made up the service area of the conference center. Graham stepped across the threshold to the corridor on the other side and looked both directions down the generic service hall but saw no evidence of Singer.

"I did the same thing," the president said as Graham came back into the pantry. "He's vanished."

"I'm sure there's a good explanation. Family emergency or something." Graham hoped his words were more convincing than they sounded to himself. "I'll see if I can get ahold of him."

Graham was still staring at the scene in the pantry, unaware the president had left until he heard his voice come over the PA system announcing that the demonstration was postponed. A renewed buzz of speculation rose in the main room, then slowly diffused into the halls as the scholars spread into the hotel.

He pulled out his phone and dialed Singer, but was sent straight to voicemail, which then announced that the mailbox was full. He quickly composed a text, trying not to sound worried. "Hey, Houdini, nice lecture. Need to work on your ending, though. Send a message from the other side." He confirmed the text had been delivered, then drifted to his room, exhausted from the effort of being social when he felt like a stranger to the world and to himself.

The dregs of the conversation with Horne nagged him at first, and he turned his phone off to isolate himself. What little energy he had left was spent wondering what happened to Singer. Hours earlier, he would have welcomed the blackness that enveloped the room. Now he lay on his back staring into it, wondering what he wasn't seeing.

THREE

Graham opened his eyes from a dead sleep, suddenly awake as a series of sharp knocks impatiently announced a visitor. A second salvo began as he reached the door and looked through the peephole. A solemn man in a dark suit and close-cropped hair stood alert, his figure warped by the fisheye lens.

"Yes, who is it?" Graham's voice was rusty with sleep.

"Dr. Graham Eliot?"

A muffled voice reached through the door as though slipping through a crack the knocks had created. Graham glanced at the clock on the microwave. 7:12 a.m. He rarely slept this late, but the repeated condolences from colleagues he hadn't seen since losing his wife and daughter brought a blanket of grief that weighed on him, making him feel exhausted despite the sleep. Still, it was too early for anything but bad news.

"Yes, this is Dr. Eliot. Who are you?"

"Special Agent John Bremmer, FBI. I need to ask you a few questions." The man held up a wallet, displaying a badge and identification to the peephole.

"FBI? Is something wrong?"

"I'd rather not say in the hallway. May I come in, please?" The clinical voice had an authority that was emphasized by the façade of politeness, making the question sound more like a formality than a request for permission.

Graham opened the door and gestured the special agent into the small sitting area—a loveseat and a stuffed chair arranged around a coffee table, next to a desk and office chair provided for business travelers.

"Thank you."

The nicety sounded robotic, reminding Graham of the impersonal demeanor of the surgeon who had treated his daughter like a machine that had malfunctioned. He had never met an FBI agent before, and he didn't know if the coldness was part of the protocol or if it was simply the man's personality.

Bremmer placed a folder on the table and sat on the edge of the loveseat, resting his forearms on his knees as Graham took the chair across from him.

"Dr. Eliot, you were friends with Dr. Andrew Singer, weren't you?"

"Yes, we were in the same doctoral program together. We've been friends since... Wait, what do you mean were friends? What's happened?"

Bremmer looked directly into Graham's eyes. "Dr. Singer is dead."

"What?" Graham involuntarily gripped the arms of the chair. "That can't... How?"

"He was found in his office." Bremmer continued to hold his stare.

"In Oklahoma City? How did he... Was it a heart attack or something?" Graham felt foolish as soon as the words left his mouth. However little he knew about the FBI, he was certain they didn't deliver news of natural deaths to friends of the deceased. "Are you here because he was killed?"

"We are in the early stages of the investigation. It's too soon to determine the cause of death."

"Why was he in his office? That's three hours away."

"I'm hoping you can help me with that. Especially since

THE WELL OF THE SOUL

you were the last person he attempted to contact."

"Me? I didn't hear from him after the session broke up." Graham had never felt so self-conscious, and he could feel Bremmer search his responses. "I tried to call him, but his phone went straight to voicemail. So I texted him, but he never responded."

Bremmer nodded, apparently confirming something he already knew. "I'll explain in a moment."

Graham squinted, trying to process the news. "None of this is making sense. Why is the FBI involved in this?"

"I'm assigned to the FBI's Art Crime Team."

"I didn't know there was one."

"We mostly deal with museum theft, some private collections. But we also help recover missing antiquities. In addition, any transportation of stolen property over state lines gives the FBI jurisdiction."

"Are you saying the mask he had was stolen?"

"That's part of what I'm here to ask you about," Bremmer said. "Are you familiar with his office?"

"Yes." Graham pictured the office of Singer's antiquities acquisition firm, a business spun off from his academic research. "I've been there many times."

"Good. I want to show you some photos from the crime scene. Nothing graphic, but I want you to tell me if you see anything unusual or out of place."

Bremmer removed a laptop from his computer bag and booted it up. Graham watched him open a dozen or so images and arrange them in a specific sequence. He realized Bremmer had ordered the images to create a panorama, each picture taken from the same position but rotated to show a different segment of the room.

He scanned each image carefully, comparing them to his memory and saw the office as he remembered it. Floor-to-ceiling shelves filled with reference books and academic works lined two walls of his office. The adjustable-height desk had piles of books on each corner, pushing up like stalagmites of information. The center of the desk held several papyri, and Graham thought he recognized them from the demonstration. A large computer monitor displayed a messaging program, though he couldn't read what was in the conversation bubbles.

Behind the desk, a row of windows floated above a three-foot-high bookshelf. A number of artifacts were scattered across the top of the bookshelf along with a power cord that had come unplugged from an upended Wi-Fi router. He worked his way down to the bottom of the picture, to the floor beside the desk. Graham pointed at the grapefruit-sized rock at the same time he noticed that it sat near a dark stain on the carpet cut off by the left edge of the photograph. In the second it took for his finger to reach the screen, he had changed what he was going to say.

"Someone used that? To hit him?"

Bremmer ignored his question. "Do you know what that object is?"

"Yeah, he brought it back from Jerusalem." Graham looked at Bremmer, who was making notes. "A rock from the Temple Mount. Part of a work-study program. First time he visited, probably twenty-five years ago. It's not worth anything, just a souvenir."

"What else do you see?" Bremmer advanced to the next image.

A portable camera stand was set up behind the door to the office. Another door interrupted the shelves on one wall, opening into an executive washroom that doubled as a small workroom. The next image showed what was left of the mummy mask sitting next to the sink, water pooled beneath it. Several pieces of papyri sat on a paper towel on the other side of the sink. The sink was full of what he assumed was the same solution Singer had used in the demonstration, framed by a ring of residue from where the bubbles had popped.

"That's what he had at the presentation. Except there were more pieces. And the large strip of papyrus he was looking at when he cut the video isn't there. Looks to me like he went back to his office to try to extract more pieces."

Bremmer looked away from the screen to Graham. "What was on the large strip?"

"I couldn't tell. No one could. It was too far away from the camera. The text wasn't clear from that distance."

"What would have made him stop a presentation like that and run out the back door so he could drive three hours to his office to do more work?"

"I've been wondering the same thing," Graham said, shaking his head. "I don't have any idea. I wish I did. Who found him?"

"Custodial staff," Bremmer said perfunctorily as he opened a new file on the computer. "I want you to take a look at some footage from the security cameras in the conference room. I'd like you to tell me who was there."

"Okay, I'll try. I'm not sure if it will help. At least half those people were strangers to me."

A window opened with two views, one showing the faces of the audience as they looked toward the screen, and one from the side.

Graham found Nigel Horne in the crowd before he found himself and saw that Nigel had put on glasses for the presentation—a vanity that would have amused him under normal circumstances. He pointed out Horne, then used him as a landmark to find himself standing a few feet away. The grainy quality of the image prevented Graham identifying anyone on the far side of the room, but he was able to point out a dozen or so other scholars.

"Wish I could tell you more," Graham said. "Not sure that's helpful."

"Any information is helpful at this point."

As Bremmer closed the windows with the video, Graham's eyes caught on one of the images of the office.

"That's odd…"

"What do you see?"

Graham pointed to the screen. "The camera stand."

"What's odd about that?"

"It's set up."

"I don't understand," Bremmer said, studying Graham more than the image.

"Part of Andrew's work was to digitize every known manuscript from the New Testament. He created a database for scholars to use. Many of these manuscripts are in private collections or in libraries that are hard to get access to. Andrew has been traveling around the world for more than ten years taking high resolution, multispectral images of these manuscripts. These pieces are so fragile that a special camera stand is needed to handle them, so they aren't damaged by the process. That's what that stand is. That camera mounted on the top takes extremely high-resolution images—fifty-megapixels, maybe more—that are then stored on a server and added to the database."

Bremmer looked at Graham expectantly. "If that's Singer's work, why is the camera significant?"

"That equipment is only for the field. There's nothing in his office to take images of. Unless…" Graham's face snapped up, his eyes locking on Bremmer's. "Did anyone check the camera?"

"You think he photographed something he extracted from the mask?"

"I can't think of any other reason it would be set up."

"May I see your phone, please, Dr. Eliot?"

"Of course." He realized his phone was still charging by his bed and retrieved it. "I totally forgot I turned it off last night when I went to—" Three dings announced incoming texts as the phone reconnected. Graham opened the messages and stared at the screen. "These are from Singer! He sent pictures. Two images of papyrus and…a strange message. It says *Alleg*." He turned the screen to Bremmer. "I think those are pictures of what he was looking at when he ended the presentation last night."

Bremmer studied Graham's face for a moment before looking at the phone, then resumed his hard stare. "Any idea what *Alleg* means?"

"No." Graham shook his head gently. "No idea."

"Can you read what's written on the papyrus?"

Graham squinted again at the screen as the words revealed their message. "Hold on. I want to double check to be sure." He retrieved his own laptop from the bedside table, opened the images on the larger screen, then opened a program and began typing Greek characters into a search box.

"What are you doing?"

"This is a database of ancient manuscripts. I'm entering the words I can make out in the order they appear. The more I add, the shorter the list of possible manuscripts becomes. If I put enough words in, there's a good chance I'll be able to tell you exactly what this is."

"But you think you know already, don't you?" Bremmer's tone hinted he had chased enough of his own hunches to recognize one in Graham. It also hinted that Graham had faded as a potential suspect and emerged as an important witness.

"I do." He finished typing as he replied distractedly. "And now I'm almost certain." Graham sat back, this time pausing to gauge Bremmer's reaction. "It's a treasure map."

FOUR

"How much do you know about the Dead Sea Scrolls?"

Bremmer squinted at the question, as if searching for a connection. "Found in the 40s and 50s about twenty miles southeast of Jerusalem along the shore of the Dead Sea. Greatest archaeological discovery of the twentieth century—one of the most important ever made. Discovered by a bedouin shepherd as he was looking for one of his sheep, if I remember correctly. You'll have to refresh me on the rest."

"You hit the highlights." Graham nodded, correcting the unimportant detail that it was a goat as he picked up the story. "The bedouin thought the goat had wandered into one of the caves that are all over the cliffs on the northwest shore. But he didn't want to crawl into a bunch of caves to look for it. He thought he could scare the goat out by throwing rocks into the caves. But he forgot about the goat as soon as he heard something break, like pottery.

"Sometimes people came across valuables hidden in these caves, so he went in to look around. He found the floor littered with fragments of broken jars, as well as a number of jars that were still intact. Most of them were empty. But inside others, he found scrolls that were almost perfectly preserved."

"Priceless artifacts," said Bremmer.

"He didn't know that. The only thing he knew was that

they were really old. He actually thought about using the parchment for sandal straps. But he changed his mind and took four scrolls to a shoemaker named Kando in Bethlehem, who sold antiquities out of his back room. Kando bought them for about a hundred dollars in today's money and told him to go back to look for more. He and a friend found another cave near the first and brought Kando three more scrolls."

"Not exactly legal," Bremmer said. "None of this was, probably."

"Yes and no. The archbishop of Saint Mark's Monastery was one of the buyers, and he did smuggle some scrolls to America, but he did it for their preservation, not his own profit. You have to remember, this was 1948, 1949. The whole area was in conflict. Israel became a state a few months after the first cave was discovered, and it was immediately threatened by the countries surrounding it. A few old scrolls were the last thing the governments were worried about."

"So where did they end up?"

"The classified ad section of The Wall Street Journal."

Bremmer lifted a finger, pausing the story. "You are telling me the find of the century was sold through a classified ad in a newspaper?"

"It's more amazing than that. By a weird twist of fate, the son of the buyer of the other scrolls saw the ad and bought these scrolls for the state of Israel for $250,000."

Graham watched Bremmer's face become progressively more incredulous. "Incredible. And that's where this treasure map came from?"

"No, not quite," Graham said. "As word of the find got out, archaeologists started looking for more caves. By the mid-50s, eleven caves had been discovered with scroll fragments in them. As a matter of fact, a twelfth cave was only recently discovered—fifty years after the last one. Anyway, in the original eleven, over 100,000 fragments were discovered. Text was found from over 900 different books, and over 200 of those were books from the Hebrew Bible. The Old Testament. Copies were found of every book except Esther."

"But they didn't discover anything new about the Bible, right?"

"That's what made them so important," Graham said. "Before the Dead Sea Scrolls were discovered, the oldest copy of the Hebrew Bible scholars knew about was from the tenth century. But every manuscript discovered in the Dead Sea Scrolls was from the first century AD or *earlier*. When the texts were compared, they were almost identical, proving the text had been copied accurately over the centuries. And the most spectacular find was one of the complete scrolls found in the very first cave—a copy of Isaiah made 150 years before Jesus was born."

"All right"—Bremmer nodded—"I get why the find was so amazing. But what does it have to do with a treasure map?"

"The third cave that was discovered was the first cave discovered by archaeologists rather than bedouin. A lot of the cave had fallen in, and manuscripts were strewn all over the floor. But they discovered—set aside from the rest—a scroll made of pure copper, which itself was rare for the time. Three sheets had been riveted together, each about eight inches tall and over two feet wide. The text had been hammered into them before being rolled up. One of the sheets had come undone and was curled up as its own roll."

"And they unrolled them to find a treasure map inside," Bremmer finished.

"No!" Graham said, tapping the air with his index finger, smiling. "When the scroll was discovered, the copper was too oxidized to open. The scrolls would've fallen apart. So, it sat unread for almost two years while scholars debated on the best way to open it. Eventually, it was coated in aircraft adhesive and baked to give it a protective coat. One of the professors built a specialized, high-speed saw and cut it into strips. When the strips were laid out in order, it revealed a treasure map. It's known as the Copper Scroll."

"Sounds like something out of a movie." Bremmer sounded both intrigued and impressed. "It's like Treasure Island."

"It's not that kind of a map. It's more of a list or inventory of sixty-four items, each in a different location. Some are near Qumran, in the area where the scrolls were found. Some are around Jerusalem, near the Temple. Some are in a valley north of Jerusalem."

"And the treasure is what—gold or silver or jewels?"

"All of the above. But there's even more than that. Sometimes it's incense or oil."

"Why would that be treasure?"

"Because they're consecrated to God. That's where the treasure probably comes from: the Second Jewish Temple. It was most likely hidden by the priests as the Romans closed in on Jerusalem to sack it in AD 70. Some scholars think it was hidden to be kept away from the Gentiles. Others think it was hidden to be used to rebuild the Temple when the right time came. There are even some Christians who think the discovery of the treasure will lead to a third Temple, something they think is prophesied in Revelation."

"How much money are we talking about?"

"Multiple millions." Graham turned back to the translation on the screen. "Let's look up just the items on the fragment. The recto contained items 17, 18, and 19. This is what the translation says: Item 17. 'In the great cistern which is in the...in the pillar on its northern side: 14 talents. °K.'"

Bremmer pointed to the end of the line on the screen. "What's °K?"

"No one knows. That's one of the mysteries. And scholars disagree on how much a talent weighs. Could be anywhere from twenty-five to seventy-five pounds, depending on who you ask." Graham opened a new tab in his browser and looked up the price of silver. "Silver is going for $18.38 per ounce, and…gold for $1,253. If a talent is twenty-five pounds, then fourteen talents equals 350 pounds. That's over $102,000 of silver or $7 million in gold. And that's just one location."

Bremmer squinted at the ancient Greek, processing the information as Graham continued.

"Item 18 says, 'In the canal which goes…when you enter forty-one cubits: fifty-five talents of silver.' And 19 says, 'Between the two tamarisk trees in the Vale of Akhon, in their midst dig three cubits. There, there are two pots full of silver.'"

"The two tamarisk trees?" Bremmer raised his brow. "So much for that location. I'm sure those trees have been gone for over a thousand years."

"Exactly. Not all the clues are helpful since sometimes the landmarks are gone."

Bremmer turned his palms up in futility. "If the Copper Scroll was opened sixty-five years ago, why hasn't anyone used it to find the treasure yet?"

"They have. In fact, one man claims to have found one of the treasures back in the 80s. But it wasn't silver or gold. All he found was one small jar of oil, possibly from the Second Temple era. Valuable, but not…Allegro," Graham said, interrupting himself.

"What?"

"Andrew was interrupted! He was trying to text *Allegro*."

"You mean *quickly*?"

"Not the musical term. *Allegro* is a man."

FIVE

"The man entrusted with the job of opening the Copper Scroll was named John Marco Allegro." The epiphany released a torrent of facts, reminding Graham of all he knew about Allegro's involvement in the Dead Sea Scrolls faster than he could order his thoughts. "He was at the University of Manchester, which is how the scroll ended up in the middle of England."

"Why would a Dead Sea Scroll scholar be based in Manchester?"

"The John Rylands Library is there—one of the most important repositories for ancient books in the world. In fact, the oldest known manuscript from the New Testament is there. A small fragment of papyrus with part of the Gospel of John. It's from the mid-second century."

Bremmer anchored his elbows on his knees, steepled his fingers, and rested his chin on his thumbs.

"Anyway, it was Allegro who oversaw the opening of the scroll and did the initial translation. But Allegro was only tasked with opening it. He wasn't the team leader for the Copper Scroll. That was a Catholic priest named Milik. The way the Scroll teams are organized, the leader of the team oversees the official translation and publishes the research.

None of the other team members are supposed to publish work before the team leader.

"Father Milik's translation is the one I showed you. However, he thought the treasure was a legend, that it never existed. But almost nobody agrees with that. There is nothing legendary about the text. It reads like an inventory, not a made-up story. It's possible Milik was trying to protect whatever is out there from treasure hunters."

Bremmer broke his pose to gesture to the screen. "The translations can't be that different. The original text is the same no matter what translation is used."

"The original text isn't quite as objective as you might think," Graham said. "There are quite a few misspellings that open the door to different renderings. Even Allegro thought Milik's translation was the better one. Just not his interpretation. Some scholars think that the list may have been written down on papyrus, then given to an illiterate coppersmith to copy because he wouldn't be able to realize the importance of the text. He did his best to copy the letter forms but made mistakes he didn't realize. Also, even though the scroll is numbered when we read the translations, it is not enumerated in the actual text. In fact, Allegro counted sixty-three, but Milik counted sixty-four items."

"So it isn't as clear cut as it looks at first," Bremmer said.

"Not quite. But that didn't stop Allegro. He got permission from the Jordanian Department of Antiquities to look for the treasure. He went to the location of every landmark he thought he could identify, but never found anything."

"What happened to Allegro?"

"He became a very controversial figure. It ended his career as a serious scholar."

"Just because he didn't find anything?" Bremmer asked.

"No. He published his translation before Milik, then cut his own deal with the Jordanians to look for the treasure. He was seen by the Scroll team as an unscrupulous opportunist. It didn't help that he renounced Christ and began writing books claiming Christianity was the product of a drug-fueled cult. It made him a popular speaker and television guest, but he was practically cast out of academia."

Bremmer looked at the images of the papyrus fragments, lost in thought, then turned back to Graham. "You think that Dr. Singer was trying to warn you that there was a treasure hunter looking for what he had found. He only had time for a short text and thought of Allegro."

"I can't think of anything else it could mean." Graham smiled apologetically.

"So let me reiterate what you're saying." The clinical tone returned to Bremmer's voice. "The fragment of the Copper Scroll is potentially so valuable that someone thought it was worth killing for. You believe the killer probably thought the scene would be investigated by people who wouldn't be able to recognize what was missing. Only one of the Ancient Near East scholars at the presentation would be able to identify the fragment and appreciate the implications of the text. And since there were numerous papyri at the scene, you think the killer thought the theft might go undetected."

"Yes, that's right." Graham felt foolish after he said it, uneasy under Bremmer's intense stare.

"You think Dr. Singer probably took the images as soon as he got to the office, then started work on the mask. And yet, the killer apparently didn't know enough about Singer's work to recognize the significance of the camera."

Graham frowned. "I hadn't thought of that."

"The implication is that the killer is working for someone else. Someone who knew enough to recognize the papyri and knew Dr. Singer had just found it."

"You're saying one of my colleagues is behind this?"

Bremmer cocked his head slightly. "Can you think of any-

one apart from your colleagues who would have the specialized knowledge necessary to recognize its importance?"

Graham looked at the translation on his computer, more
to move his eyes away from Bremmer than to study the text
again.

"If you're right," Bremmer continued, "then you need to
help me understand one more thing. Why would anyone kill
for a copy of a treasure map that already exists and that people
have already used?"

Graham leaned toward his computer and arranged two
windows on his screen. One showed the text he copied from
the image of the papyrus, the other contained the text of the
Copper Scroll with the published translation beneath each
word.

"Look." Graham pointed to the top of the Copper Scroll
translation for item 53. "'Next to them under the corner of
the southern portico at the tomb of Zadok under the pillar
of the covered hall: vessels of offering of resin and offering of
senna.'" He moved his finger to the top of the text from the
papyrus. "Now listen to this."

He began reading the papyrus text, haltingly, as he translated it into English. "'Next to them under the corner of
the southern portico at the tomb of Zadok *one cubit* under
the pillar of the covered hall: vessels of offering of resin and
offering of senna.'" Graham looked at Bremmer. "Hear the
difference?"

"One cubit," repeated Bremmer. "That was missing from
the Copper Scroll translation."

"Right. Now look at item 54." Again, he pointed to
the text of the Copper Scroll. "'Next to them at the'—this
part was damaged or is unreadable—'at the top of the westward-looking rock toward the garden of Zadok under the
great closing stone which is at the conduit: devoted things.'"
His finger moved to the text from the papyrus. "Here's what

Singer found. 'Next to them at the *rear of the tomb* at the top of the westward-looking rock toward the garden of Zadok *two cubits* under the great closing stone which is at the conduit: devoted things.'"

"Rear of the tomb. Two cubits," Bremmer said, repeating the differences. "What's it mean? Why is this list different from the Copper Scroll?"

"Because of item 64." Graham scrolled the translation down and read the final entry. "'In the underground cavity, which is in the smooth rock north of Kohlit whose opening is toward the north with tombs at its mouth, there is a copy of this writing and its explanation and the measurements and the details of each item.'"

Graham turned to Bremmer. "This isn't a copy of the Copper Scroll. I think it's the last item listed in the Copper Scroll—the Master Scroll."

SIX

"The Master Scroll." Bremmer sounded as if he were testing the words. "You're saying this is the key to everything in the Copper Scroll?"

"That would explain why it has more detail."

"Maybe. But if it's true, tell me why a cryptic map to a massive treasure would be hammered into copper, but the key to the map be written on papyrus and thrown away to be used in a mummy mask?"

"Remember," Graham said, "one theory for the Copper Scroll is that it was written on papyrus and copied onto copper. The same could be true for the Master Scroll. Maybe it was hammered into copper before being hidden at that location, and this was the text that the smith was given to work from."

Bremmer nodded, though Graham thought he looked less than convinced as he continued.

"It also explains Andrew's behavior at the presentation. He recognized text from the Copper Scroll, then saw the additional information. He knew he couldn't reveal the discovery in that way, or it might be abused." Graham paused for a moment, unexpectedly arriving at the obvious. "And he was right."

"Which means," Bremmer said, "the rest of the scroll with

the other sixty locations is still in the mask, right?"

"Probably not. I've never heard of a complete document of that length being recovered. Papyri were scavenged from the trash, which meant they were probably damaged and already in fragments. There may be another piece or two, but even that is unlikely. Even if there were more, it doesn't mean they'd be in the same mask."

Bremmer sat back, distancing himself from the computers as he gestured at a conference program sitting on the side table next to him. "Okay, so let's talk about who could have done this. We're talking about a pool of suspects made up of conservative Christian academics."

A pang of guilt stung Graham as he admitted he wouldn't identify himself that way anymore. "Not everyone interested in biblical artifacts is religious, even in the Ancient Near East Society. Many antiquities dealers are in it purely for the money. They're mercenaries, opportunists, businessmen, or pirates. Depends on who you ask and what's at stake. Kando is a great example. And some are even outright frauds."

"Like what happened a few years ago with the James Ossuary."

"That dealer was eventually acquitted of forging the inscription that caused so much trouble," Graham said. "But, yes, questions still hang over that ossuary, and that dealer, too. And the private collections that Andrew would try to access in order to photograph—they're often held by people who don't care at all about their religious significance. They only care about the monetary value. Wolves among the sheep, as it were."

"That's exactly what we're talking about." Bremmer pointed at Graham. "Can you think of anyone at the conference who might be the wolf? There might even be more than one."

Graham sighed heavily. "You should have your team at the scene look for a document in Andrew's office that shows the provenance of the mask."

"Already done." Bremmer opened his phone and read from it. "It came from a dealer in Egypt."

"Which one?"

"I can't share that."

"I could probably guess," Graham said. "Ikraam Jabir, in Alexandria. Goes by the name Maalik."

Bremmer shifted slightly, giving Graham the impression he was right.

"We've both bought a number of things from him," Graham continued. "He's a case-in-point of the morally ambiguous world of antiquities dealers, but I have a good relationship with him."

"How many people knew what Dr. Singer was going to demonstrate beforehand?" Bremmer asked, changing focus.

"I assume everyone there. Word had gotten out in the last year about what he was doing. His method was proprietary, but the last thing he wanted was for more cartonnage to be destroyed through experimentation of others trying to replicate his method. For the good of the field and the preservation of artifacts, he knew the responsible thing to do was to reveal his process. It was probably the most anticipated talk of the conference. Why?"

"Because the odds of a homicidal treasure hunter accidentally being in the audience is pretty low. If his topic had been kept quiet, then the circle of suspects would be smaller. But for now, the investigation has to include all the people in the room. Whoever is responsible was there."

"The wolf." Graham shook his head in disbelief. "I'm still trying to buy that part of the theory."

"Do you have another explanation? Someone had to be in the audience who had the ability to recognize what was on the screen, the ability to act, and the ability to follow Dr. Singer and break into his office. Or, he may have known where the office was and guessed that's where he was going. And he had to be prepared to take the life of another human being. Either the killer is one of your colleagues in the audience or he was hired by one of them."

Another sigh escaped Graham, conceding he didn't see any other options. "Can we look at the security footage again?"

Bremmer brought the video window to the front and hit Play. Graham focused on the view showing the faces looking toward the camera, this time through a filter of suspicion. He felt somewhat guilty, as if he were accusing innocent people of murder, but he couldn't deny the logic that Andrew's killer was probably in the room.

He scanned the rows of faces back and forth starting with the front row at the bottom of the screen and working his way up, to the rear of the room. The lights in the conference room dimmed for Singer's presentation before Graham reached the back of the room. The pixelated noise of digital video shot in low light turned the picture grainy, obscuring detail. Movement along the back wall caught his eye, and he watched the form of a man take his place at the far end of the room.

"What is it?" Bremmer hit the spacebar, pausing the playback.

Graham pointed at the screen. "Something seems off about this guy, but I'm not quite sure what it is. He just doesn't seem like an academic."

"Tell me why."

"Well, mainly because he looks like he cares about his appearance a bit too much. Too fashionable for this crowd. No professor I know wears glasses like that. And I guess he kind of moves differently. Like an athlete. Don't you guys have a program that could bring out some more detail?"

"Maybe," Bremmer responded automatically, distracted by the frozen image as he zoomed the screen. He pressed the spacebar again, and the man's face came to life.

Graham hunched closer to the screen. "His lips are moving. But who is he talking to?"

The man on the screen blinked twice in strong and exaggerated twitches.

"What's he doing?"

"It's almost like a tic of some kind. Hmm." Bremmer became lost in thought and paused the video once more.

"You should probably call the Israel Antiquities Authority and let them know what happened. They'll want to be on the lookout if someone really tries to hunt for the treasure."

"The IAA? I thought you said Allegro got permission from the Jordanian government to look for the treasure."

"That was before the Six-Day War. Jerusalem and the area on the western shore where the scrolls were found became part of Israel after Allegro's search. Jordan still has the Copper Scroll, but the locations of the treasure are now in Israel."

"You've been very helpful," Bremmer said as he stood. "Thank you, Dr. Eliot."

Graham tried to hide his surprise at the abrupt end to the interview. "Well, let me know if I can help you with anything else."

Bremmer handed Graham a business card as he reached the door. "If you think of something more, you can contact me here. Thank you again."

Graham closed the door and was hit with a wave of conflicting emotions that made him lean back against it. Andrew was dead. Murdered—though Bremmer wouldn't say the word—by a colleague. He bowed his head under the weight of the thought. The pose reminded him of how he used to pray. Now all he could offer was silence to a God who wasn't there.

SEVEN

Graham turned away from the door to find the fragment waiting for him on the laptop. He looked again at the incredible detail of the image, and then the shapes began to turn into words. He realized that he had translated only one side, and that was on the fly without writing anything down.

He moved the laptop to the desk and opened a blank document for his translation. After sizing the document to take up the lower half of the screen, he moved the image of the papyrus to the top left quadrant and Milik's Copper Scroll translation to the top right. Then he started comparing the Milik translation to the fragment, using it as a guide. The image on the screen contained the text near the end of the list, so Graham typed the heading *VERSO*, indicating the text was from the backside of the fragment. Below it he typed 53, keeping Milik's numbering. Wherever the fragment had additional material, he put the translation into capital letters so he could easily reference the difference. He opened the second image, and repeated the process, then looked at the completed work.

> *VERSO*
> *53. Next to them under the corner of the south-*
> *ern portico at the tomb of Zadok ONE CUBIT*
> *under the pillar of the covered hall: vessels of*

offering of resin and offering of senna.

54. Next to them at the REAR OF THE TOMB at the top of the westward looking rock toward the garden of Zadok TWO CUBITS under the great closing stone which is at the conduit: devoted things.

RECTO
17. In the great cistern which is in the COURT OF GENTILES AT THE END OF THE DOUBLE GATE, in the MIDDLE OF THE FARTHEST pillar on its northern side: 14 talents. °K

18. In the canal which goes FROM GIHON when you enter ON THE LEFT 41 cubits: 55 talents of silver.

19. Between the two tamarisk trees in the Vale of Akhon WHERE THE STREAM LEAVES THE CLIFFS, in their midst dig three cubits. There, there are two pots full of silver.

Graham opened a new browser and did an image search for the tomb of Zadok. He knew it was in the Kidron Valley on the east side of the Temple Mount. Actually, several tombs were there, cut into the rock face that began just south of the Garden of Gethsemane on the Mount of Olives. Allegro had searched the southern-most tomb, which had been left unfinished.

Graham opened his cloud drive, searched through the

theological library he kept there, and found a PDF of Allegro's book *The Copper Scroll*. He ran a text search for *Zadok* and started reading. Allegro assumed that *Zadok* was a variant spelling of the Hebrew word *zadduk*, meaning *just*. He then identified *Zadok* as James, the brother of Jesus who was known as The *Just*. Graham agreed with Allegro's thinking, then went to the next link in Allegro's chain of logic.

According to tradition, James had been martyred by being beaten to death after he was thrown from the highest point of the Temple and was buried near that spot. Allegro reasoned that since the unfinished tomb was in line with the southern wall of the Temple—east of the highest point—it was where James was buried, since it was the closest tomb. That was the location he investigated for items 53 and 54.

What puzzled Graham was why Allegro hadn't searched the tomb next to it. Although it was called B'nei Hezir, the name was relatively recent, coming from an inscription found in 1865 on the lintel above the entrance. Before then it had been called the Tomb of James.

He moved to the next item, number 17. The Court of Gentiles was the name of the outermost area of the Temple Mount, the only area where anyone was allowed in the Temple complex—even non-Jews. Graham opened a new PDF, this one of a map of the Temple Mount created from surveys done in the 1860s by British engineers Charles Wilson and Charles Warren. What interested Graham wasn't the plotting of the buildings, but the documentation of what was beneath them.

The engineers knew that the Temple Mount began as a smaller, square platform that created a plaza around the Temple at the peak of Mount Moriah. Different rulers added to it, and eventually the entire hill was enclosed by a wall and filled in. But as it was built, cisterns were created to store water for the Temple services, as well as to wash away the blood from the sacrifices, and to provide drinking water for worshippers. Some of the cisterns were fed by an aqueduct, but most collected rainwater.

When Warren and Wilson were sent there by the Palestine Exploration Fund, they were able to establish enough goodwill with the local authorities to become some of the only people known to have ever been allowed into the cisterns, and the only ones qualified to make a trustworthy survey of them. Over 150 years later, Graham studied the map they created showing thirty-six cisterns.

Before the Temple was destroyed, the main entrance to the complex was through two tunnels that enclosed stairways leading from the bottom of the southern wall to the platform surface in the Court of Gentiles. One tunnel was entered through a double gate, the other a triple gate. Together they were known as the Huldah Gates. The gates had been bricked up by the Templars during the Crusades, and the Double Gate's tunnel had been repurposed as a basement of the al-Aqsa Mosque, part of its stairway still connecting it to the surface of the Mount.

Graham located the Double Gate's shape on the map and found the exit on the Temple Mount was just southeast of Cistern 8. Its warped puzzle-piece shape formed the largest of the cisterns and sat in front of the entrance to the mosque. He did an image search for a high-resolution aerial view of the Temple Mount and zoomed in on the area. Each cistern had been enclosed in what looked like a stone pedestal capped with a steel lid painted green and secured with a padlock.

Item 18 used the Gihon Spring as a landmark, and Graham opened a modern survey of the site, documenting a network of tunnels spidering out from the spring. One of them had been cut by King Hezekiah in the eighth century BC in order to bring the water supply within the city walls so that Jerusalem could survive a siege planned by Sennacherib. It had famously been discovered by Edward Robinson in 1838, then cleaned out and explored by Warren thirty years later, who traced it back to its source—the Gihon Spring.

The last site, the Vale of Akhon, was west of where the Copper Scroll was found, and Graham was certain its landmarks had to be long-gone by now.

As he stared at the text, guilt extinguished his academic curiosity, and he closed his eyes in pain. Andrew was killed for finding what Graham had just read. The interview with Bremmer hadn't left any space for loss to work its way into him. But now he felt the familiar touch of its cruel fingers.

Yet, he couldn't fully suppress the exhilaration of discovery. Based on his translation, three of the sites had never been searched. Allegro had gone to the wrong tomb. Graham guessed that was because the traditional tomb was clearly empty with no obvious places to hide treasure. And instead of assuming whatever was there had been found centuries ago, Allegro justified looking in a more promising hiding place.

As for the Gihon Spring, a large part of the network of tunnels had not been discovered and excavated until twenty years after Allegro's death. Then there was the cistern under the Temple Mount, a place no one had ever been allowed to explore. Graham leaned back as if making room for the implication. The treasure might still be out there.

EIGHT

The staccato bass and funky drums of Peter Gabriel's "*Digging in the Dirt*" burst into the silence, scattering his thoughts. Graham had made the intro of the song his ringtone, an archaeological joke using one of his favorite artists. He looked at the screen, saw Nigel Horne's name, and answered as he shut his laptop.

"Graham, have you heard?" Horne's voice was breathy with shock. "About Singer?"

"Yes." Graham sighed. "I'm still trying to wrap my head around it."

"We were just with him. I can't believe he's gone. Especially like that."

"I know." Graham's voice was remote, and he felt more like an observer of his life rather than a participant. "It's surreal. I've known him for twenty-five years. Now he's just... gone."

"I talked to him just before the lecture. He was his normal self. Not a hint of anything amiss. Who would do such a terrible thing?"

"Actually," Graham said, "the FBI came by earlier to ask me the same thing. That's how I found out."

"I spoke to them as well," Horne said. "I don't think I knew anything helpful, though. The agent didn't stay long."

"Yeah, same here," Graham said, hoping to end the call before Horne shared a Bible verse. Or worse, offered to pray. "I hope they're able to solve it quickly. Forgive me, Nigel, I need to go. Take care."

"You, too, my friend. Let me know if you learn anything more. See you soon."

Graham reopened his laptop—the translation still displayed like a portal into a hidden world. But before he could enter, Peter Gabriel sang from his phone once again. This time he saw a long string of numbers as he picked up.

"Doctor. Thank you for speaking. I am calling from the Israel Antiquities Authority. My name is Chaim Yaniv. I am the director of the Robbery Prevention Division." Yaniv's heavily accented voice imposed a strange inflection that lilted upward in unexpected places, shaping statements as if they were questions.

"What can I do for you, Dr. Yaniv?"

"Please, no," Yaniv said, sounding embarrassed. "I did not take a doctorate such as you. A master's degree only."

"I'm sorry Mr. Yaniv, but this is not a very good time to talk. Can I call you back?"

"Special Agent Bremmer from your FBI has called me at your suggestion. He shared with me the terrible news. Thank you for making us aware of the situation." Yaniv hesitated. "I am very sorry about Dr. Singer."

"Thank you for saying so, Mr. Yaniv. And you don't need to call to thank me. We want the same thing and need to look out for each other."

"Just so, Dr. Eliot. That is the reason I am calling you. I would like you to investigate the locations listed in Dr. Singer's scroll."

Graham suppressed an incredulous laugh. "Me? You don't need me. You have a whole organization for that work. The IAA has plenty of people already who could look into this."

"Ah, but it cannot be a project of the IAA. Bremmer sent me the images of the fragment. I have read it. Two of those locations are in areas where there is great strife between Palestinians and Jews. And another site is on the Temple Mount itself. If the IAA initiated digs in these places it could cause rioting. Remember when Prime Minister Netanyahu authorized the creation of a northern exit from the tunnel that runs along the Western Wall? Arafat started a riot over it, accusing the Jews of trying to appropriate the Muslim Quarter. Eighty people died for no reason."

"I remember," Graham said.

"So you see why the IAA cannot do it. In fact, it is better if the investigation is not led by a Jew at all. We do not want another intifada. Also, the findings—if there are any—would be contested. Muslims will say they are biased in order for the Jews to prove Jewish history, and that could provoke a riot as well. It cannot be looked into by the police or the military because they have no training for this kind of thing. They might do harm to the sites."

Graham began to agree but was interrupted as Yaniv continued.

"Ever since Arafat revised history to deny the Jewish Temple ever stood on the Temple Mount, it has made it much more difficult to work in that area."

"Incredible anyone took him seriously," Graham said, trying to appease what sounded like a pet rant about to be unleashed. "I actually have a pamphlet from the 60s that the Muslim guides sold to tourists that mentions how the Haram al-Sharif was the site of Solomon's Temple."

"Just so, Dr. Eliot. They have proven they cannot be trusted with our history. That is why we need you. You can do the excavations with a license granted by us, just like any normal dig. You are trained and have done it before. There is nothing suspicious about it. You will not attract any attention. You also already know about the scroll, so it keeps the number of people who are aware of its existence to a minimum. It is exactly the kind of cover that is needed."

The polar opposites of discovery and loss, of opportunity and obligation clouded Graham's thoughts, keeping him from responding quickly. He broke the pause with a sentence he didn't know how he would finish. "Mr. Yaniv, I—"

"The IAA will pay all expenses," Yaniv said, apparently interpreting the silence as a need for more persuasion. "We can even find a way to contribute to your research, depending on what is found. But, as you know, the Antiquities Law does not permit us to pay finder's fees."

"That's not the issue."

"You will also have unrestricted access to the finds and the right of first publication."

"Mr. Yaniv, I can't do it. I can't miss Dr. Singer's funeral. He was too good a friend." The words evoked the image of the bloodied rock, eclipsing Graham's vision.

"Forgive me, please, Dr. Eliot. I do not mean to seem insensitive. I understand your friend's death is difficult. But please consider that the best way to honor Dr. Singer's life and work may be to pursue the man who kept him from completing it, rather than attending a ceremony that will not bring justice or prevent more crimes from being committed."

"Which is another reason not to go," Graham countered. "This is no ordinary dig."

"All the more reason to leave now, Dr. Eliot, and beat this thief at his own game."

"*Killer*," Graham spat the word. "Not thief. I'm not prepared to confront a murderer."

"Ah, you would not have to."

"Of course I would. Either I'd be following in his footsteps or acting as bait. Neither option is very appealing to me, Mr. Yaniv."

"Please, you do not understand. The IAA employs officers and reservists from the police and military. I have an ex-Mossad agent who will protect you as well as act as your assistant."

Graham was impressed by the idea of having a bodyguard from Israel's famed national intelligence agency.

"I also have a young Palestinian man to help dig," Yaniv said, "a looter who works for the black-market dealers. He is an informant to me. He hears things in places my ears cannot go, but where the killer might."

A sigh slipped from Graham.

"Please, Dr. Eliot. We have an opportunity here to make a truly significant contribution to our field, recover priceless cultural treasure, and hopefully bring about justice to Dr. Singer."

"Mr. Yaniv…" Graham paused, formulating his words, convincing himself to say them. "I'll be there as soon as I can. But I'll need to make a stop in Alexandria first."

"Egypt? Why?"

"I need to speak to Maalik."

"The man is a snake." Yaniv's laugh revealed a contradiction of affection and suspicion.

"Maybe," Graham said, "but knowing it is half the battle. And as far as snakes go, I'd pick him over most others."

Graham ended the call and pulled up his email. He sent a note to Maalik asking if he had any cartonnage available and told him he'd visit the shop in the next day or two. He sent another to a dealer in Jerusalem with the same message. Then he opened a browser, booked a flight to Alexandria, and another from there to Tel Aviv.

NINE

Six hours later, Graham melted into a business class seat on the Turkish Airlines jet, exhausted from the flurry of logistics it took to put him there. He had arranged an emergency leave from his post at Calbi University. The theology department head, who had recruited him to the school and had been a relentless champion of his work, saw an opportunity for both healing and justice. But what was most persuasive—he told Graham—was that for the first time in over two years, he heard purpose and engagement in Graham's voice despite the latest layer of grief.

Because he was flying east, there was no time to go home to Anaheim first. He outfitted himself at the REI in the mall next to the conference center, selecting shirts, pants, and waterproof hiking shoes for several days of expeditions. The business casual of the conference had no place in an ancient cistern.

He had planned to continue his research on the flight, but as soon as he boarded, an aggregate of stress, grief, and adrenaline created an exhaustion that overtook him. He spent the first leg of the flight asleep, out before the plane had finished boarding.

A rough landing shook him awake, and Graham spent the taxi to the gate shedding a disorientation that made him feel as if he'd been drugged. He felt the presence of Alyson and Olivia and realized he had dreamed about them yet again, though the details disappeared as he tried to bring them into focus.

He deplaned and walked into Chicago's O'Hare Airport. After passing through security and customs for international flights, he had an hour and a half before the flight to Istanbul. He bought a smoothie and an energy bar, then found a charging station at the gate. He opened his laptop, started a new document, and pasted the text from item 17.

> *In the great cistern which is in the COURT OF GENTILES AT THE END OF THE DOUBLE GATE, in the MIDDLE OF THE FARTHEST pillar on its northern side: 14 talents. °K*

He clicked Charles Wilson's 1865 book *Ordnance Survey of Jerusalem*—one of several PDFs he downloaded from his cloud library for the trip—and jumped to the description of Cistern 8, then copied it below item 17.

> *Cistern No. 8, north of al-Aqsa, commonly known as "the Great Sea," descended; 43 feet 2 inches deep, from 3 to 6 inches of water; the entrance to this is by a flight of steps leading down from a hole on the northern side of the workshops east of al-Aqsa; it is the largest of the series of cisterns, and the roof is partly supported by stone pillars left for the purpose when the excavation was made; the shape is peculiar, especially a small circular chamber in the north-west corner, the floor is uneven, and was partly dry when the cistern was visited; a conduit cut in the rock was seen coming in from the east, but it could not be reached; there have been a great many mouths,*

> *but only three are now in use; the roof is princi-*
> *pally of rock, but part is of large flat stones and*
> *part vaulted.*

He opened Warren's 1884 work, *The Survey of Western Palestine*, and found a similar description and added the additional information to the page.

- It was the largest on the Mount.
- Arabs called the cistern *Bir el Aswad*, or the "Black Well."
- The top of the cistern began five feet beneath the surface of the Mount.

Graham had no idea how he would put the information to use, but cataloging as many facts as he could about a site before he arrived had always served him well, giving him the ability to better adapt when something unexpected happened, as it always did.

He locked his fingers, rested his chin on his knuckles, and closed his eyes to process what he had read, but quickly became distracted as he remembered a fascinating twist in Warren's career. After his mission for the Palestine Exploration Fund ended, he returned to London, and—following a losing bid for parliament—served as Commissioner of Police of the Metropolis. It was Charles Warren who oversaw the investigation into Jack the Ripper, and his failure to catch the serial killer led to his resignation. Graham hoped his own part in a murder investigation would be more successful.

The insistent beep of an electric cart moving through the terminal broke his reverie. He started a new note, copying the text from item 18.

> *In the canal which goes FROM GIHON when*

*you enter ON THE LEFT 41 cubits: 55 talents
of silver.*

He knew the Old Testament mentioned a tunnel hewn
from rock by Hezekiah to connect the spring to a pool within
the city walls. He opened his Bible software and did a search
that took him to 2 Kings 20:20 and 2 Chronicles 32:30. The
accounts weren't full of detail, simply stating that Hezekiah
blocked the water of the Gihon Spring from one outlet and
created another. That meant there were at least two tunnels
leading from the spring, which was critical to Jerusalem as the
ancient city's only water source other than rain.

The tunnel had been discovered by the pioneering archaeologist Edward Robinson in 1838, though he didn't
recognize what he had found. The tunnel was almost entirely
clogged with rubbish and fill, but it wasn't cleared out until
nearly thirty years later by Charles Warren, who speculated it
was Hezekiah's. Confirmation came in 1880 when two boys
playing in the tunnel found an inscription inside the southern mouth that confirmed the site, turning a minor incident
in Old Testament history into a major confirmation of the
Bible's accuracy.

A new excavation of the area began in 1997 after the
foundation of an ancient Canaanite tower protecting the
spring was discovered while the area was being cleared to
make way for a new visitors' center. That led to the discovery
of several other tunnels as well as an underground reservoir.
Over fifteen years later, the work had finally been completed.

As Graham jotted down notes, it occurred to him that
as the first person through the cleaned-out tunnel, Warren
would have discovered any treasure that had still been there.
Yet Warren's books and correspondence didn't mention
anything like that. And if the treasure did indeed still exist, then he assumed the recent extensive excavation would

have unearthed it. But the directions from the text found in the mummy mask were so specific that he felt compelled to follow them, even if they led only to an empty niche. That in itself would vindicate the map to some extent.

He made another entry, pasting the text for items 53 and 54. Below it, he copied a diagram from the Israel Antiquities Authority's report of their 2001 excavation of the site. Item 53 mentioned a pillar under a covered hall. He looked at the diagram and easily found the only area it could refer to. Item 54 was marked by the rear of the tomb, and Graham noted two or three possible locations to search.

His phone pinged, notifying him of a text message from Bremmer.

"Dr. Eliot, I'm sending you a picture from the conference. Can you identify the people in it?"

"Will do," Graham texted.

Another message followed, this one containing a picture. Two men stood close together, their faces large enough in the frame that Graham assumed it was a selfie. Behind and to the side of them, a third man had walked into the shot. The exposure automatically adjusted to the two main faces, leaving the man in the background in relative darkness. His face was turned slightly to one side, and his eyes—the whites exaggerated by his dark complexion—looked at something out of the frame on the left side of the image.

Graham tapped the microphone icon, activating the text-to-speech feature. "The guy on the left is a colleague at Calbi. The one on the right is at Dallas Theological Seminary. The guy in the background looks like Freddie Mercury."

"Recognize the name on his tag?" Bremmer replied.

Graham wasn't surprised Bremmer didn't acknowledge the reference to the singer for Queen and smiled to himself as another text arrived. A cropped and zoomed image of the name tag hanging at the end of a lanyard displayed the name

Yari Karanlik.

"Don't know him," Graham texted. "Check the list of at-tendees? It should say what school or organization he's from."

"We did. It's not there."

"Actually, it may not be a name."

"What do you mean?"

"*Karanlik* is Turkish. It means *half dark*, or *shadow*."

TEN

Twenty-six hours after leaving Dallas, Graham landed at Borg el Arab Airport in Alexandria, Egypt. He had always loved visiting the city, though the revolution of 2011 had kept him away for a few years.

Despite the grand visions evoked by its namesake, the Hotel Helena was quite modest, which was one of the reasons Graham liked to stay there. The thought of Constantine the Great's vast empire being memorialized by using his mother's name to rent rooms not much bigger than the beds they contained appealed to his sense of humor. But the rooms were clean, and—more importantly—the hotel was a short walk from one of the most notorious markets for antiquities in the world.

The Souk El-Attarine was only a few blocks away, and yet it was a world apart. Graham stepped out of the hotel and found himself facing Saint Catherine's Cathedral, one of the last reminders of the city's rich Christian history. According to tradition, Mark the Evangelist ministered here, overseeing the church until he was martyred by being tied to a rope and dragged through the streets. Church Fathers Clement, Origen, Athanasius, and Cyril all defined and defended the faith from here. And Catherine died for it, beheaded after the wheel she was to be martyred on fell to pieces at her touch.

He turned left and crossed one of the main streets through the city center, wondering if it was part of the route of Mark's torture. The Roman Catholic presence disappeared as soon as he stepped onto the other side, into a Muslim neighborhood. Tired, colonial-era buildings battered with age and neglect crowded each other, many with the architectural wounds of missing sections of plaster or masonry. An incongruous speckle of satellite dishes covered the roofs like a layer of technological scales. Graham walked into the man-made canyon, taking cover under a canopy of umbrellas shielding the sun.

Two blocks later he turned left again and found the souk. Jews had been the main population of the market for many years, but almost all had moved to Israel now. Over 200 years before Jesus was born, there were so many Jews in Alexandria that the chief priests in Jerusalem commissioned scribes to translate the Hebrew Bible into Greek for them, a translation called the Septuagint.

The scribes who did the work reorganized the books, dividing several of them to make thirty-nine books out of twenty-two while keeping the text the same—the difference between the Old Testament and the Tanakh. Now the Alexandrian Jews struggled to survive in the hostile environment that was the wake of the revolution.

Graham entered El-Attarine's illogical maze of narrow streets, back alleys, and obscure passageways. The ancient market was a warren of merchants selling anything they could get their hands on, whether it was modern or ancient, authentic or knock-off, and everything in-between—part antique mall, part flea market, part farmer's market. And all of it spilled out of the shops and stalls into the ancient streets.

Traditional Egyptian housewares were interspersed with Edwardian-era furniture, jewelry, and knickknacks that had been abandoned or auctioned off a hundred years earlier by

British fleeing the country during the previous revolution. Clotheslines spanned the passageway, holding rugs, scarves, and clothes overhead. Furniture, pottery, lamps, hookahs, statuettes, clocks, and an infinite variety of baubles completed the thicket. The smell of spices wove together with the sweet aroma of pastries, cardamom-flavored coffee, produce, fish, and the food of street vendors. Snippets of Egyptian pop music intermittently broke through the bazaar's ubiquitous sound of bartering.

Graham usually loved exploring the market, but this time, he dodged the barkers trying to entice him and twisted through the souk with purpose. After a few wrong turns, he found himself at a door nearly hidden by the wares on either side of it. A sign hung on the door speaking a single word like a whisper in the chaos: Maalik. It literally meant "owner of things," providing him with an ironic nickname given that his right of possession had been questioned more than once.

Graham stepped into a small room lined with several ramshackle shelves stuffed with figurines, small lamps, brass cups and pots, and a clutter of miscellaneous ornaments. A bramble of hanging lamps, their chains draping like vines, hung in a twisted metal cloud over the top of the room. A tiny desk of stained plywood—pieces chipped away on the edges from being knocked into—stood in the far corner of the room. A small, fatigued rattan chair sat in the corner and squeaked with protest as a man rose from it, his face blossoming with recognition.

"Mr. Graham!" The man's heavy accent turned the *r* into a *d*. "*Nawwart Masr!*"

The traditional greeting told Graham he had lit up Egypt, and he gave the traditional reply in English. "Your light is enough, Maalik."

"It is good to see you, my friend," Maalik said, embracing him.

"It has been too long."

Maalik's white, short-sleeved button-down shirt was tucked into black dress pants, giving him a clean, collected look that contrasted with the tangle of the shop. His large, dark eyes had the shape of sadness, but twinkled with optimism and more than a little mischievousness.

"You look like you just came from the showroom," Graham observed.

He knew Maalik had another shop nearby, but in a more modern building. That was where most of the actual antiquities were, as well as his office. Unlike the shop in the souk, the showroom was immaculate, spacious, and well-lit, and the meticulously cataloged inventory of artifacts available on the floor-to-ceiling shelves was visited by collectors from around the world. Graham didn't know for certain, but he suspected that some of the most valuable pieces were probably hidden in a back room of the souk shop, available only on the black market.

"Yes, but business is not what it used to be. The Arab Spring has scared away too many people. Everyone is suffering. More like Arab Winter." As he spoke, Maalik extracted another chair from behind the desk, and they sat down. "I thought things would stay the same. You know, like the Who song. The way things were wasn't great, but it's far worse now."

Graham had almost forgotten Maalik's love of Western culture—especially the music—and his habit of quoting rock lyrics as if they were proverbs of ancient wisdom. "I'm sorry to hear that. But you have an excellent stock of nice pieces that are still valuable."

"Ah, but for how long? Every day I wonder if this will be the day the new government will confiscate my collection and sell it for themselves. Especially since I am a Copt. They have no tolerance for Christians. They only want to preserve

Islamic history. They don't care about the rest. And they don't care much about the smuggling as long as they are bribed into blindness."

"Smuggling doesn't seem to bother *you* very much, either." Graham smirked, triggering a laugh from Maalik

"Who am I to withhold treasures from those who want to care for them? These things are the property of the world—of time. Jim Croce had it all backwards. You cannot put time in a bottle, but you can put a bottle into time. And if you leave it long enough, it will fill with money. I simply charge a delivery fee."

Graham laughed at the mix of logic and larceny.

"And when they come to rob me of my antiquities, then all I will have is this." Maalik made an expansive gesture to the shop with a look in his eye that dared Graham to believe him.

Graham smiled, then let it fade as he changed the subject. "You heard what happened, right?"

"To Dr. Singer? Yes." The spark left Maalik's eyes, leaving only the sadness. "Your FBI even called to ask me questions."

"I guessed the mask came from you," Graham said. "That's why I'm here."

"I could have saved you the trip. I could have told you on the phone or through email."

"After what happened to Andrew, I didn't think that would be the safest thing to do. Do you have any other masks or cartonnage from the same find?" Graham studied Maalik's eyes, looking for any sign of veiled truth.

"There were no other masks. In fact, that was the only thing from that find that I had. If there was anything else, I do not have it."

Graham continued to stare hard at the dealer's face. "Please, Maalik. It's important."

"I tell you the truth, my friend." He brought his hands

together as he spoke, weaving his fingers in front of his chest, as if to pray, then bobbed them once to emphasize his words, hammering them into place.

"If you come across any more cartonnage or hear of another dealer that has some for sale, please let me know." He hoped his request left the door open for Maalik to invent a cover story for unexpectedly coming into more.

"Why is this so valuable to you suddenly?" Maalik asked. "These are paper masks of unimportant people. And yet you fly halfway around the world to ask me about them to my face."

"I'm sorry. I can't say yet," Graham said, suddenly aware Maalik was studying him as well.

"But you are not FBI…"

"No, but I'm trying to help them all I can."

Maalik frowned theatrically.

"I'm sorry, Maalik. I'll tell you soon, I promise. Just not now."

"You have always treated me well, so I must make do with that." Maalik nodded with a shrug. "Of course, you know that if I came across more cartonnage, the increased interest would naturally be reflected in the price."

"Won't get fooled?" Graham smiled, anticipating Maalik's recognition from the same Who song he'd quoted earlier.

"Not again. The casbah must rock!" Maalik said, wind-milling his arm across an air-guitar before bursting into laughter.

Graham was still smiling as he picked his way back through the Souk El-Attarine and stepped into the lobby of the Hotel Helena. He heard a door close above him as he started up the narrow flight of steps but was too preoccupied to give it any thought. Almost immediately, a man appeared on the landing and pushed past. Graham reached his door— the only one on the landing—and was met with a sense that someone had been in the room. He stood alert just inside the threshold, hypersensitive to every sound.

After a moment that felt like an hour, he slowly moved deeper into the room, walking without a sound. A thin bead of light emitted from the barely-open lid of his laptop, and he stared at it until the screen went into sleep mode a few seconds later. Graham pivoted around the room, looking for other signs of a search, but found nothing.

Had a cleaning person been here? Possibly he had interrupted a thief. Or was he being followed? The question sounded paranoid to him even without being spoken aloud. After all, who knew enough about the situation to follow him? Who did he know that even had the ability and resources to do it? And even if someone had tried to open his computer, there was no way to access the MacBook Pro without his fingerprint.

He double checked the doors and windows to make sure they were locked, turned off the light, and lay back across the bed. He closed his eyes and thought of the ridiculous part he found himself playing. And—like one of Maalik's quotes—a song from the soundtrack of his youth came into his head. He made Jackson Browne's confession his own as he fell asleep.

Graham, the pretender.

ELEVEN

Although Jerusalem was only 300 miles from Alexandria, the flight connecting them required a circuitous 1,400-mile route through Istanbul to avoid the political tension. By the time Graham stood by the baggage carousel at Tel Aviv's Ben Gurion Airport, he was wavering with fatigue, unaware of the man who approached him until he felt a hand touch his shoulder.

"Excuse me. Dr. Eliot?"

Graham recognized the odor of a smoker without a cigarette and turned to find a tall, athletic middle-aged man wearing a deep blue polo shirt embroidered with the logo of the Israel Antiquities Authority over his left breast. Despite being clean-shaven, the shadow of a beard already tinted his chin, framing a serious smile as he offered his hand.

"Daniel Harel. I'm with the IAA."

Graham returned both the smile and the handshake, then followed him to an SUV for the forty-five-minute drive to Jerusalem.

"Sorry about the smell, Dr. Eliot." Daniel choreographed his apology by making wafting motions with one hand. He then lowered the windows of the car and blasted the air conditioner to get rid of the smell of cigarette smoke. "I'm trying to quit."

"Don't worry about it. And please call me Graham."

The man nodded appreciatively. "Daniel."

As they entered the highway, Graham glanced in the opposite direction from Jerusalem, toward Joppa, Tel Aviv's oldest neighborhood, the biblical city of Jaffa. Jaffa was the port where Jonah had boarded a ship to avoid being sent by God to Nineveh. Now Graham was going to Jerusalem—the holy city—while avoiding God. Just like Jonah.

"Yaniv told me I would be working with a Mossad agent. Is that you?"

"There are a few of us, but yes, I am ex-Mossad."

"How did you end up with the IAA?"

"When I was very young, my parents built a house in the new territory in Jerusalem. I was born during the Six-Day War. Many houses were built there quickly for Jews to move into. But one of the homes near us was delayed because the builders uncovered a first-century tomb when they were digging out the foundation. There were several discoveries like that in my neighborhood as I grew up. That's how I became interested in archaeology."

"Quite an introduction," Graham said. "You were literally surrounded by it."

"I seriously considered making it my career, but the Gulf War happened, and I decided to serve my country. I grew up watching my country defend itself every day. Sometimes I wondered if Israel would even exist when I was an adult. Defending it is just a part of who I am," Daniel said. "I wasn't looking for a change, but I had friends in the reserves who did work for the IAA, and that led to me being introduced to Yaniv."

Graham suspected Daniel wanted to ask about the expedition, and Graham wanted to ask about the sites he planned to visit, but he didn't know how much he should say until he met with Yaniv. The route to Jerusalem was strewn with so much history, however, that they did not lack for conversation.

Jerusalem rose from rugged hills in contradictions. It was where God had chosen to dwell with his people, making the remote backwater the center of the universe. It was an embattled city of peace in a promised land filled with broken promises. It was a city where God had died, and the dead came to life.

They reached the northern part of the city, and an interchange fed them south, through modern Jerusalem to the Old City. Graham tried to imagine how the city had looked when Titus approached from the same direction in the spring of AD 70.

Titus had waited until Passover to lay siege to Jerusalem, knowing that every able-bodied Jew was required to attend the Temple for the feast. It made it easy for him to trap the Jewish zealots who had led an insurrection against Rome for four years. When Titus appeared on the northern horizon, the Jews camping outside the walls for the eight-day long festival pushed into the gates, bloating the city with over two million people—more than triple its normal size.

When the siege finally ended six months later, more than a million people had died. Most of the trees from the hills around the city had been cut down and used for crosses to crucify as many as 500 escapees per day. Those who remained within the walls became victims of starvation, disease, infighting, Roman swords, and even cannibalism. More than 100,000 Jews were enslaved by Rome, some used to complete the colosseum. Another 100,000 were sold into slavery to other countries.

But the most tragic victim was the Temple itself. Titus had been so captivated by its beauty that he wanted it preserved for Rome and ordered that it should be left unharmed. The day after the order was given, the Jews attacked the Roman garrison on the edge of the Temple Mount but were pushed back into the inner courts of the sanctuary. During the battle, a Roman soldier disobeyed the order and hurled a flaming timber through one of the doors, setting the interior on fire. The jars of holy oil inside burned so hot that the Temple became an oven fed by the wood paneling on the walls. Titus's calls to extinguish the fire were ignored.

According to Josephus—a Jewish general captured by the Romans, and eyewitness to the siege—the only thing greater than the flames was the stream of blood that came from it. And it happened on the anniversary of the destruction of the First Temple by the Babylonians 410 years earlier. With the Temple lost, Titus decided to raze the building, and had its massive stones thrown from the edge of the platform, unknowingly fulfilling a prophecy made by Jesus almost forty years earlier. In 1968, many of the Temple's blocks were discovered along the base of the southwest corner of the Mount, and still lay in place as part of an archaeological park, one of Graham's favorite places to visit.

As the Babylonians approached the city in 586 BC, the priests hid the Temple treasures. It was the last time anyone saw the Ark of the Covenant. As the Romans approached the city in AD 70, the priests again hid the Temple treasures. As Graham approached the city today, he thought about how it had been reduced to ruin, and yet had not only risen again, but still held its treasure. The Master Scroll changed that. Now the best way to protect the treasure was to find it. And it was up to him to do it.

TWELVE

They exited the highway north of the Old City and followed the ancient wall to the northeast corner. Directly across the street on their left, a hexagonal white limestone tower stood on a hill, overlooking the Temple Mount and its surroundings. Two wings expanded the building in a straight line on either side of it, while two others reached at forty-five-degree angles, anchored to the base of the tower like spokes to a hub. Behind the tower, two parallel wings created a courtyard, giving the complex the shape of a warped asterisk.

"I've always thought this place looked like a fortress," Graham said absently as the Rockefeller Museum came into sight.

"The architect must have been a prophet," Daniel said. "During the Six-Day War, Israel used that tower as a lookout after they captured it. There was a battle here."

Graham hunched forward to see up the hill. "The first time I was here I found bullet holes still in the stone of one of the cloisters."

From the road, Graham could just make out the bas-relief image of Asia meeting Africa hanging above the entrance, connecting the angled wings to funnel visitors inside. He had spent hours in its library, and many more marveling at how much history had been recovered during the British Mandate between the world wars—the timespan from which the museum actively collected items. Some of the finds even came from the tombs that were discovered on the site as the museum was being built in the 1930s.

Daniel passed the ramp that led up to the main entrance and continued around to the private entrance at the back of the museum. Graham knew that the building was more than the archive of the Mandatory period. It was also the headquarters for the Israel Antiquities Authority, though that partnership was soon coming to an end. They had long ago outgrown their space, and a new building was being constructed near the Israel Museum and Bible Lands Museum.

They entered through a side door into a part of the building Graham had never visited. The unadorned halls fed into officious and utilitarian rooms. A generic office sign identified one of them as the Antiquities Robbery Prevention Division and they stepped through the open door, into a reception area. An administrative assistant looked up from a computer screen and smiled. She opened her mouth to speak, but a man's voice sounded instead, coming from the open door to the inner office.

"Please come in!"

A slender man in the same deep blue IAA shirt as Daniel made his way around the desk, offering his hand before he was close enough for it to be shaken. Dark, intelligent eyes welcomed Graham from behind small oval lenses, both streetwise and academic.

"Shalom, Dr. Eliot. I'm Chaim Yaniv."

Graham returned the greeting of peace, but before he could add anything else, Yaniv's smile turned empathetic.

"I do wish our meeting was under better circumstances."

"Thank you." Now that the work was beginning, Graham struggled with guilt over feeling excited about it, and he appreciated Yaniv for recognizing his conflicting emotions.

"I never met with Dr. Singer. I knew him only through his work. I hear he was a good man."

"He was. Very." Graham was still unnerved by the use of the past tense for his friend.

They took their places around a wooden desk that looked as old as the building and was too large for the room. The surface of the desk not claimed by the usual office trappings was strewn with photos showing a variety of artifacts and locations. One wall of the office was filled with a whiteboard covered in Hebrew words and names written in different colored markers joined together by colored lines and arrows. The opposite wall held a bookcase overflowing with archaeological reference works, most of which Graham recognized from his own collection. A framed display hung in the space between the windows behind the desk, containing an impressive collection of ancient coins, papyri fragments, and bullae.

"Fakes," Yaniv said. "Lies made of metal, clay, and leaves."

"They did an excellent job."

"Yes, they were done by a true artist. Too bad he was a criminal." Yaniv sighed and shook his head, sounding regretful as if the forger missed his calling. "Most archaeologists dig for truth. Or at least what truth left behind. But me, I dig for lies." He placed his elbows on the desk, crossed his arms, and leaned forward. "Tell me, Dr. Eliot, what are your thoughts about this…treasure map?"

"I assume you've seen what Dr. Singer found."

"Yes, the FBI—Special Agent Bremmer—sent it to me."

"Well, according to my translation, I have identified three of the four locations it mentions. Two have been excavated, but no one has ever connected any of them with the Copper Scroll list." As he spoke, Graham removed his laptop and opened his notes. "The location in the Vale of Akhon is still a mystery."

"That is no surprise." Yaniv sounded unimpressed and twitched a shoulder in a dismissive shrug.

"No," Graham said, "but one location uses the Gihon as

69

the reference point that leads to somewhere else in the tunnels."

"That is a surprise." Yaniv leaned back. "Those tunnels have been cleared out and have been open to the public for years now. Surely one of the excavations would have found something."

"I thought the same thing. But the map is specific enough that it is still worth checking." Graham pointed to a place in his translation on the screen. "The tomb of Zadok has very definite descriptions as well, but I don't think anyone has looked in the right tomb."

"What do you mean?"

"After Allegro searched for these two items in the unfinished tomb next to the Tomb of Absalom, I don't think anyone thought to question the location. It seems to me that since zadok means just, we should be looking in the tomb of James, on the other side of Absalom's Tomb."

"B'nei Hezir," Yaniv said.

"Exactly."

"But that one has also been thoroughly excavated."

"Only by people who didn't know what to look for or where to look," Graham said, answering the same objection he had at first. "My guess is you're probably right and there's nothing there. But we should still look."

"And then there is the Temple Mount," Yaniv said, exchanging a look with Daniel.

"Yes," Graham said. "Cistern 8."

Yaniv sighed, visibly deflating. "Just outside al-Aqsa Mosque. Do you know how hard it will be to get in there? Impossible."

"But just imagine being the first people to see it since Wilson and Warren," Daniel said, his face lit by the idea.

"You read about that?" Graham asked.

"Warren's book." Daniel nodded. "The etchings of him

exploring underground Jerusalem fascinated me as a boy. As good as any story you could make up. If only they had been able to take a camera with them."

"And even they didn't get to explore it fully," Graham said. "Who knows what's down there?"

"We should start with B'nei Hezir." Yaniv tapped his desk, turning practical. "That is the easiest to enter and examine."

"I agree," Graham said. "It would be a good place for testing the map—or at least my translation—to see if we're on the right track."

"It is also the easiest site to close without drawing a lot of attention," Daniel added.

"Hezekiah's Tunnel will take a bit more time to arrange." Yaniv rocked back and spoke to a random spot in the ceiling. "We will leave Cistern 8 alone for now. I will have to think about it to see if it is even worth trying."

"I will tell my digger to be ready to start tomorrow," Daniel said.

"And I will make sure the site is closed beginning tonight and all day tomorrow," Yaniv said reassuringly. "I will put a guard at each entrance."

"We'll be there at dawn," Daniel said.

Yaniv checked his watch. "It is just after 4 p.m. I am sure you are tired of traveling. We have a room for you at the Promised Land Hotel." He stood up, signaling the meeting was over. "If there were such thing as luck, I would wish it on you. But *HaShem* has no need of luck." Yaniv's use of the phrase *the name* to avoid using the word *God* told Graham that Yaniv was serious and conservative in his faith. "Peace upon you both."

THIRTEEN

Daniel guided the SUV around the irregular block into a small parking lot hidden behind the buildings along the street, revealing a four-story hotel. Graham's sense of direction had always been good, and as he oriented himself, he realized they were just on the other side of the garden behind the museum, a shorter walk than drive.

The call to afternoon prayer began as they unloaded the car, the Arabic voice floating above the parking lot in long, sustained syllables punctuated with quick bursts of consonants. It seemed to be coming from a bullhorn that added a fuzz of distortion to the voice. Other, more distant calls transmitted the same words, though delivered at a slightly different pace and pitch, blanketing the air in a discomfiting dissonance.

"I am always surprised by it when I haven't been here in a while." Graham looked into the sky as if trying to see the sound. "It's so eerie. And yet, there is something beautiful about it."

Daniel gave a noncommittal "Hmm" that Graham took to mean he agreed only with the eerie part. The exchange broke the spell of the prayer and freed them to walk up the steps, past a cat stationed at the entrance like a doorman. It ignored them as they pushed through the revolving door and into a clean, bright marble lobby trimmed in dark wood. Daniel had already checked them in, and minutes later, Graham looked over the northern wall of the Old City from his balcony.

"Incredible view! Everything is so close."

To his left, Graham saw that the tower of the museum framed the edge of his panoramic view. He scanned right slowly, creating a parade of landmarks: the Mount of Olives, the Dome of the Rock on the Temple Mount, the domes of the Church of the Holy Sepulcher, the Tower of David, and the modern city on his far right.

"Hard to imagine that Jerusalem was entirely within those walls until a hundred and fifty years ago," Graham mused.

"As someone who grew up here, I have seen many walls go up, and others torn down," Daniel said. "What is hard for me to imagine is that there are still walls to the Old City at all. Especially since they've been leveled and rebuilt so many times." He tapped the balcony rail, closing the topic. "Speaking of walls, I'll be on the other side of this one. Right next door, if you need anything. But right now, I need to pick up our digger. He's staying here as well so we can get an early start."

"Thank you, Daniel," Graham said, shaking his hand. "For all your help today. And for being willing to join me on this…" Graham paused, too embarrassed to say *treasure hunt*. "For whatever happens next."

"Are you joking? I feel like a boy again on a treasure hunt!" Daniel's infectious smile spread to Graham's face. "Sleep well. Shalom."

Graham turned back to the room, glad for the space that had been missing from the Hotel Helena. Judging by the dated exterior of the building, the room had been recently renovated, for which he was thankful as well. He set up his computer on the bistro table near the balcony so he could enjoy the view as he worked, but after connecting to the Wi-Fi he felt restless and decided to visit the other dealer he had emailed before leaving Dallas.

Although Jerusalem's history had been of special interest to him since college, the first time he visited the Old City he was so excited by the experience that he frequently blanked out when it came to the historical importance of many of the locations he visited. Features and sites he studied in books and online went unappreciated, and he returned home with an overwhelming love for Jerusalem. This love mingled with regret as he realized the number of opportunities he'd missed. Since then, he had developed the habit of reminding himself of its history as he moved through it.

With Daniel's words still fresh in his mind, he fixed on Herod's Gate as he approached it from half a block away. The entrance—one of only seven to the Old City—had recently been renovated by the IAA. It had actually been built by Suleiman the Magnificent 500 years ago, 1,500 years after King Herod's death. Suleiman had rebuilt the entire city wall, replacing the one that had stood for 700 years. The wall Titus had destroyed was only one in a series that began when King David made the city his capital.

Just before he entered the passage, Graham wove his way through the cluster of vendors and looked up at the rosettes carved in the stone that gave the entrance its Hebrew name: the Flower Gate. At the other end of the long passage was the neighborhood in the Muslim Quarter that gave the entrance its Muslim name: *Bab al-Zahra*.

Inside the gate, the stalls of merchants created their own wall, saturating every available space, dividing visitors into narrow walkways along the perimeter. He took the branch to the right, walking up a stepped path that gently curved to the left, then straightened out to guide him deeper into the city.

As always, Graham was entranced by the ancient feel of

the Old City. His sense of irony was piqued as he thought of how this part of what he called the *Old City* was what Jesus had known as the *New City—Bezetha*. Alleys and alcoves splintered off into capillaries he could explore only with a glance as he navigated to one of the most misunderstood roads in the world.

The Via Dolorosa commemorated the route Jesus walked from his condemnation before Pontius Pilate to his cruci-fixion. As Graham stood on the corner—the Monastery of Flagellation to his left, and the Ecco Homo Convent on his right—he thought of the millions of pilgrims who had tried to retrace the last steps of Jesus beginning as early as the mid-fourth century.

He wondered what would happen to their faith if they learned the street they walked wasn't the original street but was built above the road Jesus knew—sometimes by as much as ten or fifteen feet. What would happen if they learned the route itself had changed many times since people started trav-eling it, and that the current route had first been walked only in the 1800s? And what would happen if they learned none of the routes had ever taken the right way and the street was, in fact, on the wrong side of town?

First-century historians Josephus and Philo recorded that the Roman governors did not stay at the Antonio Fortress—the traditional route's starting point—when in Jerusalem, even though the building on the north side of the Temple Mount was used as the Roman garrison. Instead, the gover-nors stayed and worked out of Herod the Great's palace, built on the west wall of the city. And the most recent archaeologi-cal discoveries—only a few years old—included the discovery of the Praetorium there, the place where Pilate probably tried Jesus. The route was off by nearly 180 degrees.

The only thing Graham considered accurate was its des-tination, the Church of the Holy Sepulcher. Even then, the tomb of Jesus had been destroyed and rebuilt so many times that only the bench in the tomb was likely authentic. Graham looked at the tourists and wondered which of them would struggle to accept the facts, who would prefer the superstition to the truth?

One fact was undeniable: the shopkeepers and street vendors didn't care about truth. They lined the route Jesus didn't walk and played the part the tourists cast them in, selling Jesus-themed memorabilia.

The thoughts made Graham feel guilty, and he silently apologized. He hated intellectual snobbery and hated it most when he saw it in himself. But his quest for knowledge also made him a teacher, and sometimes he became frustrated when the demonstrably false was taken as unquestionably true.

He turned right and passed under the misnamed Ecco Homo Arch. Given that it was built by Hadrian a hundred years after the crucifixion, it was not where Pilate presented Jesus to the mob. But the merchants in the stalls congesting the street with jewelry, icons, garments, and ornaments gave the impression that Jesus had carried his cross past their ancestors.

As he turned left at the intersection, Graham stumbled on the heels of a tourist who had stopped suddenly in front of him. He had gotten distracted by how the woman's bright red baseball cap was one of at least a dozen that swarmed around him. He'd been trying to figure out where the group was from when he tripped.

He tried to apologize to her, but she was captivated by the building on his left and didn't seem to hear him. Graham saw that he was standing outside the third station of the cross, marking the spot where Jesus stumbled for the first time under the weight of the beam he carried. He almost laughed but choked it back when he saw the reverence the red caps gave the spot.

Graham looked back to see if he had blocked anyone behind him and spotted a soldier on the roof at his post next to an Israeli flag and a security camera. He wondered if he had just provided some comic relief to whoever monitored the street. He turned forward again and traveled the block that separated the east leg of the Via Dolorosa from the West. The zigzag was marked by the fourth station, where the road's tradition said Jesus encountered his mother, though the meeting was not recorded in Scripture.

Graham crossed the street and passed the fifth station, where Jesus stumbled again, and the cross was given to a bystander name Simon to carry the rest of the way. It was also where several antiquities dealers kept their shops in the Old City.

Less than a minute later, he stood before an arched stone doorway that opened beneath a modest sign hung perpendicularly for maximum visibility in the crowded street. The simple, white background cleared a visual space in the chaos to announce *Avraham Antiquities, Authorized Antiquity Dealer*. The address and hours appeared below it, as well as a telephone number in a different font, an indication the sign had been edited, and a cell number handwritten with permanent marker, giving it the unintended aesthetic of a ransom note.

Graham slipped through the door and into a tastefully appointed room with floor-to-ceiling display cases of lightly stained wood supporting glass shelves. The ceiling was paneled in matching wood, though the florescent tubes that lit the shop marred the elegance as much as the marker on the sign outside. Coins, oil lamps, figurines, busts, bowls, Roman glass, and a few daggers lined the shelves. Although the definition of an antiquity included any item produced prior to 1700, most of this collection tried to find some connection to the Bible.

"Dr. Eliot. What a surprise." A cultivated voice with only the hint of an accent crossed the room, just loud enough to convey enthusiasm without violating the decorum of the shop. "So good to see you."

"Shalom, Ravid. Good to see you, as well."

Gideon Ravid abandoned his post behind the counter. The slender man moved with a graceful economy that emanated calm and control. His brown dress pants and white dress shirt matched the decor perfectly without looking intentional. Thinning hair, mostly faded to gray, lay perfectly in place, framing a sober face that warned anyone looking into it not to waste his time.

Graham shook his hand warmly. "You haven't changed a bit. You look as timeless as the items in your shop."

"I wish the same could be said of you, Dr. Eliot." Ravid's smile melted away as he spoke. "I am very sorry to hear about your family. I can see your wife and daughter in your eyes even now."

"Thank you. I appreciate that."

Ravid held his gaze, and Graham decided to keep the conversation moving. He looked around the empty shop and was about to comment on it, but he changed his mind when he realized what time it was. "I'm so sorry. You must be trying to close for the day."

"Please," Ravid said generously, "my door is always open to you."

"You are very kind. Did you get my email?"

"About cartonnage? Yes. But I am afraid I have nothing for you. Would you like me to make some inquiries?"

"No, no, I don't want to spark any interest. But will you please let me know if you hear something from one of the other dealers?"

"Absolutely. Understood."

"Haven't come across a collector who calls himself Yari

Karanlik, have you?"

Ravid's incredulous laugh answered the question before his words. "The *Shadow*? My whole world is shadows. Almost anyone in this business could go by that name."

"Except for you, of course." Graham smirked. "Listen, I don't want to be a bother. I'll come back, when we both have more time."

"I would like that very much. Shalom."

Graham retraced his route, and—after a plate of falafel and hummus at a sidewalk table across from the third station of the cross—made his way back to the hotel. He climbed the stairs to the roof to watch the sunset, taking advantage of an amenity advertised in the lobby. The sound of *Maghrib*—the sunset prayer—received him as he stepped onto the terrace. Warm lights lit the Old City wall. Behind it, the gold-plated Dome of the Rock floated over the former spot of the Holy of Holies like a sleeping sun.

He stared into the darkness at each location he planned to visit as night coated them. The question was whether any of them would reveal their secrets in daylight.

FOURTEEN

Half an hour before dawn, Harry Nilsson's piano pounded Graham awake with the intro to "Gotta Get Up," the song he'd programmed as his alarm. After a quick shower, he looked for Daniel in the lobby and found him already waiting for him, smoking outside the entrance. By the time he had pushed through the revolving door, Daniel was stabbing his cigarette out on a trash can.

"Shalom," Daniel said, with a guilty look that was anything but peaceful. "I promise I'm trying to quit."

Graham was about to tease him when the sunrise prayer began, distracting him. He wondered if Daniel's lack of reaction was a resigned acceptance of the status quo as the flourishes of a dozen different muezzins overlapped each other at different volumes. A windowless, white van with extended height and length waited at the bottom of the steps. Graham assumed it belonged to the IAA and started for it.

"We can't go yet."

Daniel's voice turned Graham around.

"Nagi's on the roof. Praying."

"Who's Nagi?"

"The digger. He insisted. I didn't know he was so devout."

Graham wondered how a Palestinian Muslim could be trusted to help a Jew and a nominal Christian recover artifacts that could corroborate the historicity of the Second Temple.

"It's okay." Daniel must have interpreted Graham's expression. "I've worked with him before."

Daniel handed Graham a cup of coffee and a paper bag.

"I don't get it." Graham glanced into the bag to see that it contained a bagel. "And thanks."

"He has to help us, or he goes to prison. We busted him at an illegal dig. There are lots of guys like him in the West Bank, more mercenary than militant. Nagi knows what to look for, and he's smart. And now he's an informant. He probably doesn't tell us about every dig he hears of, but he gives us enough to keep himself out of jail."

The prayer time ended, and a moment later a man in his early twenties shot out the revolving door with an urgency that made Graham certain he was Nagi. He swallowed the last of his bagel and chased it with the coffee as the man came up to the van. His long-on-top, short-on-side haircut combined with his faded jeans, black zipper hoodie, and hiking shoes made him indistinguishable from most of Graham's students.

"Graham Eliot, Nagi el-Hashem." Daniel made the introduction as they started down the steps.

"Shalom." Graham said it from habit, then realized his mistake.

Nagi froze and looked hard at him for a moment with intelligent eyes before smiling unexpectedly. "*Wa alakykum issalam.*" He held out his hand to shake as he translated his own words, not knowing Graham had understood. "And peace be upon you." Then, seeing the embarrassment on Graham's face, added, "Don't worry about it."

Daniel followed the roundabout at Herod's Gate until it fed them toward the Rockefeller Museum.

"I don't get to do many daylight digs," Nagi said from the bench behind them. "I usually get picked up after dark and work until dawn."

"A hard day's night," Graham said.

Daniel chuckled. "You should be sleeping like a dog." He looked at Nagi in the rearview mirror as he said it.

"Okay," Nagi said flatly. "Whatever."

The van turned right, onto a road that crossed the Kidron Valley, the wash that separated the Temple Mount from the Mount of Olives. Before Graham could decide how to respond to someone so young that they didn't know who the Beatles were, Daniel drove past the Church of All Nations, the entry to the Garden of Gethsemane. The van slipped into an opening in the wall on their right, barely wide enough to fit through. Normally, it was closed to traffic, but a soldier had been stationed at the gate to admit them.

Daniel navigated carefully down a steep, unpaved road with a low wall that descended to the base of Absalom's Tomb at the foot of the bluff. He parked in front of Zechariah's tomb, told the others to stay put, and climbed the embankment to the foundation of the tomb.

An Israeli soldier dressed in black fatigues, armed with a machine gun, stood outside a doorway cut into the rock in the wall next to the tomb. An iron gate was shut behind him, and two ribbons of orange crime scene tape with the pattern of the IAA logo formed an x across the frame.

Daniel showed his ID, and after a brief exchange, walked back to Graham's window.

"We're good. There's another guard at the top entrance in the cemetery. Both gates have been secured since yesterday evening."

Graham and Nagi followed Daniel to the back of the van to unload the equipment. Graham slung the backpack containing his laptop over his shoulder, grabbed a duffel bag holding work lights, then headed up the hill behind Daniel. He nodded a greeting to the soldier as he walked up a small flight of metal steps leading into a passage cut into the rock.

Graham quickly surveyed the iron gate that caged the space and wondered what the builders of the tomb would have thought about something so ugly being bolted to their hard work.

"They had to install this in the 30s." Daniel nudged the gate open with his foot. "There's another at the other entrance. The place was filled with rubbish. People used it as a dump for over a thousand years." He kept walking up the stone steps as he spoke. "And as a latrine."

"Thanks for that," Nagi said sarcastically.

"It could be worse," Graham said. "This is where King Uzziah supposedly came after he contracted leprosy."

He stepped out of the passage into a portico about fifteen feet long and nine feet deep and set the bags down. To his right, a square opening connected to a small hall that served as the antechamber for the burial chambers. Ahead of him was another iron gate blocking a flight of stairs, leading down from the top of the bluff. Oddly, the flight stopped four feet above the floor of the portico.

"That's one of the reasons we came from the bottom," Daniel said, anticipating a question from Graham. "And because we would've been more exposed. Strange, isn't it?"

Graham walked to the steps and touched the bottom one as Daniel continued. "The theory is that the stairs originally came all the way down. But when the portico was completed, the builders realized they had made a mistake and put the stairs in the wrong place. So they cut away the bottom part of the stairs."

He turned to examine the main opening in the portico. Two Doric columns, formed by carving away the stone, stood evenly spaced. Half columns were sculpted as decoration on either side of the threshold, making it appear from the outside as if four pillars supported the tomb. A black iron railing spanned the gaps between the columns, presumably as a safety measure to keep people from falling off the fifteen-foot drop.

Graham climbed over the waist-high railing, stepped to the edge of the bluff, turned back to the tomb, and looked up at the entablature. He could barely see the inscription that identified it as the tomb of the priestly sons of Hezir. Above the writing, a frieze ornamented the façade.

He stared across the valley at the Temple Mount's massive eastern wall and tried to picture it as it had appeared to Jesus, without the fill and debris at its base that raised the ground level to where it was now. The tiered colonnade of the Royal Stoa that held the market on the southern end of the platform would have added another hundred feet to the looming edifice. Parallel to the wall, the Kidron Valley descended south, making the southeast corner the highest part of the Temple.

Graham fixed on the spot where Jesus had been tempted. And from which James was thrown, martyred for believing his own brother was God incarnate. Now Graham was preparing to dig up James's tomb to look for treasure that was generated—in part—by the market Jesus famously overturned.

"That's all of it." Daniel set the last bags down as Nagi pulled a portable generator up the top step.

"What do you want us to do?"

Graham opened his laptop and called up the diagram of the tomb made during the last excavation fifteen years earlier. He glanced from the screen to his surroundings and back again several times as he stepped into the antechamber. Sunlight reflected into the dank trapezoidal space that the survey drawing indicated was twelve feet wide and about fifteen feet deep. Each of the three interior walls had a gap that communicated with a burial chamber filled with shadows.

"Let's put up a light here, near the back chamber, and two more inside," Graham said.

All three men pulled stands, lights, and cables from the duffels, then began to assemble and connect them.

"So, Nagi, what kind of stuff do you usually find?" Graham asked.

Nagi looked at him with suspicion and then looked at Daniel, who started laughing.

"It's okay, Nagi. I'm not going to arrest you. It's not like we don't already know."

Nagi returned a sarcastic *thank you* look, then turned back to Graham.

"Coins, oil pots, clay seals. That's what's usually there."

"Tell him how we met." Daniel's big smile broke open before he could finish the sentence.

Nagi answered with another exasperated face. "Really?"

"He was stealing a wine press!" Daniel's laughter bounced off the stone walls.

"I don't understand. You mean like a stone floor where grapes were crushed? How can you steal that?"

"It's not as hard as you think," Nagi said, struggling to sound rational as he defended himself. "Just takes a while to dig it out."

"Which is why we found you."

"*That time…*" Nagi gave a cynical smile to Daniel, then turned to Graham. "You'd be surprised how many rich people here have things like that. They put them in their gardens."

"What if someone finds out they have them?" Graham tried not to sound as indignant as he felt. Nagi wasn't the real culprit; it was the buyers who created the market.

"They have connections, I guess. They just buy their way out of trouble."

Although Graham thought it was a simplistic explanation tinged with resentment, he had to admit that there was probably truth in it. He had, after all, just come halfway around the world to dig up treasures for people with connections that would keep him out of trouble.

FIFTEEN

The harsh illumination of the work lights bluntly exposed dimension and detail of the oddly shaped antechamber diagramed on Graham's laptop. Three burial chambers branched off the room, one from each wall. Although he was sure only the back room factored into the Master Scroll, curiosity compelled him to look in both side chambers.

He removed a light from the stand, entered the chamber on the left, and found a wraparound bench carved into three sides of the wall. Two long, narrow niches that looked like the mouths of stone ovens were cut into the back wall, and a third was cut into the right, all level with the bench. Graham recognized them as kokhim, where bodies were laid to allow the flesh to rot away.

"Any ossuaries?" Nagi asked, trying to peer into the room from behind, looking for stone boxes the bones would be placed in once they were clean.

"No, but two of the kokhim are wide enough for two bodies, which is interesting. And there are a couple of beer cans."

"Besides," Daniel said sarcastically, "didn't you hear? James's ossuary has already been found."

The infamous bone box had been discovered not far from

where they were, though it had been in the hands of a dealer since the 70s—decades before its existence was made public in an exploitative television documentary. What made it important was an inscription roughly carved into one end of the box: *James, son of Joseph, brother of Jesus.* Even though they were three of the most common names in first-century Palestine, the three of them together made it newsworthy on the remote chance that it was archaeological evidence of Jesus's existence.

But the announcement spawned a controversy around whether the inscription was authentic, especially the last phrase. The IAA claimed *the brother of Jesus* had been forged. And even though a seven-year-long trial found the dealer not guilty, the court added that the acquittal should not be taken to mean the inscription was authentic, only that there was no proof the collector did it.

"I've never understood why the Jews went to so much trouble," Nagi said. "Why not just bury them in the ground?"

"Most of the time they did," Graham said. "Just like now. At least the poor did." He kept talking as he crossed the antechamber to the room on the right. "But if they had the money, they would preserve the bones as a form of respect for the body God had given them, especially since most of them believed in a bodily resurrection on the last day."

"Anything?" Daniel asked as Graham looked in the second room.

"Couple of Stars of David spray-painted on the wall. Otherwise, it's empty. Four kokhim, and two of them are double-wide. Hezir must have had a lot of sons."

Graham entered the back chamber, another cavity with a wraparound bench and several kokhim. A small passage opened from the rear left corner of the chamber. He shimmied across the bench and held the light in front of him.

"It's an acrosolium."

"What's that?" Nagi's questions revealed his knowledge

was almost entirely practical, lacking technical terms.

"It's where a shelf for a body is cut along the wall, like a berth on a train or a tour bus. One on each wall. No kokhim. It's more exclusive since it's not as efficient." Graham slid back into the room. "It's for rich people. Probably what Jesus's tomb in the Holy Sepulcher was, though just one bench is left there now."

Graham looked around the empty chamber wondering where to start.

"I don't know what you think you're going to find," Nagi said skeptically. "If there ever was something worth finding here, it was found a long time ago. There's nowhere to hide anything."

"You're probably right." Graham walked to the portico and grabbed his laptop.

"What's up with this?"

Graham looked up to see Nagi studying an orange metal casing the size of a cashier box bolted to the end of a yellow pole designed to pivot at different angles. A pair of small wheels were attached to the back corners, while larger wheels were mounted to an attachment extending from the front face. A white fiber optic cable ran from the side of the box to a control unit fixed to a harness.

"GPR," Graham said. "Ground-Penetrating Radar."

"You're playing with the big boys now, Nagi." Daniel patted Nagi's shoulder and smiled. "Your metal detector is a toy compared to this. This is real science, not treasure hunting."

Graham smiled at the friendly jibes as he turned back to his laptop and read the text from the fragment.

> *Next to them under the corner of the southern portico at the tomb of Zadok ONE CUBIT under the pillar of the covered hall: vessels of offering of resin and offering of senna.*

Graham walked to the iron railing between the two pillars and looked down at the rock floor. The stone in the area between the northern pillar and the wall was much rougher than the rest of the portico, lacking the smooth art of a master mason. He guessed the scarring and pitting was the byproduct of the demolition of the misplaced bottom steps after the rest of the tomb was completed. Between the two pillars, a slight depression sunk into the floor, about a foot square. Another depression, twice the size, lay between the northern pillar and the wall. He guessed they were artifacts from the process of hewing the tomb from the solid rock.

"Let's take a look at these two areas," Graham said, pointing out the squares. "But first we'll have to take down that railing."

"No problem." Daniel headed for the tools even before he finished replying.

Graham used his phone to take pictures of the area, documenting the site from different angles and distances. By the time he finished, the other two were at work dismantling the railing.

"I'm going to start taking a look at the other location."

He picked up his laptop and read the next location's description, mumbling the words as he walked back into the tomb.

> *Next to them at the REAR OF THE TOMB at the top of the westward-looking rock toward the garden of Zadok TWO CUBITS under the great closing stone which is at the conduit: devoted things.*

He positioned himself at the back wall while keeping a straight line of sight to the portico. After spinning around, he studied the entrance to the acrosolium—literally the rear of the tomb. The scarring around the threshold looked like the best place to investigate. It was where a stone would have been used to seal the opening.

Graham reached for a whisk brush and used it to clear off the area. He stepped back onto the floor, strapped on the harness for the GPR, and turned it on. After positioning the antenna contained in the orange box at one edge of the room, he looked at the monitor. Stratified snow filled the screen, giving no indication of a cavity below. He slowly guided the antenna down the side of the room, then reversed direction, walking slightly offset from his first pass, as if he were mowing the lawn. The visual noise on the screen remained consistent as he moved. No indication of a hollow area in the rock. He focused his concentration as he neared the spot in the room he had marked mentally, but it was broken by Daniel's voice.

"Looks like we got something over here."

"Gotta hit!" Nagi repeated.

"Not a hit. A reflection feature," Daniel said. "Hits are what your toys find."

As he walked to the front of the tomb, Graham unstrapped his harness and set it down. Daniel pushed the GPR several times over the smaller of the depressions he had marked out.

"Did you get a profile from the area around the reflection?"

"Yes, several meters of depth penetration," Daniel answered without looking away from his monitor. "The apex of a reflection hyperbola is right here." He stopped moving the box and nodded. "Do you want to process the data to be sure?"

Graham took the handle of the GPR and repeated Daniel's movements, staring at the feedback on the screen. "There's a reflection there, for sure." He kneeled and moved the antenna out of the way to inspect the stone beneath it.

"I think we have enough to go on without taking the time to process it."

"So what is it?" Nagi asked, looking at the screen. "What are we even looking for, anyway?"

Graham, Daniel, and Yaniv had all decided it was best to keep the Master Scroll a secret—as well as its items—and tell Nagi only what he needed to know when they got to each location.

"This location may have some stone vessels," Graham said. "Possibly incense."

"You mean like from the Jewish Temple?"

"Maybe. We're not sure. We won't know until we find out what's underneath."

"But you think you know already," Nagi said. "And I still don't understand what the big rush is."

Graham ignored the comment as he examined the depression, then traced its lip with his fingers. He looked around and found the tool bag within reach, grabbed a rock pick hammer with a chisel edge on the reverse side, and tapped the lip. Several flakes immediately chipped away.

"Looks like some kind of mortar." He stood up and looked at the others. "My guess is we'll find a seam if we chip the rest of it away. I think this recessed area is some kind of seal."

Daniel stood up, looking out at the portico. "We should put up a tarp as a screen in case anyone gets curious."

Nagi squinted in confusion, following Daniel's gaze across the valley.

"Good idea," Graham said, moving toward another bag of tools. "I'll set a datum point."

He chose the inside corner of the base of the northern pillar as the reference for any measurements he took. He drew a quick diagram on his iPad and took several pictures of the depression with the ruler aligned to one edge of the square.

"All right," Graham said. "It's ready for you guys. Try to find the seams. I'm going to see if I can find anything at the other spot."

He strapped back into the harness and continued his systematic survey of the floor. As he reached the threshold of the chamber, the background noise on the monitor changed. A shape pushed its way into the snow, growing larger as he neared the center of the opening. He scrutinized the signal of reflected energy but wanted to check himself. He continued through into the next chamber and the shape receded. Graham reversed himself and went through the other direction, and again the shape grew.

Daniel's voice came from the front of the tomb. "Find something?"

"Metal!"

SIXTEEN

Graham kneeled down and touched the floor, moving his hand across the stone. The surface was mottled, stained with wear and weather, and smoother than the portico floor, with no obvious seams or depressions to investigate.

"There's definitely something there," Daniel said, staring over Graham's shoulder at the barber pole patterns in the middle of the screen. "Amazing."

"Daniel, can you hand me the pick hammer and the meter scale, please?"

Graham spoke as if in a trance, moving his hands across the boundaries he had detected. The hammer came into his peripheral vision, and he took the handle without focusing on it.

"Thanks." The word was dull with concentration.

He gently tapped near the fingertips of his left hand, which held a point on the perimeter, then tapped either side at various distances. He thought the sound on the outside of the boundary was more solid and grew more hollow on the inside. But it was subtle enough to make him question whether he was simply hearing what he wanted to hear.

He placed the meter scale along the perimeter, then stood to take reference photos of the spot. After he finished, he kneeled over the spot, raised the hammer, and let it fall under its own weight, merely guiding the head.

On the third strike, a crack splintered through the rock. The fourth blow knocked loose a shard of rock, exposing a faint groove.

"Theeere it is…" Graham drew his words out in a combination of relief and anticipation.

"What is it?"

Nagi's raised voice from the portico surprised Graham for a moment, and he realized he almost forgot about the other site in his excitement.

"Mortar. I think we have a seam over here, too."

As Graham used a stone chisel to chip away the seal, Daniel used a can of compressed air to blow away the dust and debris from the groove, progressively revealing a precisely cut, square stone, about two feet on each side.

"That's some nice work," Daniel said, looking at the tight seam with admiration. "If I didn't know there was something underneath, I might think it was just some scoring left from the way they built the place."

"It'll be a trick getting it out," Graham said, pulling the bags of tools closer to see what the options were.

Nagi came from the other site to see the discovery and looked at the seal with the least intimidation of the three. "We can do it."

"He means without breaking it," Daniel said, referring to the damage illegal digs often caused.

Graham placed a handful of jimmy wedges on the face of the stone—flat strips of metal, ten inches long and an inch and half wide, that tapered to a point. He pulled out a crack hammer that looked like a miniature sledge, setting it next to the wedges. Lastly, he extracted a heavy, three-foot-long slate bar.

Slotting the end of a wedge into the seam about a quarter of the distance from one of the corners, Graham then added another the same distance from the other corner. He used the crack hammer to tap them into position, making them stand like stakes in the stone.

"Okay, Daniel, I want you to take the slate bar and try to pry the seal from the middle of the seam. Once you make progress, Nagi and I will hammer the wedges in."

Daniel nodded, reached for the bar, and centered himself over the seam as Nagi grabbed the pick hammer and shifted to a wedge.

"It's going to be hard to get enough leverage to start," Daniel said, setting the tip of the bar into the groove.

Graham lifted the crack hammer. "Use this."

Daniel took the hammer and pounded the angle of the L-shaped bar, forcing the point of the short side into the split. He pounded again, the brittle sound of metal-on-metal reverberating off the stone. He gave the hammer back to Graham, then pulled the top of the bar, putting as much of his weight on it as he could. After several seconds of sustained force without movement, he let up, took a breath, and tried again with no result.

"One more time," Daniel said.

He pulled back on the bar a third time, hanging, making his whole body a counterweight as he bounced, jolting the bar in spurts.

"It moved!" Graham immediately tapped the wedge slightly deeper, prompting Nagi to do the same. "That worked. Keep going!"

Daniel gave the bar another series of bounces that allowed the wedges to go even deeper. One more round raised the stone just enough for Graham and Nagi to add wedges into the seam's sides. They repeated the process until Daniel's bar finally slid the edge of the six-inch-thick stone onto the floor. It took all three of them to push it clear of the hole, which had been carved with a lip that kept the stone from falling inward. The effort reminded Graham of trying to lift the slate bed of his pool table during a move. The iron bar had left a number of bite marks in the edge of the cavity, but the damage was minimal.

They peered into the opening at a bed of palm leaves, dried and brown, but mostly still intact. Graham pulled out his phone, took several pictures, then handed it to Daniel.

"Let's get some video as I uncover this. Nagi, grab some sample bags and a bucket, please."

Daniel waited for Nagi to set the equipment next to Graham. Then he nodded. "Rolling."

Graham gently lifted a stack of palm leaves and sucked in his breath. A hewn, stone jar with the diameter of a large dinner plate was filled to the brim with a mound of silver coins. They were dull with age, catching the light as if being awakened from a 2,000-year-old sleep. He reached for a coin, lifted it up for the camera, then brought it close to his face for inspection. He spoke aloud as he examined it, making verbal notes for the video.

"It's a Hebrew shekel. Obverse contains a cup with an ornamented rim—probably the offering cup of the first fruits— and some writing." He paused as he turned the coin to expose the Hebrew characters to better light. "It reads, 'Shekel of Israel…year 3.'" He flipped the coin over. "Reverse displays a sprig with three branches, probably pomegranates. It says… 'Jerusalem the Holy.'"

Graham replaced the coin and grabbed a handful, sorting through them quickly. "They're all the same. Probably about AD 68."

"How can you tell?" Nagi asked.

Graham glanced up at him, surprised to hear genuine interest in the voice of a looter. "Year 3. Of the Jewish revolt. It started in AD 66, so 68 was the third year." Graham handed a coin to Daniel. "If these really are the 'consecrated things' then this was probably from the Temple treasury." He held a coin flat in his palm for Nagi to get a better look. "The Temple only accepted Jewish money, so when Jews made their offerings they had to convert their Roman currency first. The people who did that are the moneychangers whose tables Jesus overturned in the market."

"Huh," Nagi grunted. "But if it's from the Temple and it's so important, why is it in that rock jar? Why not some gold pot? Or even a fancy clay one?"

"That's a good question. I assume they had so much gold and silver that they had to divide it into as many vessels as they could. But they couldn't put it in a clay pot because it would make the money impure."

"Really?" asked Nagi. "Why?"

"Leviticus, chapter 11, if I remember correctly. It's part of the purity laws. It says clay jars make anything in them unclean. So putting the silver from the treasury in a stone jar makes sense. Or like the jars at the wedding at Cana, where Jesus turned water into wine. Those were for water used in ritual cleansing."

"So many laws." Nagi grimaced. "How could anybody ever keep them all?"

"They can't," Graham said, answering the rhetorical question. "That's what so many of the Temple ceremonies were for—to atone for failing to keep the law." Graham stood up. "The Temple was everything. That's why its treasure was hidden. So it could be rebuilt if the Romans destroyed it. Because without the Temple the Jews believed they couldn't appease God."

"Wait a second." Nagi held up his hand. "You guys are looking for treasure? From the Temple?"

Graham and Daniel exchanged looks.

"Daniel, can you bag the coins and pull up the jar? Nagi and I have some more treasure to find."

SEVENTEEN

The white tarp Daniel had erected to hide their work diffused the light at the front of the tomb, giving the site a softness after the harsh lights and sharp shadows of the first location. A gentle current of air moved through the portico, a welcome break from the dank stillness of the interior rooms. By the time Daniel finished bagging the silver shekels, Graham was chipping away the last of the mortar from the depression. While Graham photographed the second two-foot-square slab, the other two brought the jimmies and slate bar over to the first site.

They repeated the method they'd used earlier, taking up the same positions by rote. As the gap in the seal widened, a thick, pungent odor escaped.

"What is that?" Nagi asked, swatting the air in front of his nose.

"I think it's incense," Graham said. "Let's push this slab off the rest of the way."

The cavity was built like the first, with a lip that held the seal in place. A layer of palm leaves covered the top, again protecting what was beneath like first-century packing material. After documenting the site and handing the camera to Daniel to video, Graham lifted away the leaves.

Four chalkstone jars waited below, completely full, though

not with gold or silver. One vessel was filled with amber pebbles, and another contained reddish brown pellets. A third held what seemed to be fennel seeds, though they were larger. The fourth contained peels of what looked like unrolled cinnamon sticks. Graham reached for one of the peels and smelled it.

"Cinnamon. Or Cassia." He lifted a handful of the amber pebbles. "And this is frankincense. These are the ingredients for incense. This is myrrh and this is spikenard." He touched the brown pebbles, then the seeds as he spoke.

"How do you know it's for incense?"

Again, Graham was impressed by the tone of Nagi's question. "Exodus. When God gave Moses the instructions for the Tabernacle, he also gave him the recipe for the incense he required. These are the four ingredients. They had to be combined in equal amounts, just like you see here. The priests must have kept a store of everything so they would never run out. This has to be from the Second Temple. Except..." Graham left the sentence unfinished as he followed a thought.

"What's wrong?" asked Daniel.

"Well, these are the ingredients for the Tabernacle and the First Temple."

"You mean God changed the recipe?" Nagi asked.

"No. The priests did. By the time of the Second Temple, they were using eleven or even thirteen different ingredients, depending on which historian you read. But these were still the core four. I wonder where—"

A loud popping sound came from the tarp, knocking away the remainder of Graham's sentence.

"Get down! Now!" Daniel barked, forcing instant obedience from Graham and Nagi. "Lie flat and don't move!"

Graham looked at Daniel from the floor and followed his eyes to the tarp. A needle of light threaded through a perfectly round hole in the white plane. Two more poked through, one after the other, making the material pop twice as Graham flinched.

"Gunshots!" Nagi said the word Graham was yelling inside his head. "Why is someone shooting at us?"

"This is Harel. We're under fire!"

Graham watched Daniel speak into his walkie-talkie. A short burst of static was followed by a voice that sounded as if its owner were cupping his hands over his mouth.

"I didn't hear anything from down here."

Another second voice followed. "Nothing up top, either."

"Three shots. Must've come from across the valley. Somewhere on the east wall. Check the cemetery. And scan the Temple Mount."

"Checking now," the second voice responded.

"How could anyone get a gun onto Haram al-Sharif?" Nagi asked softly.

Graham pictured the soldier at Zechariah's tomb looking through binoculars. After a silence that made him wonder if anyone was still there, the voice returned.

"Nothing in the cemetery along the wall."

"Nothing on the top of the wall either," reported the other guard. "Maybe it came from a car as it passed."

"Good thinking. I'll check to see if there are any video cameras on that stretch past the east wall. Keep looking." Daniel put the walkie down and looked across the valley. "That does make sense. If the shots were from a moving car it probably means that accuracy was not their highest priority. It's like whoever did it meant to scare us, not kill us."

Graham remained frozen, as if they were still under fire. "What it means is that someone is watching us. They knew we were here."

"I can understand why someone might try to scare you out of here for the silver," Nagi said. "But I'd gladly give them the incense. That stuff is nasty."

"Let me get some help over here," Daniel said, punching a number into his phone. "We need to get this stuff back to the Rockefeller. There's nothing else to find, right?"

"We hit both places we came to see," Graham nodded. "Why couldn't they just throw rocks into the cave like the Dead Sea Scroll bedouin?"

EIGHTEEN

Although Kidron Valley meant *dark valley*, Graham felt exposed and vulnerable as Daniel negotiated the narrow access road to the gate across from Gethsemane. From his side-view mirror, he watched the olive-green military police jeep escort them, thankful for how quickly they had arrived to protect them as they loaded their finds and gear. It accompanied them all the way back to the museum before peeling off.

Daniel steered through a restricted gate on the corner of the building farthest from the entrance, into a courtyard with a loading dock. Graham deflated with relief as the SUV slowed to a stop parallel to the platform.

Yaniv stepped out from a loading bay and jumped off the dock, hurrying to the car. "Is everyone okay?"

"We're fine," Daniel said without emotion.

"Just another day in East Jerusalem." Nagi shrugged.

"No, we are *not* fine," Graham said pointedly. "You guys might be used to getting shot at, but I am not."

"I understand, Graham," Yaniv said, putting a hand on his shoulder. "But you are safe. Someone was watching over you."

"Yeah, watching through the site on a gun," Graham sniped.

Yaniv ignored the sarcasm and started for the rear of the van. "Come, show me what you have found."

Graham's complaints died away as he watched for Yaniv's reaction. Daniel had pulled away the packing blankets, uncovering the five stone jars and bucket of white sample bags full of shekels. The four jars of incense had been moved so quickly that they still contained their spices.

"That is quite an air freshener you have." Yaniv worked open a sample bag. He held up a shekel, turning it in the sun as he examined it, waiting to speak until it was back in the bag. "This is an amazing discovery," he said, looking at the find, then toward Graham. "You have done some excellent work here. Please, let us go to my office."

Minutes later, Graham dropped into the same chair he'd used the day before and sighed heavily. "I can't do this, Chaim. You need to find someone else. I'm going home."

"Please, Graham," Yaniv said, patting the air as if to calm it. "What you are doing is too important. Your discoveries today are proof."

"In fact," Daniel said, taking a seat, "we are lucky we were shot at." He'd already unloaded the truck and sent Nagi back to the hotel.

"Interesting," Graham said. "I don't *feel* lucky…"

"Daniel is right. Whoever shot at you was only trying to scare you."

"Mission accomplished."

"But do you not see? He gave himself away. Now we know he is there, that he is watching."

Daniel gestured at Yaniv as he looked at Graham. "We can factor that into our plans for the other sites. And we can use it against him."

"How so?" Graham squinted.

"Whoever this guy is—Karanlik, or The Shadow, or whatever—knows we're going to different sites. He probably has a general idea of where the sites will be because he has the same list. What he doesn't know is which one we are going to next.

And the locations on the list are somewhat open to translation. I suggest we close several sites to hide which one we are actually interested in."

"That makes sense," Graham conceded.

Daniel glanced at Yaniv before going on.

"The next site we want to go to is Hezekiah's Tunnel, so that's the one place we *shouldn't* go when we leave the hotel."

"Qumran. Cave 12," Yaniv said, picking up the argument. "He'll think the discovery of the first scrolls in sixty years could be related to what we're looking for."

"Everything will be done out in the open," Daniel said. "We won't try to hide anything. We want him to see us leave the hotel, and we want him to see where we're going. Once we get there, we can become lost among the other workers at the site and change clothes, so he won't recognize us. Then, one at a time, we can get into a different van to come back. That will strand this guy twenty miles away so that we can do our work without him bothering us."

Graham could feel their eyes on him as he stared at the floor, processing the plan. He began to speak several times but pulled his words back before they could make a sound, resulting in a long pause. When he finally found his voice, he was surprised by how calm he sounded.

"Actually, that's a pretty good plan." The words came slowly, and he didn't look up until he finished. "When do you suggest we do it?"

"Tomorrow," Daniel said. "He won't expect us to move that quickly. It'll help keep him off his guard."

"Maybe we should wait until evening to start, like Nagi does," Graham said, warming to the plan. "It seems to give him cover most of the time."

"Yes, but they are working at unknown locations anyway," Yaniv said. "Hezekiah's Tunnel is a popular place to visit for tourists. If there was activity there at night, it would be unusual."

"It would draw attention, not shield us from it," Daniel agreed. "The best cover is daylight."

"Go back to the hotel," Yaniv said. "Rest. You will need to be ready for another long day tomorrow." He stood and escorted them into the hall.

"I think I'm going to walk back," Graham said, moving the opposite direction as Daniel. "Clear my head a bit."

As he drifted through the galleries, his gaze slid across the artifacts, feeling an affinity with the archaeologists who had preserved the history on display. He reached the Tower Room, just inside the entrance and was struck by the exhibit, wondering if it was providence or his subconscious that had guided him here.

Replicas of reliefs he'd seen at the British Museum covered the walls just as they had in the palace of Sennacherib, king of Assyria. He glanced at the museum label, reminding himself of when the excavation of Nineveh had taken place. 1847. The beginning of the Golden Age of archaeology. The discovery was only one of many important finds in Iraq, and it saddened Graham that the current political situation made further discoveries impossible.

The reliefs depicted the sacking of Lachish, thirty-five miles from Jerusalem. The siege was recorded in 2 Kings 18 and 2 Chronicles 32. Sennacherib extorted eleven tons of silver and one ton of gold from Hezekiah, promising the safety of Jerusalem in exchange—an amount that required stripping the gold overlay from the doors of the Temple to pay. However, Sennacherib acted in bad faith and attacked Jerusalem despite the ransom, but not before sending a spokesman to Jerusalem to deliver a message. *No god of any nation or kingdom has been able to rescue his people from my power or the power of my fathers. How much less will your God rescue you from my power!*

What Sennacherib didn't know was that Hezekiah had been preparing for the siege. Below the spot where the envoy delivered the warning, Hezekiah had dug a tunnel to connect Jerusalem's primary water supply, the Gihon Spring, to a pool within the city walls. Sennacherib boasted that Hezekiah was trapped like a bird in a cage, but in the end, the siege failed.

Now Graham was preparing to go into the tunnel that had brought Jerusalem salvation, hoping that he was as prepared for his enemy as Hezekiah had been for Sennacherib."

NINETEEN

A cemetery of tombs built above the ground surrounded Graham like altars awaiting offerings. They ribbed the ground to the edge of the bluff as if delineating the boundaries of death. The valley on the other side separated the cemetery from the Temple Mount, and Graham gravitated toward it. Just beyond the last tomb, he found stairs hewn from the rock and he descended soundlessly into the darkness.

An iron gate built across the bottom step hung from its hinges unlatched, cantilevered above the floor four feet below. Graham dropped the rest of the way into the cave and found himself standing in the portico of the tomb of B'nei Hezir. The gate to the lower stairs stood in front of him, locked. He turned back again and saw that the gate he had just come through had closed and locked without a sound—an observation that left him strangely unconcerned.

He moved across the portico and through the antechamber to the rear of the tomb. As he crossed the threshold, he looked down to where the treasure had been buried and saw no evidence that it had been excavated. He wondered vaguely how he could see perfectly without any work lights while he hunched into the burial chamber at the back of the room.

Then he saw them.

At first, they were nothing more than different shades of shad-

ow. But something drew his eyes to the kokh on the far side of the room, to the mouth of a double-wide niche.

Two bodies lay side-by-side on the slab, each enshrouded in its own sheet of linen. And one form was so small that it could only be a child. He froze, the sight making him as still as the bodies he stared at.

Until one of them moved.

Cold fear blanketed him, and Graham abstractly wondered if his motionlessness had somehow been part of a transaction that took the life from him and instilled it into the corpses.

He watched the larger sheet ripple as a hand beneath it fisted the material and began to pull it down. As it moved, the second sheet began to do the same. Graham remained inanimate, somehow becoming more calm on the outside as he became more panicked on the inside.

But before the faces were unveiled, he already knew who they belonged to.

"Olivia! Alyson!"

Their faces—more serene than he'd ever seen them in life—turned to him. They reached their arms out of the tomb, trying to grasp him, craning their necks to see him better. Graham reflexively mirrored the gesture, but the more he stretched out his arms, the farther away he became from them, pulled backward without moving. Pulled into blackness. Until they were gone.

TWENTY

Graham awoke with a violent gasp, as if he hadn't taken a breath since lying down. He hated these dreams, and sometimes dreaded sleep. He wanted to see his family again more than anything in the world, but the dreams were often so real that—in a small way—he experienced their loss all over again.

"Alyson…" He whispered her name, knowing there would be no reply. But somehow saying her name was the closest thing he knew to touching her ever since the cancer had robbed him of her. The doctor called it Juvenile Myelomonocytic Leukemia. Alyson had been only three when it was discovered.

Graham sometimes thought of the time she asked who Jim was, and why Jim was trying to hurt her. She had overheard her parents talking about JMML, the abbreviation the doctor had used. He only had five years with Aly, and two were spent watching her waste away until she was gone. It was almost a year since she'd died, and her absence was so profound that it had perversely created a presence, like a shadow that cast itself over most of his thoughts each day.

He looked at the clock—1:10 a.m.—and closed his eyes. He knew it would be futile to try to go to sleep. Instead of trying, he sat up against his pillow, pulled the laptop from his bedside table, and completed his notes from the dig at B'nei

Hezir.

He was surprised he had spent the whole day in a tomb without connecting it to death, let alone Olivia and Aly. But the association had obviously not been lost on his subconscious. There had been days—weeks, even—when he would have welcomed his own death, either joining them in the afterlife or ending his torture in oblivion. He didn't want the memory of that dark place to be his last thought before sleep and decided to distract himself by reviewing his research on Hezekiah's Tunnel.

The diagram of the tunnels connected to the Gihon Spring included a legend indicating the extensive excavations done over the last fifteen years. Two Canaanite era tunnels left the spring cave, the first to the southeast, and the second due south. Hezekiah's Tunnel—known as Tunnel 8—exited the spring cave to the west and meandered southwest to the tip of the City of David.

One of the most significant discoveries from the recent digs was an enormous rock-cut pool. It was situated between the second Canaanite channel and Hezekiah's Tunnel and connected to each. A passage that descended from within the ancient walls of the City of David added a final tunnel to the web, but it was the one shaft Graham had excluded as a possibility based on the clue.

> In the canal which goes FROM GIHON when you enter ON THE LEFT 41 cubits: 55 talents of silver.

When Graham first read the text, he assumed it led to a place in Hezekiah's Tunnel. But the diagram revealed it could just as easily refer to Channel 2, or even Tunnels 3 or 4—the connecting passages to the rock-cut pool. In that case, the location might be in or near the ruins of a house built on the site after the pool fell into disuse. Another possibility was that the start point might be the beginning of Hezekiah's Tunnel rather than the spring source.

Graham didn't think there was any place to hide treasure, especially since the debris and fill in the abandoned reservoir had been cleaned out so recently. Then he reminded himself of the shekels and incense they had recovered the day before after 2,000 years of hiding just inches away from countless visitors. Plus, he had instructions for where to look.

His eyes burned, losing focus, signaling that he couldn't resist sleep much longer. The adrenaline of the dream had worn off. He set the laptop back in its place on the bedside table, and before the display put itself to sleep, Graham was out, this time welcoming the darkness that pulled him under.

TWENTY-ONE

"*Digging in the Dirt*" burst from Graham's phone, abruptly ending the little rest he had been able to salvage. The clock displayed 5:14 a.m., but his annoyance evaporated with the realization that the alarm would have gone off in one minute anyway. He looked at the phone for a moment, wondering if he should answer. Usually, he let *No Caller ID* calls roll to voicemail, but nothing about his life was usual right now.

"Hello?" Graham said hoarsely.

"Graham, my friend, it is Maalik. I am very glad to hear your voice." Maalik's anxious words sounded anything but relieved.

"Maalik? What's wrong?" Graham sat up on the edge of the bed.

"Danger is following you. You must be careful."

"Maalik, please, slow down and tell me what happened."

"Someone called to ask about cartonnage. Just as you said. But he was very specific. He only wanted cartonnage from the same find as the mummy mask I sold to Dr. Singer."

"What did you tell him?"

"I said I wish I *did* have more. I could make a fortune!"

Graham waited for Maalik's laugh, but none came. "Was his name Karanlik?"

"He left no name. But I think he may be near you."

"What makes you say that?"

"I could hear the call to prayer in the background. I noticed because it wasn't time for prayer here for another hour."

"Which means he might be here, in Jerusalem." Graham pictured the shots penetrating the tarp at B'nei Hezir.

"He called the day after you came to see me. I would have called sooner, but I left town myself. On business. I had just hung up the phone and was about to call you when it rang again. And this time it was the police. They told me someone had broken into my showroom."

"Maalik, I'm so sorry." Graham knew that the list of possible suspects would be long—including the Egyptian government itself—but he felt certain he could narrow it down to whoever was after the treasure. "What was taken?"

"That is the great mystery. Nothing. The shop had obviously been searched—even the safe was open—but nothing was missing. I have security video of the whole thing. Whatever he was looking for, he did not find it."

"What did the guy look like?" Graham asked, recalling the image of Karanlik that Bremmer had sent.

"Young, but not like a student. Well-dressed. He tried to keep his face turned from the camera, but what I could see looked like that comedian. Sacha Baron Cohen."

"Or Freddie Mercury?"

"Yes! Of course! But how did you know?"

"Is there any way you could email me a screenshot from the video?" Graham wanted to get it to Bremmer at the FBI as soon as possible.

"Certainly, my friend. I hope it can help you. But there is more to tell you. After I left the shop, I went back to my place in the souk. I don't have any security camera there. The door was open, and it had been searched as well. Things everywhere. Quite a mess. More than normal. But they did not discover the place where I keep certain special items.

And even if they had, they would have been disappointed if they were after more cartonnage from the same place as the mask. Someone knows we have spoken. And with the police involved, I could not take the chance they would be listening to my calls. This is a prepaid phone. I am just now able to feel safe enough to call you and let you know."

"I am so sorry to have gotten you involved in this, Maalik. I know it's hard enough for you right now. Please let me know if there is anything I can do for you."

"Please do not start singing James Taylor to me."

"Actually, *You've Got a Friend* was written by Carole King."

"Ha! I always forget. You got me on that one. Keep yourself safe, my friend."

Graham texted Daniel that he was running late, then took a quick shower to clear his head and think before executing the next phase of the plan. Five minutes later Maalik's email with the screenshot appeared in his inbox. He copied it into a text message and sent it to Bremmer with an explanation of what had happened to Maalik.

Next, he called Yaniv and—after apologizing for the early hour—repeated Maalik's story.

Yaniv listened without comment until Graham finished. "Are you having second thoughts again about going through with this?"

"No. If anything I'm more committed now. I can't let people get hurt because of me and not do anything about it. Plus—as you said—this is too important. I want to end this, and I want to find the treasure—if there is any more to find."

"I am very glad to hear you say it. I have closed all the sites we talked about yesterday. They are expecting you at Qumran. And I have stationed guards at both entrances to the Gihon Spring, as well as the exit at the Pool of Siloam."

"Excellent. Thank you, Chaim." Graham was about to

end the call when a question stopped him. "Do you know if any silver was discovered in the latest excavations at Gihon?" The question of how so much wealth could be hidden in Hezekiah's Tunnel without being discovered bothered him, making the premise of the expedition suspect.

"Off the top of my head, I do not think so, but let me check. Hold on."

Graham could hear the soft taps of a computer keyboard conjuring up information.

"About 200 bullae and Egyptian scarabs, and 10,000 fish bones. But no silver. In fact, there were no coins of any kind. Does that help you?"

"I'm not sure. Thanks for checking. Got to go meet the others and get going."

"*Yasher koach*," Yaniv said, wishing him strength.

"Thanks. I'm going to need it."

TWENTY-TWO

Daniel and Nagi waited on the steps outside the front door in a cloud of Daniel's latest failed attempt to quit smoking. Daniel handed Graham a bagel wrapped in foil and a Diet Coke.

"Sorry about the late start."

"What's going on?" Daniel gave him a searching look.

Graham wasn't sure how to answer around Nagi. "Let's get on the road. I've kept us long enough."

It took an hour to cover the thirty miles between Jerusalem and the shore of the Dead Sea. Halfway there, Graham looked back to see Nagi lying across the bench asleep, made doubly oblivious by a pair of earbuds. He kept his voice low while he told Daniel about his early morning phone calls. As he finished, Daniel turned the van off the road, onto an unmarked trail that led to the site of Cave 12, where the Dead Sea Scrolls had broken their sixty-year silence.

The rugged cliffs of the area were pocked with caves, and Cave 12—like its eleven cousins—gaped anonymously among them. A cluster of three vans and a truck marked the end of the road, and Daniel added their van to the others. The rest of the journey would have to be taken on foot.

They slung on backpacks containing the clothes they would change into and set out on the half-mile hike that took them midway up the slope. Although the main work at the site had been completed, it was still being studied, and they found a crew of nine people outside the entrance to the cave.

After the site leader introduced himself, Graham crouched down to look into the mouth of the chamber. The opening was surprisingly small, and he wondered how many other holes in this porous region held secrets waiting to be told. He took his backpack off, then crawled inside, pulling the bag behind him.

The cramped space and floor covered with scree made it difficult to change his shirt and pants, but he emerged a few minutes later, his altered appearance augmented by the addition of a scarf and an orange hardhat with a headlamp. Different enough—he hoped—to throw off anyone who might be watching from a distance. If Daniel's plan worked and they were being surveilled, they wanted to create the illusion they were still in the cave, that other workers were leaving. That would give them time to reach their real destination without being followed.

Nagi and Daniel underwent similar transformations, and began the hike back to the vans, accompanied by the site leader and one other person to disguise their number. Once they were at the lot, the leader swapped keys with Daniel, pulled a couple of empty backpacks from the van to make it look like he was retrieving some equipment, and sent the others on their way in a different van than they had arrived in.

"Think it worked?" Graham couldn't help feeling exposed again as they crossed the desert wilderness.

"No idea," Daniel said. "But at least we'd be able to easily spot anyone following us out here."

An hour later, Daniel drove up the Kidron Valley until the road came to a dead end at the old entrance to the Gihon Spring. This had been the main access to Hezekiah's Tunnel until a few years earlier, when the visitor's center in the City of David—at the top of the slope, just south of the

Temple Mount—reopened the original access to the spring. Now tourists walked to the spring using the same tunnel the ancient citizens of Jerusalem had used. From there, they had the option of walking through Hezekiah's Tunnel itself, to the Pool of Siloam.

The blocky spring house stood completely unmarked, strangely anonymous amidst the surrounding homes given the historic significance of the site. Daniel worked the van around cars parked on the street, then through the opening into the small lot, and backed into a space near the door. Graham noticed a black cat napping on top of a small structure of abandoned scaffolding. A low, graffiti-tagged wall fenced a flight of steps that descended steeply into a peaked arch twenty feet below the surface. At the bottom, an iron gate closed the passage, and a soldier stood in its shade, making it look like an ancient dungeon.

Daniel skipped down the steps, identified himself to the guard, then jogged back to the surface as the soldier unlocked the gate.

"Let's get the gear inside as quickly as possible," Daniel said in an urgent rasp. "I don't like being out here where we can be seen."

He opened the back door of the van, pulled out the closest two bags, and trotted down the stairs again, this time entering the spring house. Graham grabbed his laptop bag and a duffel and followed Daniel, nodding to the guard and exchanging *shaloms* as he passed.

Daniel waited on an irregularly shaped landing at the bottom of the steps, inside the gate, and Graham and Nagi set their equipment down next to his. The pointed arch of the passage continued to the ceiling into the cave, creating a vault that protected access to the spring when it was still being used for drinking water. Directly in front of him, a narrow, ancient stairway dropped another fifteen feet or so along the right wall of the landing. An iron railing had been artlessly bolted into the rock floor along the ledge on the left side of the stairs. A stone trash can and a white plastic patio chair sat against the left wall, crowded next to a second iron gate that stood open in the corner.

"That's new." Graham stuck his head through the threshold but didn't step through it.

"That leads to the observation platforms in the pool, and to the towers that were discovered," Daniel said. "From there, Warren's Shaft system leads all the way to the original entrance at the top of the hill."

"That's a long walk for water," Nagi said, staring at the surroundings. "Makes you wonder how they even found the spring in the first place."

Graham smiled to himself. Nagi's curiosity reminded him of his students, and he wished opportunity and education could have put Nagi's natural abilities to a more honorable use.

Daniel moved past Nagi, patting him on the shoulder. "Come on. Let's get the rest of the gear while he sorts out what to do next."

As the others brought the rest of the gear, Graham walked to the edge of the stairs, pulled his iPad out of his bag, and studied an image with two diagrams—one, a top view of the paths of the tunnels, the other a cross section. The sound of the spring reverberating off the walls of the chamber gave the air a watery shimmer, and Graham knew they must be near the source.

"That's all of it," Daniel said, setting down the last of the tools. "Now what?"

"Well, there's a couple of possibilities," Graham said. "But let's leave everything here while we look around and figure out where to focus our attention."

Daniel handed a flashlight to Graham and kept one for

himself, using it to gesture to the steps. "Lead the way."

Graham took one step down and stopped, reading the warning sign on a ledge above the stairs forbidding candles, children under five, baby carriers, pregnant women.

"Either of you guys claustrothobic?"

"You mean claustro*phobic*?" Daniel smiled cautiously.

"No. Claustro*thobic*. Says it right here." Graham pointed to a misspelling in one of the bullet points and read it aloud. "The entrance is forbidden to those who are claustrothobic."

"Good thing none of us are wearing thobes," Daniel said, referring to the traditional Arab tunic.

"Nice," Graham deadpanned.

"Or maybe it's a fear of dragons." Nagi's comment turned the other two around. "What? Don't you know where we are?"

"What are you talking about, Nagi?" Graham asked, unable to tell if Nagi was joking or not.

"A dragon lives in the cave where the water comes out of the ground. Whenever it's awake, the water stops. And when it falls asleep, the water overflows and goes into the tunnel."

Daniel looked at Graham, eyebrow raised, but Graham was smiling at Nagi.

Nagi shrugged. "Arab myth."

"There's a story like that about this place in the New Testament, too," Graham said. "The other end of this tunnel feeds the water into the Pool of Siloam. In Jesus's day, people used to go there who were sick or lame. They went to wait by the water because they believed every once in a while an angel would stir it, and the first person to touch it after that would be healed."

"Maybe the angel and the dragon ran each other off," Daniel said.

"Actually," Graham motioned down the stairs, "the spring ran them both off. There was probably a kind of natural siphon created by the passage that the water followed through the rocks. It made the flow of water intermittent, and that made it look like the pool rippled on its own every once in a while. Sometimes the water even dried up long enough for the level in the pool to visibly drop. But at some point in the last 150 years or so, the rocks shifted and now the flow is steady. No more angels to heal us, or dragons to attack us."

"Great," Daniel said. "Now all we have to worry about is snipers."

TWENTY-THREE

"Let's start from the spring and see where each possible tunnel leads us," Graham said. "Nagi, keep an eye out for anything that looks interesting to you. You may see something we miss."

Graham descended the ancient steps cut into the stone, which were well-lit by a permanently mounted work light. Halfway down the twenty-foot-long passageway, an iron gate hung open across the entrance to Channel 2. A sign mounted above it showed an arrow pointing left, and a label identifying it as the Canaanite Tunnel. Graham glanced into the channel without stopping. The top part of the sign pointed ahead to Hezekiah's Tunnel, and after ten more feet he came to the cave where the water poured out of the rock. A heavy grate spanned most of the surface above the water, bridging the way to a rectangular exit cut into the wall fifteen feet away. All three crowded into the cave and looked into the shallow water that sounded like a bath being drawn.

"The Gihon Spring is our start point," Graham explained, raising his voice above the sound of the water. "The spot we're looking for is about sixty feet from here."

"Where are you guys getting this stuff from?" Nagi knitted his brow as he looked from Daniel to Graham.

"You wouldn't believe me if I told you."

"That's the truth." Daniel snorted.

Graham pointed to the rectangular exit. "That's the start of Tunnel 4, and it funnels the water into Hezekiah's Tunnel, so that's where we'll measure from. Who's got the—"

Before Graham finished speaking, Daniel pulled out a reel coiled with 100 feet of engineer's measuring tape that had been clipped to his belt. "Here."

Graham took the reel, wedged the end into one of the hinges of the gate, then stepped through the exit and into the tunnel. An opening that Graham identified as Tunnel 8—Hezekiah's Tunnel—appeared on their left after about thirty feet.

He continued down the rectangular tunnel—just barely wider than his shoulders, and only a few inches taller than he was—feeding the tape until the ruler displayed the sixty-foot hash mark, then stopped to investigate the spot. Water rose almost to their knees, the current gently pushing against them. The rock was smooth, without a single niche, not even one small enough for one of the tiny oil lamps so common in the antiquities shops.

"Nowhere here to hide anything. Let's try again." Graham took a step in the direction they had just come from, shepherding the other two back toward the cave. But as they took an unusually sharp turn created by the start of Hezekiah's Tunnel, Graham stopped. "Actually, let's measure from here, just in case, since this is where Tunnel 8 starts. Maybe everything from here to the spring doesn't count since it's really more of a connecting channel." He didn't sound convinced by his own reasoning, but the others followed his lead.

After measuring from the new spot, they again found themselves at a location with no place to conceal even a few coins and walked back upstream to the spring cave.

The third time, Graham took a route that turned into Tunnel 4, and they were immediately encouraged by the presence of several niches and cavities in the wall. But after scouring the area around the right distance, they found no obvious places to explore.

"Best place so far," Daniel said. "We should come back here if we don't find anything anywhere else."

"Sounds like a plan," Graham responded flatly and headed back to the spring for the next attempt. Once they were back on the grate above the water, he repeated the clue by heart.

> *In the canal which goes FROM GIHON when*
> *you enter ON THE LEFT 41 cubits.*

"The canal that originally carried the water from here is back up the stairs." Graham pointed to the bottom of the steps with a sideways tilt of his head. "And it was on the left as we came in, which is the entrance that was used when the scroll was written."

"Scroll?" Nagi arched his brow. "You really did find a treasure map, didn't you?"

Graham answered with a knowing smile, but he left the question unanswered as he handed Nagi the end of the tape measure. "Here. Hold it on the bottom step."

He climbed up six steps and turned into Channel 2. It had been built 800 years before King David was born and was probably the route David and his men used to attack Jerusalem and capture it from the Jebusites, an event recorded in 2 Samuel 5. It was a jagged route, part natural fissure and part gashed into the rock without the skill that had hewn Hezekiah's Tunnel. When the tape showed thirty feet, another tunnel opened to the right. Graham recalled it as Tunnel 3, the passage that led to the underground reservoir. He continued another thirty feet and again found himself with nowhere to dig.

"Anything?" Nagi's voice followed them down the channel.

"It's a bust," Daniel yelled back. "Just like the first spot."

"Stay there," Graham said. "I'm going to try Tunnel 3."

Daniel took the cue and led the way back to the offshoot, halfway back on the left. He stepped past it to allow Graham to go first and nodded to him. "After you."

Thirty feet in, Graham stepped into a chamber with no ceiling, and he knew he was standing in the lower part of the recently discovered pool. It was a rounded area about the size of a small private swimming pool and dropped like a diving well from the floor of a much larger rectangular pool, carved out of the rock, more than fifty feet wide and thirty feet long.

Another opening in the lower pool cut into the wall to their right—which Graham knew was the other end of Tunnel 4—and led to the spot they had marked to return to if nothing else looked more promising. Forty feet above Graham, a walkway entered the pool from the foundation of the tower. Over 2,500 years ago, a wooden platform had extended out over the pool, and people lowered their buckets into the water from there. Now a series of modern platforms connected by stairs descended in levels to the floor of the upper pool.

Graham looked for the remains of the house that had been discovered there, but the side of the lower pool was too tall to climb, let alone see over.

"Go get Nagi and start bringing the gear down. And see if you can find a ladder anywhere around here."

"I have a better idea." Daniel pointed to the lowest platforms. "We can go in through the new exit, onto the walkway, and climb over. I think there may even be a ladder built into the frame."

Graham followed Daniel back down the tunnel to the pile of equipment. They each grabbed a GPR antenna and harness while Nagi carried Graham's backpack and a duffel of tools. The other side of the newer gate stepped down onto a small metal grate landing that fed down three more steps to the right before entering the upper part of the Canaanite reservoir.

A sleek, modern wooden walkway framed in glass and industrial metal beams gave Graham a much better perspective of the pool than he had had a few minutes earlier. He was glad to see aesthetics had entered the minds of those who restored it, rather than the brute functionality that had so often informed the preservation of earlier sites. It created an overlook for the lower pool, while looking up gave him a true appreciation for the enormous space.

After observing the view, he stepped onto the next highest platform and found part of it had a thick glass floor, allowing him to look directly into the ruins of the stone house that had been discovered there. Although it was an interesting way to view the site, Graham felt like he was levitating through someone's home, a ghost from the present haunting the past. He walked to the edge of the platform and leaned over the low glass wall, looking for the easiest way to access the floor below.

"Over here," Daniel said.

Graham saw that Daniel had stopped above a ladder built into the metal structure. He set his gear down next to Daniel, slung his legs over the glass barrier, and descended the ladder. Daniel handed him the GPR units before joining him. Graham strapped on his harness, connected the cables, then scanned the floor of the pool.

The ground was strewn with rocks, scattered by time, the slow collapse of the house, and the excavation. He noted several places to search, but none of them made him hopeful.

Daniel turned in place as he surveyed the ground. "Where do you want to start?"

"Not sure. But I doubt we'll find anything."

"I thought the same thing yesterday," Daniel said. "And

yet we found niches in what looked like a completely empty tomb."

"You're right"—Graham nodded—"but this time we're looking for a lot more silver."

"Silver?" Nagi leaned over the glass wall. "As in shekels again? How much are we talking about?"

"Fifty-five talents."

"Which is…?"

"Depends on which scholar you ask. But it's at least a thousand pounds." Graham looked back at the pool trying to envision how much space it would take to contain so many shekels. "Maybe as much as 4,000."

"Four. Thousand?" Nagi paused between the words for emphasis. "But where would they put it all? And even if it had been here, they would've found it during the excavations."

"I thought the same thing, Nagi. But we need to check it out anyway." Graham looked around the pool, trying to manufacture optimism from the success of the day before. "If it's in jars like we found yesterday, then we're looking for at least ten of them."

Graham took the area near the house, while Daniel went to the opposite end of the chamber. Nagi moved rocks out of the way for the antenna, alternating locations.

After fifteen minutes, Graham stopped. "Nagi, could you grab the other GPR, please? That's the cart-looking thing with the bigger orange box."

"Sure thing."

Daniel walked over to Graham and took off his harness. "Think there's some cavity that's deep enough to need the bigger antenna?"

"It's possible." Graham shrugged. "Or maybe another chamber with an access that hasn't been discovered yet. I doubt the team that cleared this place out was looking for any hidden cavities, so it's worth a shot. If there is something here, we'll have a better chance of finding it even if we can't dig for it today."

Nagi reentered the pool carrying a frame that looked like the handle of a lawnmower. Two large wheels were mounted on either side of one end near a control unit. The other end held an orange metal box—an antenna twice the size of the one they had been using. He gently handed it down to Daniel, who unfolded the extension holding the wheels into a frame resembling a figure *4* set on its angle, making it look like a modified wheelchair without the seat. Graham checked the cables running from the antenna at the front to the control unit near the handle at the back.

Before switching it on, he maneuvered it to the spot where he had searched with the other GPR. Daniel and Nagi watched as Graham began pushing the antenna, studying the monitor. He began his switchback pattern as Nagi and Daniel again cleared rocks out of the way to make room for the work. Graham had covered half of the room before the silence broke.

"Do you really think there might be—" Nagi's voice suddenly disappeared.

Along with the light, filling the pool with inky blackness.

TWENTY-FOUR

While the instantly dark room blinded Daniel and Nagi, Graham's monitor almost blinded him with light, making him squint and look away from what was now the only light source in the room.

"Everybody okay?" Daniel's unflappable voice sounded reassuring, accustomed to the unexpected.

"I'm good," Graham said.

He detached the harness and turned the monitor to illuminate the area directly in front of him, softly lighting all three faces.

"Looks like something blew," Graham said it more as a preface than an observation. "Didn't think the GPR pulled enough juice to pop the circuit."

"Me either," Daniel said. "Nagi, you're closest to the ladder. Think you can get back to the entrance and find the breaker box? The guard might be able to help you."

"I can try."

"Do you still have your flashlight?"

"I left it at the entrance when we brought the gear down here since it had lights."

"I did the same," Graham said. "Here, take this." He offered the harness to Nagi and unplugged the antenna.

Nagi held it screen outward and moved to the ladder. He

lifted it to the platform, climbed up to it, and picked it up again. Graham and Daniel watched Nagi's silhouette as the electric bloom floated through the pool, up the steps, and out of the chamber.

"See anything?" Daniel called up to Nagi almost immediately after the light turned the corner, his voice seemingly amplified by the absolute darkness.

As if in response, a clatter of thin metal and plastic dropped onto stone sliced through the black.

"You okay, Nagi?" Graham stood completely still.

The silence that followed the fall was broken by footsteps descending the metal stairs into the pool.

"Nagi, is everything all right?" Graham asked again more urgently.

But the only response was more footsteps crossing the platform. Graham listened to them coming closer and thought they sounded too sure, too purposeful for someone walking blindly. The nearer they came, the more he grew convinced it wasn't Nagi.

"Who are you?" Daniel commanded the void, apparently arriving at the same conclusion.

The steps immediately stopped, and Graham pivoted to face the spot.

"This is a closed site. Identify yourself." Daniel spoke as if he had the advantage over the unseen visitor.

In response, a click cracked the air, immediately followed by the pop of compressed air. Graham placed the sound on the platform, close but out of reach.

Less than a second later, a grunt of surprise pushed its way out of Daniel, and Graham heard him stagger as if crushed under a weight.

"Dart!" Daniel said, the word barely more than a burst of air. A gasp punctuated the word, then let loose two more. "Tranq gun!"

Graham heard Daniel's body fall just feet away and realized that whatever he had just imagined happening was about to happen to him as well. He crouched down in a panic, feeling the ground as if it contained a clue about where to go. He extended a leg backward, felt the edge of the lower pool with his toe, and immediately improvised a plan. If he could slide over the edge into the lower pool, he could escape through one of the tunnels.

Another crack in the air shattered the plan, this time followed by a stinging sensation on his left shoulder. He reached for the dart planted in his body, but by the time he pulled it out, it was too late. The hole it created allowed the blackness of the pool to pour in like liquid night. He felt himself beginning to swirl as the dark cold of tranquilizers wrapped around him, then began subtracting him, until he was gone.

TWENTY-FIVE

The sound of rushing water greeted Graham as he awoke, as if it had eroded his unconsciousness, leaving him entangled in contradictions. He opened his eyes, but he couldn't see anything; he heard the rapid water inches from his face, but he wasn't wet; he heard the sound bounce off of the rock walls of a small cave, but he felt metal. He tried to push himself into a sitting position, discovering that his hands couldn't move. Plastic ties threaded through a metal grate and around each wrist, just enough binding to restrain him. He pulled against them twice, but his body was still shaking off the induced sleep and felt weak. But at least he knew where he was: the Gihon Spring.

The realization made him look around the space even though he knew it would be useless, and he imposed his memory on it, envisioned it as if it were full of light. As he scooted himself around, he felt his feet touch something else on the walkway, and it occurred to him that he might not be alone.

"Daniel...Nagi..." His voice was thick with the dregs of the tranquilizer, and it was lost in the water's constant purl. He tried again, louder, but—at the same time—tried not to attract the attention of his assailant if he was still close by. After getting no response, he tried once more, this time jostling the body with his foot at the same time.

"Wake up!"

Hours of seconds passed with no sign of life. He shook the body again, this time more forcefully, and knocked loose a groggy groan too low pitched to be Nagi's.

"Daniel!"

A boom thundered into the cave, interrupting Graham with the hollow sound of something heavy dropped onto a sheet of wood. Several blows from an unseen hammer striking metal drove spikes of sound into the blackness, making him fully alert.

Graham strained the silence for more clues, trying to understand what was happening. But the next sound he heard came from inside the cave.

"Graham. That you?"

"Daniel. Good to hear your voice."

"What was that?"

"I'm not sure, but I think the entrance to the spring cave just got blocked off."

"Great. Where's Nagi?"

"I don't know. I assume he's around here, but he's not awake and I can't feel him with my feet."

Graham heard Daniel move, material sweeping across the grate. "I think I just found him, but he's still out. The good news is that I still have my knife. I can feel it strapped to my shin."

"Good man. Cut us out of here."

"Gimme a second. Have to curl myself up to reach it."

Graham heard Daniel grunt with effort as he contorted himself, then heard a sigh of relief.

"Got it?"

Darkness scattered in a narrow cone of light spreading from Daniel's hand to land against the wall of the cave. It moved awkwardly across the water, onto the walkway, stopping on Graham's face. The beam started waving wildly as Daniel's wrists twisted. In the ambient light, Graham spotted a small black stick that looked like a magic marker glowing from one end.

"Where did that come from?"

"I slipped it in the sheath with my knife," Daniel said. "I was lifting my ankle up to my hand to grab it when the dart hit me. It's actually a Kubotan."

"What's that?"

"A weapon. One of the ends has a point. Not very sharp, but enough to do harm. And it's a pen, too. The cap is the light. Disguises it," Daniel explained as he adjusted the angle of the beam to see the plastic ties. "I need to put this down to get the knife, but I don't want it to fall through the grid. Put your foot on top of it to hold it steady."

Graham did as he was told, and this time could see Daniel bring his ankle up to his chest and pull the knife out of a sheath wrapped around his calf.

"Israeli Army knife," Daniel said. "Kept a few things when I left the service."

After trying several different angles, Daniel found one that gave him the leverage to saw through the tie while keeping the risk of cutting himself to a minimum. Graham watched Daniel free himself, then step around Graham, slip the blade under the band of thick white plastic, and quickly pull up, slicing it easily.

"Thanks. I owe you one."

"Actually, that's two. If you count yesterday. And we're not out of this one yet." Daniel scanned the walkway with the flashlight as he talked, locating Nagi near the alcove that served as the entrance to the cave. His body lay facedown, unnaturally twisted, looking lifeless.

"Nagi!" The name escaped Graham reflexively. "Is he alive?"

Graham wanted to get closer to him, to try to shake him awake, but Daniel was between them.

"He's breathing. It's shallow, though. He must've gotten it worse than we did." He maneuvered to Nagi's wrists, which were bound to the grid just as theirs had been. "Shine that light over here so I can cut him loose."

A few seconds later, Nagi's hands were unbound, but stayed where they had been tied.

Now that they were free, Graham pointed the penlight past Nagi, to the entrance of the cave. A thick sheet of plywood blocked the passage that led up to the landing of the old entrance. The bottom edge was wedged between the first and second steps, and the top corners had splintered away as it was forced into the irregular arch of the ceiling. The rude seal looked fairly insubstantial, nothing more than an inconvenient hindrance that could be removed. But its mere presence rattled Graham with a fear he struggled to suppress.

"What about the other side?" Daniel's practical tone gave Graham a sense of assurance that this problem had a solution.

The exit of the spring was barred by an old gate, padlocked shut to a latch bolted into the rock wall. Graham rattled the door, creating a metallic staccato that confirmed its sturdiness.

"Surely the guard will see that barricade and know something is wrong," Graham said.

"My guess is they tranq'd the guards as well. No way they could trap us in or even get to us without taking out the guards first." Daniel pressed a hand against the plywood and patted it. "The question is how sturdy this thing is."

After dragging Nagi to the other side of the grate, Daniel moved back to the plywood. He stretched his arms across the entrance, bracing himself, then unleashed a powerful kick against the board, just below the center.

"You look like Samson pushing the pillars of the Philistine

temple," Graham joked feebly.

Daniel rocked himself back to kick again, then sent his leg into the wood like a battering ram. "I feel more like Samson with his hair cut off. This thing is not moving. It must be braced on the other side somehow."

As if he doubted his own words, he kicked again with a ferocity that was the first sign of frustration Graham had noticed. Daniel turned back to the cave and leaned his forearms against the rail, frowning in concentration. Graham joined him and pointed the light at the water. He stared idly into it, leaving Daniel to his thoughts. Then he saw it.

"The current!"

"What?" Daniel asked.

"I imagined the water coming into the pool from a crack or hole in the floor. But it looks like it's coming from under the steps."

"Of course," Daniel said, slapping the railing. "I can't believe I didn't think of it. This walkway didn't used to be here. It was put in during the excavation of the pool. Before that, people just stepped right into the water. But just before they put the walkway in, a couple of kids swam under the stairs. That's where the water comes out—underneath the bottom step."

"That's crazy. There'd be nowhere to go."

"It's completely insane. And yet they found an air pocket that was big enough to stand up in. They had taken their flashlights with them, and when they came up, they found a room under there. Turns out it's where Hezekiah closed off the water to channel it to the tunnel he built."

"Incredible."

"It looked like the place was also converted to a mikveh. Some scholars think it's mentioned in the Talmud, that one of the high priests in the first century used it to purify himself there on the way to the Temple."

"I don't remember hearing any of this," Graham said.

"There were so many discoveries being made here during the excavation that it was hard to keep up with the progress. Anyway, the point is that when it was excavated, they found a passage that led outside. It's easy to miss."

"And you're thinking that you can swim under the stairs, into the room, go out the passage, and then come back down here through the old entrance?" Graham asked, following the train of thought.

"Not me. You." Daniel gave Graham a crooked smile.

"Why me?" Graham flinched. "You're the one trained in this kind of stuff."

"I'm too big to fit." Daniel glanced down at Nagi's limp body. "And he's in no shape to do it. That leaves you."

Graham looked at the water undulating under the steps, sighed, and shook his head as he accepted the task. "So how do I do this?"

Daniel smiled reassuringly. "The room on the other side isn't very far. It's under the fifth or sixth step. Take the flashlight; it's waterproof. Drag your free hand across the top of the rock until you feel it open, then follow it up. I'll be in the water right behind you. If your feet don't disappear within thirty seconds, I'll grab your ankles and pull you back out. You can hold your breath that long, but I don't think you'll need to. Once you're in the room, the way should be obvious."

"You make it sound easy."

"Don't think of it as easy or hard," Daniel said. "You need to change your mindset. Think of it this way: It has been done before. And it was done by kids who had no idea what they were doing or what lay ahead. Plus, they had no way out because the entrance hadn't been excavated. If they could do it, you can."

"Okay. Let's do this before I lose my nerve." Graham

handed Daniel his phone, wallet, and hotel key, then bent to take off his hiking shoes.

"You could leave those on. You should be okay since you're going through a stream, not into a pool. Plus, you might need them on the other side."

Graham stood, climbed over the railing, and stepped into the narrow space left now covered by the grate as Daniel followed. The frigid water came up past the middle of his calf, just below his knees. He waded as far as he could, but several feet of walkway covered the area directly in front of the step. He dropped to his hands and knees and let out a *whoop* as the cool water soaked into him. The walkway hovered a foot above the surface of the stream, giving Graham and Daniel the room to crawl to the opening without putting their heads under water.

Graham paused at the first step, looking at the square opening barely the width of his shoulders. He shined the light into the aperture and cocked his head to see what was inside.

"Can't see anything down there," Graham said.

"Ready?" Daniel's voice came from directly behind him, not giving him the chance to rethink the plan.

Graham took a deep, intentional breath, then released it. He took another, and as soon as his lungs were at capacity, he dropped into the water and pulled himself into liquid black yet again.

TWENTY-SIX

Before Graham had a chance to orient himself, he felt Daniel's hands on his ankles, thrusting him into the stone shaft. His momentum was amplified by a rush of panic at the unexpected push, and he reached his right hand up to the top of the tunnel to try to slow his progress. But the ceiling of the passage disappeared, and his hand reached upward, out of the water. He pushed himself forward and up, exhilarated, into the room found by two kids on a lark.

He stood up cautiously even though the flashlight showed the rectangular room to be about twenty-feet high. Once he felt safe, Graham leaned back down to the water, over the hole he had just climbed through, and yelled, "I made it!" He wasn't sure Daniel would be able to hear him and thought for a moment about how to signal that he was okay. He held the flashlight under the water, pointed it in the direction of the cave, then switched it on and off several times.

He stood up again and this time took in the details. A worn, wooden ladder reached to the top of one of the walls on the narrow end to an opening that could only be the passage to the outside. The opposite wall was made of an aggregate of rough stones, distinct from the smoother blocks of the rest of the chamber. Graham wished he had time to study them, but assumed the rough stones were the work of Hezekiah's men trying to quickly reroute the water.

Graham climbed the ladder into a long passage that led to a narrow, surprisingly insubstantial door. The lack of a knob or handle gave the impression there was a padlock on the outside. He kicked hard, aiming his heel where a knob should be, and the door flew open with only the slightest brittle splinter of protest.

The journey to this point had disoriented him, confounding his normally excellent intuitive navigation, and he had no idea where he was based on the view from the threshold. The ground outside the door was at the bottom of a steep hill rising on his left. On his right, a wall extended from the edge of the door another twenty feet. He walked out into the late-afternoon sun, passed the end of the wall, and looked for anything familiar. Ahead of him, he saw the valley of the monument tombs, where they had searched the day before. It was enough to fix his position.

Turning right, he found himself at a small courtyard next to the Gihon Spring House. A trail of wet footprints documented his path as he walked through the courtyard, and into the dead end of the street they had driven in on. The sloshing sound of his steps as he began to trot across the parking lot made Graham realize how strange he must look, and he hoped the scattering of people in the street didn't notice the conspicuously soaked American running through their neighborhood.

He aimed himself at the stairs of the old entrance but stopped at a pile of metal poles near the front of the IAA van. The derelict scaffolding that had been standing when they arrived was now in a pile. And the board that had been lying across the top was gone.

After registering the change, he rushed to the top of the stairs and saw the guard crumpled at the bottom, between the last step and the gate. He took the ancient, uneven steps two at a time, and knelt beside the soldier. His breathing was shallow, like Nagi's had been, but he was alive.

Graham reached over the soldier and rattled the door, verifying it was locked. He looked down at the soldier, wondering where he had put the key. The man was a walking armory: machine gun, pistol, bulletproof vest, nightstick. And based on where Daniel kept his knife, there were probably more weapons Graham couldn't see. A short burst of static came from the vest, followed by a male voice speaking Hebrew. Graham unclipped the palm-sized walkie microphone from the left shoulder of the guard, raised it to his mouth, and spoke as quickly as he could in Hebrew.

"This is Doctor Graham Eliot. I'm with the IAA. I'm at the entrance of Hezekiah's Tunnel, the old one, at the Gihon Spring House. There is a soldier down, and two people are trapped inside. We need help…"

The walkie-talkie fell to the ground, and he ignored the pop of static as he released the button. His eyes fixed on a spot about four feet inside the gate, on the light glinting off the key.

He stuck his arm through the gate, knowing he couldn't reach it before he even tried. But the attempt gave him an idea of how far he fell short, and how long of a tool he would need. The walkie-talkie squawked again, and he looked down to see the answer sitting next to the mic: the night stick.

He slid it from its sheath, and after scooting the key close enough, Graham drew it under the gate and opened the lock.

The immovability of the barricade became clear instantly. Several metal poles held the plywood wall in place. One end of each pole was wedged against the wood and the other against the vertical edge of a stone step. He guessed it had been built from pieces scavenged from the wrecked scaffolding.

"Daniel, I'm inside!"

"Good work." Daniel's muffled voice leaked through the

makeshift wall. "Can you get us out of here?"

"Working on it."

Graham wove his way down the stairs, crouched, and placed a shoulder under one of the poles. He pushed up on his legs sharply and scraped the end of the support a couple of inches up the step. After a second push, the pole jumped free and clanged onto the stone.

"You okay?" The closeness of Daniel's voice gave Graham a sense of progress as well as an adrenaline boost.

"Fine. Almost done."

He shoved another support out of place, this time loosening the tension enough for the wall to become wobbly. He placed a foot on a third pole and stomped it to the ground, causing a fourth pole to drop as the plywood slowly fell toward him. He grabbed an edge of the board, rocked it to the side like a door, and revealed Daniel on the other side.

"I think you missed your calling." Daniel smiled.

"Can we go now, please?" Nagi appeared behind Daniel, giving him a poke to move him forward.

"Nagi! I was worried about you." Graham reached past Daniel to put a hand on Nagi's shoulder.

"Just a little headache." Nagi shrugged. "Let's get out of this place."

Daniel started up the steps, but at the landing, turned into the passage that led to the pool platforms.

"Daniel, where are you going?"

"We should see what this guy did after tying us up. See if he found anything. Grab a couple of those torches."

"Good thinking. Nagi, stay here with the gear. Rest a little bit more." Graham picked up the flashlights they used to explore Hezekiah's Tunnel and followed Daniel back to the pool.

Several rocks had been displaced from the house, and several other large stones in the area had been moved, encircled in fresh boot tracks. Other tracks looked recently added to the dirt floor in areas they hadn't explored. The two smaller GPR antennas still lay where they had left them, but the larger one was gone. As they tried to analyze their attacker's work, the lights in the pool exploded to life.

"I called for help," Graham said. "They must've just shown up."

Daniel visibly relaxed. "I'm not sure there is much left to…"

Graham turned his head in the same direction. "What do you see?" But as he finished the sentence, he already knew the answer. A section of the white fiber optic cable of the GPR was draped over the edge of the lower pool.

They hurried off the platform and found the antenna below them at the bottom of the lower pool's curved wall. A few small rocks were scattered across the floor, and more footprints patterned the dirt.

"Doesn't look like he found anything," Graham said, relieved.

"Actually, he found the one thing he wasn't supposed to." Daniel said it while still looking into the depths of the dry pool, then turned his eyes to Graham. "He found us."

TWENTY-SEVEN

Midway up the steps from the pool room to the old entrance, Graham stopped, wondering if they were about to walk into another trap. The bags of equipment they had left at the landing were gone. He changed his grip on the metal detector, preparing to use it to defend himself.

"What's wrong?" Daniel asked, trying to look past him.

Graham raised a hand, signaling silence. He turned his head while keeping his eyes forward and whispered, "The gear's gone. So is Nagi."

Daniel raised his eyebrows just as the sound of footsteps echoed in the old entrance, coming toward them. The shadow of a head and shoulders appeared on the floor and spilled across the landing, followed by Nagi stepping into the space.

"Nagi!" Graham said. "I'm so glad it's you."

Nagi turned to look into the passageway, confusion wrinkling his face. "Uh, yeah, it's me. Why are you just standing there?"

Graham walked the rest of the way into the room. "Thought you might be the guy who came after us. I'm a little paranoid right now."

"It's all right. I loaded the van. The guard helped me. He's outside with the others that just showed up."

"You shouldn't push yourself," Daniel said. "You were

drugged pretty heavily. You should go rest in the van. Let Graham and me get the GPR."

"Okay. Thanks. If you're sure you got it." Nagi took a step backward, then paused.

"Go," Graham ordered with a smile.

As the van rumbled onto the dilapidated street, Graham dialed Yaniv. After a quick report, they agreed to meet at the Promised Land Hotel's restaurant to debrief. But first, Graham had to get cleaned up.

He walked self-consciously through the lobby in damp clothes caked with dust and smelling like a cellar. He gave the man behind the front desk an apologetic glance as he hurried past. Once in his room, he stood in the hottest shower he could tolerate and tried to wash the day away.

An hour after leaving the Gihon Spring House, he found Yaniv and Daniel waiting for him. Except for two tables of tourists recounting what they had seen that day, the restaurant was empty. A long buffet bisected the dining room, and Yaniv and Daniel had taken a table at the far corner, away from the other diners. The sight of food made Graham realize how hungry he was, and by the time he joined them he had a full plate.

Yaniv motioned to an empty seat. "Graham, I am so glad you are okay. Thank goodness you were not hurt."

"Thank Daniel. We'd still be there if it weren't for him."

"That's not true," Daniel said. "You did all the work." Daniel looked exhausted, and Graham knew he must look the same.

"The important thing is that you are all well," Yaniv said, looking back and forth between the two. "I must agree with Daniel that this man—Karanlik—was not trying to kill you. He could have easily done that. No, I think it was to scare you. And to keep you out of the way as he searched the pool."

Graham nodded as he swallowed a bite of lamb. "I think

you're probably right. What I think we were wrong about is believing there was a chance there would still be anything there. The excavation was so thorough that if anything had been there, it would have been found. But they didn't find any hint of the silver. Not a single shekel. According to the report, they didn't even find evidence that anyone had been in the pool for 1,800 years. Maybe more."

"Yes, I have thought the same," Yaniv said. "But come to think of it, it was only the upper pool they discovered. The deeper pool where the GPR was left was found a hundred years ago by—oh, what was his name? Very English sounding...Parker! Montagu Parker."

TWENTY-EIGHT

"Montagu Parker found the lower pool?" Graham recoiled, recalling snippets of Parker's infamous expedition.

"Oh, yes," Yaniv said. "It is hard to believe something important came out of his work—if you can call it that. Yet he found it when he cleaned out Hezekiah's Tunnel and Warren's Shaft."

"Mmm." Daniel held up a finger as he swallowed. "Back up a second. I'm lost. An archaeologist was there before? And I thought Warren cleared the tunnel."

"Just so. But in the years after Warren's work, debris had begun to fill it again. Parker had to clean it out for his own exploration."

"But Parker was not an archaeologist." Graham watched Daniel's expression become incredulous as he explained. "He was a treasure hunter. Guided by a couple of spiritualists. He was a British aristocrat with the time and money to chase what fancied him. He was approached by a theologian—Juvelius was his name, Finnish, I think—who claimed he had found a code in the book of Ezekiel. The code was so specific that he was able to draw a map showing the exact location of the Ark of the Covenant."

"And people believed him?" Daniel sneered.

"Well, what Juvelius *really* wanted was for people with

money to believe him. He couldn't fund the expedition himself, and he was too controversial to get a permit even if he could finance the work. So he went to London and convinced several people with both money and social standing to back him. And the main supporter was Montagu Parker. If I remember correctly, he was a captain in the British Army, and the son of an earl. Became Lord Parker later in life. He used his title and connections to raise the money from other important families and finance the project. It legitimized the request for a permit, and the Ottoman government granted it."

"Even though he had no training?" Daniel asked.

"Money made that irrelevant. Juvelius promised everything would go to the Ottoman Empire. But at the same time, Parker promised to pay dividends to his financiers based on what he found."

"And what did he find?"

"Trouble."

Yaniv chuckled, then elaborated on Graham's answer. "Yes, he did almost everything wrong. He made a bad impression by arriving in Jaffa on a yacht owned by one of the backers. Then the team took up luxurious rooms in one of the hospices on the Mount of Olives. He did not understand how much sludge and fill needed to be cleared from the tunnels. It cost a great deal more time and money than he had planned."

"Wasn't anyone policing the cultural property being discovered?" Daniel threw his hands into the air. "This was the Golden Age of archaeology in Jerusalem. And no legitimate archaeologists objected?"

"Most certainly they did," Yaniv said. "So Parker invited Hughes Vincent, an archaeologist who was also a Catholic priest, to accompany the crew and properly document their finds."

"But if he was looking for the Ark of the Covenant, why

was he in Hezekiah's Tunnel?"

"The map Juvelius drew assumed the tunnel had been altered," Graham said. "He thought there might be a passage that had yet to be discovered that led under the Holy of Holies. To the Well of Souls."

"The cave that supposedly lies beneath the Dome of the Rock?" Daniel frowned dismissively. "That's just a legend, isn't it?"

"No one knows for sure," Yaniv said. "All we know is that the cave—the prayer room beneath the rock itself—has a marble floor that is said to sound hollow when it is knocked on."

"According to the Talmud, it's the center of the world," Graham said. "Sir Richard Burton himself once visited it and wanted to lift the slab he saw in the floor but wasn't allowed to."

"Muslims believe it is where the souls of the dead gather on Fridays to worship Allah."

Graham was impressed at Yaniv's ability not to make a face while explaining what must be blasphemous to him.

"And that's where Juvelius said the Ark had been hidden?" Daniel said skeptically. "In a place no one had ever seen, and where no one was allowed to look?"

"That is one way to put it." Yaniv smiled. "However, if it was hidden in a place people were allowed to see then it would not be hidden, would it? Interestingly, there was one person who claimed to have seen the Well of Souls. Ten years before Wilson and Warren made their survey of the Temple Mount, there was an Italian architect—Pierotti—who claimed to have followed a conduit into the chamber under the prayer room."

"He went from Hezekiah's Tunnel?" Graham asked.

"No. He was allowed to enter several cisterns. The conduit he followed connected to a cistern north of the Dome of the

Rock. But he also claimed there was a conduit that led all the way to the Gihon Spring."

"So there is a tunnel," Daniel said.

Yaniv opened his hands in an empty shrug. "Perhaps. Unfortunately, his maps and descriptions did not agree with what Wilson and Warren saw—especially of the conduits. Warren made note of the discrepancies between what they found and what Pierotti recorded. Not surprisingly, Juvelius's maps were even less reliable than Pierotti's. And yet Parker *did* actually find passages hidden behind walls in the tunnel that had been made to look exactly like the cave walls—much like the cavities in the floor of B'nei Hezir that you found yesterday."

"I still wouldn't trust them," Daniel said. "So what happened when the tunnels didn't take him where he wanted to go?"

"Here's where it gets interesting," Graham said, leaning forward. "Parker spent three years without finding anything he promised to his backers, and they grew impatient. He even began to wonder if Juvelius's maps were reliable."

"Understandable," Daniel said.

"But all along Parker also relied on an Irish mystic who said he saw the location of the Ark in a séance. So he decided to skip the tunnel entirely and go directly into the Well of Souls from the prayer cave."

"But how could he possibly do that?" Daniel shook his head emphatically. "There is no way to get permission to dig under the Dome of the Rock. There would be riots."

"There were," Yaniv said. "But not at first. Parker thought he found the perfect moment to do a quick exploration. A time when Jerusalem was most distracted: Passover. The Jews are busy celebrating the feast, the Christians are celebrating Easter, and most importantly—"

"It's *Nebi Musa*." Daniel sat back, his brow bent in

thought.

"Exactly," Yaniv said. "When Palestinian Muslims make a pilgrimage from Jerusalem to the traditional site of Moses's tomb, just beyond Jericho. Parker bribed the sheik who oversaw the Temple Mount to allow him and his crew to excavate at night during the week of the festivals."

Daniel leaned forward again. "The Muslims let infidels desecrate a holy place?"

"In any religion God's chief rival is not the devil," Yaniv said. "It is greed."

"There is not enough money in the world to bribe a Muslim to allow digging on the Mount."

"You'd be surprised, Daniel. Charles Warren bribed the Muslims guarding his dig on the Mount by letting them eat his pet lizard." Graham laughed at Daniel's pained expression. "It's true! He was going to take it back to the zoo in London. Instead, he used it to get in good with the guards. He promised them another—one named *Warren*—if they looked the other way while he dug under al-Aqsa Mosque."

Daniel laughed, half in disgust.

Yaniv arched both eyebrows while closing his eyes. "Anyway, Parker dressed his team as Arabs and began to work in the prayer room cave under the Dome of the Rock."

"And they got away with it?"

"Oh no," Yaniv said with a satisfied frown. "They were discovered. But how they were found out is in dispute. One version is that their work awoke a guard who had not been bribed. The guard ran out of the Temple Mount, into the streets, screaming the news that the sacred site was being profaned. Another version is that there was a spy on the team who made sure Parker wouldn't recover anything if it looked like they were getting close to discovering something. Whatever happened, Parker and his team found themselves at the center of a riot. He fled to Jaffa and sailed his yacht into international waters as fast as he could."

"But what did he find?" Daniel glanced between Yaniv and Graham.

"No one knows," Yaniv said. "According to the newspapers, they found incredibly important and valuable items from the Temple, possibly including the Ark of the Covenant—though the papers did say that particular claim was unlikely."

"It was worldwide news when it happened," Graham said, "but the reports of it didn't bring any clarity. Some papers reported that he had found the Ark of the Covenant and made off with it. Other reports say he found it but had to abandon it. If he did find it, then he never used it to pay back his investors."

"But what does any of this have to do with Hezekiah's Tunnel?" Daniel asked again.

"If the silver had been hidden in the lower pool, then it would've been Parker who discovered it." Graham saw comprehension spark in Daniel's eyes.

"Right," Yaniv said. "We know they found pottery and seals—items such as that—but there is no record of the silver. If there had been, it would have been seized by the Ottoman government and documented by Père Hughes. And yet—"

Graham exchanged a glance with Daniel as they waited for Yaniv to break his reverie.

"Parker fled Jerusalem so quickly that he left behind two sealed chests. He hoped to come back for them, but he never did. Eventually, one was turned over to the government, but the other was never found."

"Where were they stored?" Graham asked.

"In a house in Silwan, the neighborhood south of the Temple Mount."

"And you think the chest had the silver in it?" Daniel asked.

"I do not know what was in it," Yaniv said. "I do not know if he found a way to smuggle it out of the country, or whether someone else stole it. I do not even know if there was anything in it worth stealing. But given that no investors were paid back, and no further bribes were paid to the government, I doubt it left with him."

"Well, as interesting as all this is, it's really not very helpful for what we're doing." Graham steepled his fingers under his chin.

"Actually, this is incredibly helpful," Daniel said. "We are obviously being watched. And we have to consider that whoever is watching may be getting his information from inside the IAA."

"A mole? Karanlik has someone inside?" Graham felt self-conscious at the words, as if he were living someone else's life.

Yaniv nodded. "I was actually wondering the same thing."

"What if we used the rumor of Parker's chest to draw this guy out of the shadows?" Daniel lowered his voice. "We could leak the news that the second chest has been located. That it never made it out of Jerusalem, and that we are about to recover it."

"Leak the news to whom?" Graham asked. "How are we supposed to communicate with an unknown person who keeps himself hidden?"

"We leak it to the department, maybe a couple of dealers who we know won't keep quiet. We could stage a dig as bait, but this time be ready for him and arrest him."

The table fell silent as they processed the idea.

"It is hard to justify proceeding to the last item with lives at stake," Yaniv said. "And maybe the next time this man might not be so patient. Might not be so willing to let you live."

"It will be hard enough getting into a cistern on the

Temple Mount. We do not need to invite anyone to kill us," Daniel said.

"All right. Let's do it." Graham felt his attention beginning to fray. "But let's not plan it right now. I need sleep first."

"Agreed." Yaniv stood. "We will meet tomorrow, at my office. In the meantime, I will do more research."

TWENTY-NINE

Black, unseeing eyes fixed their stare on Graham from the bottom of the sink. He had awoken parched, risen to get a drink, and found the painted face of a mummy mask looking up at him. Cracks and stains textured and discolored the gold, giving a dull, metallic complexion to its passive countenance. It occurred to him that he held the same expression on his own face, creating a reflection without a resemblance.

The whisper that floated up from the mask began so softly that he thought he was hearing the sound bleeding through the wall from another room. As its volume grew, it became clear that the words were coming from the motionless lips of the mask. But as the syllables became more distinct, he realized it was a language he did not know.

Bubbles began to spill out from under the mask like substance-less pebbles pushing up from the drain. They framed the mask, then climbed its edge and began to cover it.

Graham reached in and pulled the mask away. But instead of a mound of bubbles, he uncovered the face of his wife.

"Olivia!"

Shock had paralyzed him, turning him into a living statue as he watched her face submerge in the soapy solution. Just before the veil of bubbles obscured her face, Graham saw her eyes open.

"No!"

His scream shattered the scene, and he found himself sitting up in bed, awake and exhausted as much from sleep as from the events of the day before. His dry mouth felt like it had been smuggled from the dream, and he shuffled to the bathroom for a glass of water. He was almost surprised to find the smooth porcelain sink empty. By the time he crawled back into bed, he felt heavy with sleep again. He rolled onto his side, put his hands beneath his head, under his pillow, and seconds later, the world disappeared.

The sound of water surrounded him, and he was confused when he opened his eyes to find himself completely dry. He could feel the grid pattern of the iron grate as his body pressed into it, and he knew he was once again in the Gihon Spring cave. His head rested on his hands, but when he tried to use his arms to sit up, he felt the plastic zip tie holding his wrists to the walkway. He pulled against the tie in sharp jerks, then resigned himself to being bound.

The cold metal beneath his hands suddenly felt fluid, and he realized the water was rising. Or was he sinking?

He rolled onto his back with his hands over his head, try-ing to keep his mouth above the surface as long as possible. The waterline drifted higher, panic rising with it. He arched his body upward, sucking in as much air as possible as his face fell beneath the surface. He tugged frantically at the ties tethering him as water blurred his vision. A moment later, the air that had been so precious only seconds before, now burned poisonously in his lungs. Breath finally exploded from his mouth, and at the same time he began to sink he also discovered that his hands had somehow become free.

He got to his feet and pushed himself out of the water, gulp-ing the air. Hair hung over his face, dripping water as he bent over, his hands on his knees. After he caught his breath, he stood up and felt something on his face. He reached for his cheek and peeled away a strip of papyrus the length of his hand. Several strings of Greek letters were inscribed across the fragment. He started to scan their shapes, but before he could make out any words, light flooded the cave, turning it completely white, bleaching out all detail.

When the light receded, he was once again in bed, the morning sun tinting his hotel room like residue from the dream. Alyson's death had broken him in ways he was still discovering, but it had weighed even more heavily on his wife. Olivia became distant, disengaging from everything she was involved in—church, friends, even their marriage. Graham pursued her, knowing she was the only person who could truly understand his grief, but she had been able to carry her burden only with the help of medication.

Six months ago, the medication itself weighed her down, causing her to fall asleep in the bathtub, accidentally letting her slip under the water and drown. At least he hoped it had been an accident. When he found her, she looked more peaceful than he had ever seen her. He attempted to revive her, but—as he now remembered it—he got the feeling that her body didn't want the life he tried to push into her.

He had believed in God for all of his adult life, having come to faith as a senior in high school, but he had no way of making sense of what happened to his wife and daughter. He had always believed God was all-knowing, all-powerful, and perfectly good. But he didn't believe that anymore. He couldn't.

No God like that could allow such things to happen, he told himself. An omniscient God would have known what was happening; an omnipotent God would have been able to stop it; and a benevolent God would have wanted to stop it. That left him only two options: a god not worth worshipping or no god at all. He chose the latter.

THIRTY

Graham awoke unrested, emotionally battered, and forced himself into action. The remnants of the dreams stole his thoughts, keeping him in a fog, rendering the present vague. Even his plate of shakshouka was tasteless, an abstract combination of eggs and tomato he barely noticed. Daniel's arrival rescued him from self-pity, and he was able to shake off the night on the short walk to the Rockefeller Museum.

They entered through the main doors of the Tower Room, and once again, Graham stopped to look at the replicas of Sennacherib's reliefs, feeling a connection to the story.

"What is it?" Daniel asked, glancing between the images and Graham's face.

"They're not just pictures anymore," Graham said. "It's a bit more real now. We survived a siege because of a tunnel at the Gihon Spring. Just like Hezekiah."

Daniel's lips turned down in appreciation. "Yes, I guess we did."

They made their way into the private area that housed the Israel Antiquities Authority. Yaniv's door was open, and they could see he was engrossed in an old file. Both elbows rested on the top of his desk, and his steepled hands supported his temple. Below his face, a dozen antique memos—yellowed with age—littered the desk before him.

"Graham. Daniel. Shalom." Yaniv smiled warmly as he stood and reached across the desk to shake their hands. "I found the file with the correspondence regarding the chests Parker left behind." Yaniv waved a palm-up hand over the paper in explanation. "Really quite interesting."

"Does it say what was in them?" Daniel asked, twisting his neck in an effort to read the memos.

"It does not have to. You have seen what was in them. One of them anyway."

"What do you mean?" Graham squinted.

"His discoveries are on display in the North Gallery."

"That's what he found?" Graham pictured the rows of display cabinets—at least half a dozen on each side of the aisle down the long room. "We just walked past them. I didn't even notice they were Parker's."

"Not all of it is what he found, of course," Yaniv said. "But what was recovered from him is there."

Daniel looked away from the memos and sat down. "You said it came from one of the chests. What was in the other?"

Yaniv smiled weakly as he shrugged. "I do not know. It disappeared."

"How?" Graham frowned. "It was an international incident, and he was a wanted man."

"I know. I know," Yaniv said, nodding. "But all I can tell you is what is in the archive. And this is it." He again waved a hand over the papers. "Let me read you the relevant parts." He searched for a specific memo and picked it up. "This is from Colonel Storrs, the military governor of Jerusalem, to Captain Mackay, the Inspector of Antiquities. Dated 19 December 1919."

"Wait," Daniel said, holding up a hand. "1919? I read up on Parker last night. I thought his expedition lasted from 1909 to 1911. That memo was written eight and a half years after the riots?"

"Just so," Yaniv said. "But this is where the papers begin." He held the yellowed sheet before him and read aloud.

> *"I beg to report that Mr. Montagu Parker, who was excavating in Silwan before the war, left two cupboards containing antiquities and deposited in them the house of Hussein Musa, Mukhtar of Silwan; also some tools—but the two cupboards of antiquities, which were sealed by the Turkish Government and Mr. Parker, still remain intact.*
>
> *Another cupboard of antiquities belonging to the French excavator Hermon Gateau was deposited in the house of Antebi and under the care of a certain Guzlan of Silwan. This cupboard is also sealed and remains intact.*
>
> *I fear that these antiquities may be tampered with and request that they may be taken under Government Control."*

"Silwan has its own *mukhtar?*"

Yaniv looked surprised at Graham's question. "Yes, the neighborhood has, in many ways, retained its identity as a village separate from Jerusalem, including its own village leader."

He set the paper facedown away from the others, then picked up another. "Five days later, Captain Mackay replied.

> *"The two sealed cupboards you have called my attention to will be visited shortly. If the seals are unbroken they had better remain so. If otherwise I will make an inventory of the contents and re-seal them officially."*

"Two?" Daniel said, leaning forward. "The first memo says there were three cupboards."

"Exactly."

"Maybe he was referring only to Parker's chests," Graham said. "The third was Gateau's."

"I thought so, too. Until I read the next memo." Yaniv stacked the second memo on the first, then skimmed the desk and picked up a third sheet. "This is from Mackay, dated 17 July 1920."

"Six months later?" Daniel asked. "Why did he wait so long?"

"I assume this was not a priority during World War I," Yaniv said. "And the time that followed was rather confusing as the Ottoman Empire ended and Mandatory Palestine was established. I am sure the new administrators had more urgent issues to sort out. The region was a mess a hundred years ago." Yaniv looked back to the memo and began to read.

> *"The two cupboards were inspected by me*
> *28.4.20 and their seals were found intact."*

Yaniv inflected his voice to emphasize two.

> *"One cupboard contains the property of Captain*
> *Montagu Parker and is deposited in the House*
> *of Hussein Musa, Mukhtar of Silwan. The other*
> *cupboard contains antiquities belonging to M.*
> *Hermon Gateau and is under the care of a cer-*
> *tain Guzlan of Silwan."*

"One of Parker's chests was missing," Graham said.

Yaniv discarded the memo and found the next. "Apparently, the chests stayed where they were for another two years. The next memo—dated 2 May 1922—shows Mackay asking the governor for the authority to take possession before the antiquities are damaged or go missing. He was told to request an order of seizure."

"I can't believe they sat there so long, completely undisturbed, just waiting to be stolen," Daniel said. "That would never happen now."

Yaniv pulled the remaining papers closer to him, then picked one up. "A week later he put in the request. It mentions only one cupboard found by Parker, and the other by Gateau."

"One?" Graham asked. "Was that a mistake or deliberate?"

"I wondered the same thing," Yaniv said, plucking up the next memo. "The order came through a week after that, citing the Antiquities Ordinance, which does not allow for private possession of antiquities discovered during excavation."

"The same policy that governed the excavation under the Ottoman code," Daniel said.

"Just so." Yaniv nodded, shuffling to the next document. "And a week later, the cupboards were seized. This says, '*The antiquities were removed without opposition or disturbance and are now deposited in the museum premises.*'"

"What exactly was in the cupboards?" Daniel asked.

Yaniv lifted one of the unread sheets. "One month later, Mackay reported back and said they found…" Yaniv skimmed the memo, reading aloud only the relevant parts.

> "*The bulk of the antiquities seized…consisted of very important primitive remains…almost entirely ceramic. Most…have now been placed in the Palestine Museum…The specimen of greatest interest is a fragmentary bowl of polished red and black ware.*"

"Not exactly the Ark of the Covenant," Graham said.

Yaniv raised a finger, signaling a point before he replied. "No, but it does document a second chest of Parker's that is not accounted for. And that makes the next memo rather interesting." As he spoke, he picked up the paper and displayed it. "This is from someone named Johan Millén, sent from Stockholm, 20 November 1922—five months after the seizure. It is addressed to the director of the Department of Antiquities.

> *"I am desirous of disposing of the collection we*
> *have stored up in Jerusalem, the result of our*
> *excavations in Mount Ophel during 1909-10-*
> *11. I should indeed be very glad if I in this could*
> *count on your exceptional expert advice, and*
> *how and where to sell it. It is now sealed up in*
> *a house belonging to the Mukhtar of Siloam,*
> *Hussein, as Pere Vincent well knows."*

"Parker's second cupboard?" Daniel leaned forward to see the memo. "So there really were three. And if he was trying to sell it five months later, then it wasn't seized."

"Exactly!" Yaniv pointed his index finger into the air again, bookending the information.

"And it has never been found?" Graham asked.

"There is no record of it."

Daniel glanced at Graham, then back to Yaniv. "Let's go look, then. What was the address of the Mukhtar's house?"

"Unfortunately, the records do not say." Yaniv shrugged. "And any records that would have it were lost."

"Which leaves us nowhere," Graham said.

"No, it is perfect." Daniel sat up, inflated with an idea. "Karanlik doesn't know where it is either. If he is following us—and he probably is—then I assume he'll try to take whatever we pretend to find. We would have undercover agents all around to watch the site while we're there, ready for him."

"Very good." Yaniv nodded. "An excellent idea. The current Mukhtar lives near the Pool of Siloam, which is also near where Parker made his headquarters toward the end of his expedition."

"That's perfect, since the Pool of Siloam is where Hezekiah's Tunnel leads to," Graham said. "Makes sense to hide the silver close by. And that ties it to the Master Scroll in two ways since the chest could contain either the items from the tunnel or the Temple Mount."

"The problem, of course, is that Silwan is almost entirely Palestinian," Daniel said.

"But there are some Jewish settlers there. They have built homes there since the war in 1967." Yaniv turned to his computer as he spoke and called up a map of Jewish occupied homes. "There is a strip of settlers at the tip of the Kidron Valley. We can see if we could pay one of the owners to let us have the house for a day or two. Give me the rest of the day to work on this. Let us meet for dinner to make the final plans."

"Do you think you still have the cupboards that were seized?" Daniel asked.

"Very doubtful. I would not even know where to look."

"I think I might."

Both men looked at Graham.

"I mean, we're faking it, so it doesn't have to be the real thing, right?"

THIRTY-ONE

Graham retraced his path through the museum and slowed as he entered the North Gallery. He scanned the rows of exhibits, then stopped when he found the name *Montagu Parker* on an object card next to an artifact.

"Graham Eliot!"

His own name startled him, feeling out of place as he looked into the display. He turned to discover an unexpected face that took a moment to place.

"Nigel Horne. Good to see you." Graham offered his hand, rallying himself to become socially present. "What brings you here?"

"Doing a bit of consulting for the IAA." Horne flicked his head toward the door that led to the offices. "How about you? Here on business, I suppose?"

"Yes, I'm doing a little consulting for them myself."

"Really?" Horne smiled. "What do they have you working on?"

Graham had anticipated the question and scrambled to invent a plausible reason for him to be there. "The *Matzevah*."

The IAA's excavation of the Gihon Spring had unearthed a stairway that led uphill to a row of four rooms. One had a series of precise *V* shaped carvings in the floor. Another appeared to be designed as an animal pen and oil press. A third had a small, raised platform and a drainage gutter—possibly an altar with a channel for the blood. The fourth room contained an object of much debate, and what could be one of the most important archaeological finds in Israel.

A rough stone slab with the dimensions of a large computer monitor had been wedged into bedrock so that it stood upright on its long side, like a fin. The surface showed evidence of having oil poured over it, just as Jacob had done to the rock he set up to memorialize the place where he had his vision of a stairway to heaven. The type of monument was common in the middle Bronze Age, which loosely spanned the time between Abraham and Moses. It was clearly a sacred site. According to the archaeologist who discovered it, it may have been the monument where Melchizedek—the mysterious priest-king encountered by Abraham—worshipped.

"The Matzevah? That was found in 2009. I would have thought you would have studied that by now." Horne's face transformed into a mask of regret. "I'm so sorry. I did it again. I didn't mean to be insensitive. Please, forgive me."

"It's okay, Nigel." Graham held up a hand, ambiguously hovering between shielding himself and giving absolution. "Don't worry about it."

"So what do you think?" Horne asked, awkwardly moving past the moment. "Is it Jacob's altar?"

"I do think it's someone's altar. But I wouldn't want to use it as a pillow."

Horne tilted his head back as he chuckled. "Is that why you're looking at this display?" His eyes glanced at the object label that had caught Graham's eye.

"What do you mean?"

"Parker. He found these things while mapping the same area where the Matzevah was found, so I assumed—"

Graham shook his head. "I actually hadn't made that connection."

"Apparently, he went right past it." Horne chuckled again.

"Well, he probably wouldn't have recognized its importance if he *had* found it. To him it would be just a rock, since it wasn't gold or silver."

"Too true," Horne said. "Think of all the things that have been lost or destroyed by people like Parker, who didn't recognize what they had."

"I guess that's what keeps people like us in business," Graham said, willing himself not to glance at the exit.

Horne looked at the floor and tapped a foot. "And there is still a city *under* this city for us to discover. Except now the political layers are as thick as the layers of dirt. But as Saint Paul says, 'What can be seen is temporary, but what cannot be seen is eternal.'"

"You got that right." Graham hoped his growing impatience wasn't as obvious as it felt. The last thing he wanted to hear were Bible verses quoted out of context.

"By the way," Horne continued, "have you heard anything more about Andrew?"

"Not since the FBI came to see me," Graham said. "I still can't believe he's gone."

"It does have a twisted irony," Horne said, raising one eyebrow.

"How do you mean?"

"Andrew would have given his life to go underground below the Temple Mount. But it was a rock from the Mount that took his life and put *him* underground." He arched both eyebrows at the observation.

Graham didn't know how to respond, taken aback by both the dark humor he didn't know Horne had, and by its truthfulness. "Well, I don't want to keep you from your work."

Horne shook Graham's hand warmly as he looked frankly into his eyes. "Not at all. Hope we see each other again."

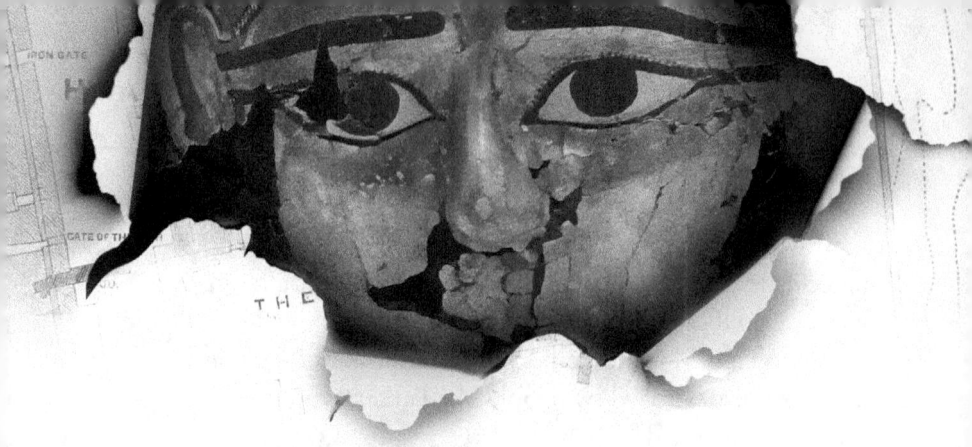

THIRTY-TWO

Escape from the conversation gave Graham a sense of freedom as he left the museum and followed Sultan Suleiman Street, along the north wall of the Old City. He continued past Herod's Gate and entered the Damascus Gate—a more direct route to Avraham Antiquities.

Two imposing towers stood on either side of an opening much larger than Herod's Gate, and he studied the recently completed restoration of the crenellated wall destroyed in the 1967 war. He descended the bowl of steps that funneled visitors from street level onto a landing crowded with vendors. Tailgating tents and bistro umbrellas filled with knock-off running shoes, jeans, and jewelry littered the space in front of the gate that had served as the primary access to the city for 2,000 years.

The gate in the 500-year-old wall was built on top of the entrance in a previous wall. Like so much of ancient Jerusalem, it was at least a dozen feet higher than when Saul passed through it and onto the highway that led to his conversion as he traveled to Damascus to persecute Christians. Graham glimpsed over the left side of the pavement and saw the arch of the old Roman gate that had been uncovered below the current entrance. An inscription in the lintel identified the city as *Aelia Capitalina*, the name Hadrian gave Jerusalem when he expelled the Jews as a result of their final revolt against Rome in AD 135.

Graham joined the aggregate of Muslims, Jews, and Christians congesting the narrow streets. Pilgrims, tourists, and vendors flowed in conflicting currents of traffic as Israeli soldiers policed the crowds.

Inside the gate, he crossed the spot where a Roman column once stood that had been used to measure the distance between Jerusalem and other cities. Now it was the beginning of Souk Khan El-Zeit, the street market that divided the Muslim and Christian quarters. Drab green and gray metal awnings made a continuous patchwork canopy over the shops and stands lining the street. As he stepped into the bazaar of vegetables, spices, cheap clothes, backpacks, beads, hookahs, bags, scarves, religious tchotchkes, and antiques, Graham rebuked himself for thinking it defaced the city. This market had been here—in one form or another—since before Jesus first visited the Temple.

After a quick plate of falafel and hummus, he continued down the street, then turned right onto Via Dolorosa, to the door of Avraham Antiquities. The sterile ambiance of the shop felt like an oasis among the clutter of the Old City. More than half a dozen customers browsed the wood and glass display cases, looking for pieces of history to take home.

Ravid stood with a couple deliberating over a shelf of ceramic oil lamps, answering questions. He nodded a welcome as Graham busied himself in front of a tray of coins that promised to be authentic widow's mites. After the sale, Graham joined Ravid at the counter.

"Welcome back, Dr. Eliot. Shalom." Ravid gave Graham a sober smile.

"Shalom. Good to see you so busy."

"Always busy." He made an expansive gesture toward the display cases, then raised a finger in exception. "But not with mummy masks."

"Nothing?"

"Not a whisper. No one has. Or at least, no one is saying so." Ravid looked past him and gave his customary nod of welcome to new arrivals.

"Ever heard about the chests left by Montagu Parker?"

Ravid's attention instantly focused entirely on Graham. "Don't insult me. Of course I have."

"Heard about the one that went missing before the government could take control of it?"

Ravid responded with a long look, and Graham sensed he was trying to anticipate where the conversation was going. "Only rumors…" Ravid said with slow caution.

"What kind of rumors?"

"It is said that Parker found the Ark of the Covenant."

"I know about that."

"But some say he found things in the tunnels he explored." Ravid glanced at his customers before continuing. "Parker was very secretive, but I heard stories from an old man who was the son of one of the diggers on the expedition. He said there were all kinds of rumors."

"About silver?" Graham asked.

"About silver. Gold. The Ark." Ravid shrugged. "But he said his father didn't see any of it himself."

"Do you believe it?"

"I hear lots of stories," Ravid said dismissively. "People think they know things. They want me to pay for their stories."

"But there really were two chests left behind by Parker at the Mukhtar's house. And one of them went missing."

"That is how all such stories end." Ravid smiled apologetically. "That is why I don't buy stories. Only things I can hold. Things I can see."

"Is one of those things an old chest?" Graham asked. "I need one. One that looks about a hundred years old."

Ravid furrowed his brow in thought. "I have many things from that time. Wait."

He disappeared into a room behind the counter, leaving Graham to monitor the shop. Graham examined a Roman flagrum—the kind of whip used to scourge Jesus before his crucifixion. Three leather cords with lead weights and sharp bits of metal on the ends were tied to a wooden handle. He was impressed with its authenticity, and equally glad to see it was marked as a replica. A genuine first-century Roman nail sat next to it, like a malignant companion. Graham sauntered to the case where the couple from earlier had selected their oil lamp. He inspected several and determined the couple had chosen well as Ravid backed through the door, pulling a large trunk.

"Is this what you had in mind?"

The antique was four and a half feet wide, three feet tall, and about three feet deep. Worn leather straps encompassed the wooden chest marred with scrapes and stains. Brass fittings had been hammered onto the corners and edges of the case, dull with neglect. Travel stickers worn partially away looked like faded tattoos, completing the effect Graham had wanted.

"Perfect! Could you please deliver this to the IAA as soon as possible? Care of Chaim Yaniv. Oh, and put it in a cardboard box or something so it can't be seen."

THIRTY-THREE

"We have our house," Yaniv said as they took what was becoming their customary corner table at the hotel restaurant. "Very close to the Pool of Siloam, not far from the current Mukhtar."

"That was fast," Graham said, working a piece of lamb from a skewer. "How'd you manage that?"

"*El'ad* took care of it," Yaniv said.

"What's El'ad?"

The question caught Yaniv in mid-bite, leaving Daniel to answer for him.

"A foundation that helps settle Jews in East Jerusalem, which is mostly Arab."

"Just so. They focus on the Silwan neighborhood, especially the area around the City of David." Yaniv gestured with his fork toward the Temple Mount. "El'ad arranged the home for this family. Not sure what excuse they gave them for wanting the house, but they provided them a room in the King David Hotel for the night."

"How could they refuse that?" Graham pictured the five-star hotel famous for hosting heads of state and celebrities.

"So, the family will not be home. We will have the chest delivered there tonight. It will be in the crawlspace beneath the house. The cover story will be that it was uncovered as work was being done on the foundation."

"Good. Glad you got the chest okay," Graham said.

"Yes, excellent work." Yaniv nodded. "It will do nicely. I have someone from the restoration department helping to put a seal from the Ottoman era on it now."

"We're on for tomorrow, then?" Daniel asked, raising his brow.

"Yes. Tomorrow morning—not too early, no need for the break of dawn—you will go to the house. A Yamas unit will be nearby if Karanlik makes a move."

"What's Yamas?"

"A secret counter-terrorist unit," Daniel said. "They specialize in going undercover in Arab neighborhoods where disturbances can flare up. Like the Silwan."

"There are 40,000 Arabs in Silwan, but only 400 Jews," Yaniv added.

"That doesn't make me feel secure," Graham said.

"The Jews in Silwan take care to protect themselves because they are so outnumbered." Yaniv bounced his fork as he spoke, accenting his words. "Their houses are surrounded by walls—some with electric fences. They have security cameras monitoring their properties. Some even have guard posts on their roofs. When you enter the neighborhood, there will not be a second when you are not being watched. And with the addition of a Yamas unit, you will have adequate protection, I assure you."

"Why not have Yamas there the whole time?" Graham asked.

"Ah, but they *will* be there before," Daniel said. "An officer will be dressed as a normal soldier guarding the gate. Four more officers will be in the house. One will be in civilian clothes, acting as the homeowner." He tapped spots on the table as he spoke, abstractly indicating positions. "The house has an excellent security system, and the officers inside will be able to monitor us at all times. Except when we're under the house, of course."

Graham processed the plan, balancing the security measures against the fact that they were necessary.

"A GPS chip is being embedded in the trunk," Daniel said. "If Karanlik does find a way to take it, then we will have his precise location. Worst-case scenario is that he will have stolen pots full of metal washers, not silver shekels."

Graham busied himself sprinkling cinnamon on a few figs, aware that Yaniv and Daniel were waiting for a response. After a swig of Diet Coke, he looked from one to the other. "Honestly—given the choice—I'd rather be at the King David."

THIRTY-FOUR

A faint cloud of jealousy followed Graham from the café to the hotel, fogging his thoughts like an internal shadow. He had worked to keep the connection he felt with Iris at bay. Even if he planned to stay in Spain longer than a few days, he knew it was unwise to encourage a relationship with someone who didn't share his faith. The difference in worldviews would ultimately cause too much conflict. And yet, when he saw the instant chemistry between Iris and Paco, he felt a sense of loss. He was self-aware enough to recognize the irrationality of his reaction, but too emotionally vulnerable to be armored against it. He craved for a connection like he'd had with Olivia and had to be vigilant not to project his need on a substitute.

He climbed into bed and pulled the sheet over his head, as if hiding from his own distractions. Lying on his back, he realized he was in the same position as the man in the Shroud. The pose reminded him of Paco's list of artistic techniques for recreating the image, and he started working his way through them, analyzing each one.

The sensation of the cloth on his face and chest made him think of Paco's idea to lay the linen sheet across a heated bas relief. The contact would scorch the material, imprinting an image. Graham felt the cloth on the sides of his head and arms, conforming to his body, and knew the technique would fail. Even if an image was left behind, it would become distorted when the sheet was laid flat. Any method that used contact to create the image—such as paint or dye on the body—would fail for the same reason. The blood and dirt would be transferred by contact, of course, but not the image.

Paco had said he was thinking about making his own red ocher paint in the same way as it had been made in thirteenth century Europe—vermilion and iron oxide. He made a mental note to see if the STURP findings mentioned iron oxide on the cloth. In his work with manuscripts, Graham grew to appreciate how strokes used in writing showed directionality and a subtle variance in the way pressure was applied at different points on the line. Again, those would be characteristics STURP might have detected if the image had been created with a brush.

Powder applied with a dry brush—another method suggested by Paco—would also leave traces of directionality and variant density. But it would also leave grains of powder caught in the weave. Yet another feature STURP may have detected or tested for.

The technique suggested by Paco that made the most sense to Graham is how light could be projected through a glass painting to discolor the cloth. It was clearly within the reach of the imagination of a thirteenth-century forger, but it had a number of practical problems. The amount of sunlight needed to create the discoloration would require multiple exposures for long periods of time. Given the changing angle of light from a moving sun, the image would be blurred. Either that or the glass would have to move with great precision and be mounted in such a way as to change the angle as well.

Graham doubted a medieval forger would have that kind of knowledge, let alone go to such trouble. What would be the upside to the effort? And even if he correctly made the calculations and the apparatus, how would the forger know to collect and apply pollen from the regions where the Shroud had apparently been kept prior to its appearance in Europe? Paco's favored method dropped from ingenious to wildly improbable.

Haunting all the methods was the question Paco himself asked: Why would an artist make a negative image if the idea was to convince people the image of Jesus had been imprinted on the cloth? It's a strange choice for someone pulling a con. Especially for one that did not bring the con man fame or fortune.

As Graham reflected on the implausibility of the methods, he became more aware of the weight of the sheet pressing against him. The perspective from beneath the linen gave him a new insight, a truth he accidentally stumbled upon. He had always thought of the Shroud as covering Jesus, when the truth was that people were the ones enShrouded. They wore the veil of sin, of unbelief, of self-deceit. They were cloaked in mortality and finitude. The Shroud didn't trap darkness, it enveloped light—Jesus.

Moses had veiled his face after beholding God's glory because the light from His countenance shone so brightly. The light was where shadow should have been. The Holy of Holies—the location of God's immediate presence on Earth—was obscured by a curtain, ultimate reality condescending to be with His people. It was this same curtain-veil-Shroud the writer of Hebrews referenced when he wrote, "We have this hope as an anchor for the soul, sure and steadfast, which reaches inside behind the curtain."

From beneath his bedsheet, behind closed eyes, Graham imagined himself bathed in light, and fell asleep.

THIRTY-FIVE

As Daniel showed his ID to the soldier Yaniv stationed at the gate, Graham scanned the compound. A cinder block wall as high as the first story surrounded the property, supporting several strands of razor wire and at least four security cameras. The modular three-story house looked like a stack of blocks, stylistically matching the other boxy houses that ubiquitously studded Silwan. Unlike most of the other houses, the walls were unblemished by graffiti, and a set of solar panels crowned the roof, distinguishing it as a recent construction.

"Go knock on the door."

"Why?" Graham glanced at Daniel. "Wouldn't that expose Yamas?"

"We have to make it look real," Daniel said. "The officer is in civilian clothes, remember? Acting like the homeowner who will guide us to where we need to go. That way it will look like we've been called to the house or prearranged the visit. We need to sell the scene to Karanlik—if he's watching."

"It's your show," Graham said, bowing slightly.

He started for the door and realized he was walking alone. He looked back to find Daniel already leaning on the van, fishing out a cigarette. "Coming, Daniel?"

"No. You're the leader of the dig. You need to look like you're in charge." He tilted his pack of cigarettes toward Nagi, apparently offering a truce.

Nagi shook his head with a smile and joined him against the van.

Graham crossed the driveway, his movements stiff with self-consciousness, and rang the doorbell.

The door was opened by a woman with a stern face framed by coils of long dark hair. Graham took in the scarf, blouse, and skirt and wondered if she was armed.

"Shalom," she said.

After Graham played his part and returned the greeting, the woman leaned across the threshold and gestured to the side of the house farthest from the gate.

"It's around here. Come."

Daniel stomped out his cigarette and grabbed a pack of gear as he and Nagi fell in behind Graham, following the agent around the corner. The security wall ran parallel to the house, creating an eight-foot-wide corridor filled with shadow. She stopped halfway down, kneeled at the door to the crawlspace, and used a key to open a padlock hanging from a latch. Graham looked at the square portal—less than four feet on each side—and wondered how they got the chest to fit through it.

"It's in there, along the wall on the right," the woman said, rising.

Graham bent down and shined a flashlight under the house, sweeping the crawlspace with light until the beam hit Ravid's trunk. "There it is."

"Want me to go pull it out?" Nagi feinted forward.

"No," Daniel said. "It wouldn't look right. We have to do everything we would normally do. All three of us need to go in there for a while. We need to set up lights, and then wait long enough to evaluate it." He looked at the Yamas officer. "Stay here, like you're curious what we're going to remove from under your house."

Ten minutes later, the three of them crouched around the chest in a pool of harsh utility light. Graham was impressed with the improvements the IAA had made to it. A heavy round paper seal had been glued over each metal latch. Writing in Arabic, Hebrew, and English declared it was property of the Turkish government, not to be opened without authorization.

A round adaptation of the Turkish flag—a red field with the white crescent and star—made the labels look vaguely like targets. Each had been distressed—the edges of the yellowed paper bent and frayed, the ink faded and scratched, conspiring to give the appearance of age. *Parker Expedition* had been stenciled on its top as well as both ends, the antiqued white paint worn almost completely away to reveal the grain of the wood underneath.

"Your guys did a great job on this."

Nagi touched one of the seals, rubbing it as he appreciated the work.

"They are good." Daniel nodded. "There are probably no better forgers than the team who restores the real things. I don't think it would survive close inspection, but it's certainly good enough for what we're doing."

"Well, can we do whatever it is we're doing any faster?" Nagi asked. "It's like a sauna in here."

"You don't have to tell me." Daniel held his arms away from his chest as best as he could in the confined space, displaying the design of sweat stains. "I'm like a living Rorschach test."

"I'm more concerned about what the shape smells like than what I see in it." Graham began to laugh at his own joke but was cut off by the voice of the plain clothes agent.

"Someone's here. A van just pulled up to the gate."

"Karanlik," Graham said.

"Right on time," Daniel said. "I told the officer at the gate to question him pretty heavily. Let him tell whatever story he worked up. Make him work for it but let him through."

Graham froze in place, futilely straining the air for fragments of the exchange. He had to swallow his surprise when Daniel tapped his shoulder. Daniel pointed to his earpiece, then held up a finger, signaling him to wait.

"Hold on," Daniel said into the mic, then addressed Graham. "The driver claims that a man hired him this morning to drive the truck here at this time to pick up a package. He said he would be given an address to deliver it to. He doesn't know who the man is. The officer says the driver seems completely clueless as well as a little nervous that he got stopped by an Israeli soldier. He's not sure this is our guy."

"Karanlik sent someone in case it was too risky?" Graham asked.

"Only one way to find out."

Daniel told the officer to let the van through, then enlisted Nagi to help him drag the chest to the hatch. Nagi lifted one side of the box onto the lip of the foundation as Daniel and Graham guided it into the opening. An inch-wide margin created a square corona as they pushed. The sound of the van's engine rumbled into the crawlspace, accented by the crunch of gravel under slow tires stopping near the hatch.

Hurried footsteps suddenly clomped on the floor above them, running to the far end of the house.

"*Someone just dropped over the fence on the other side of the yard," Daniel whispered. "They watched him on video from inside.*"

"*The van was a decoy?" Graham asked.*

"*Looks like it.*"

Cries of protest tangled with sharp, authoritative commands came from the opposite corner of the property. Again, the three men froze, listening. A crack of wood broke their concentration as the end of the chest exposed to the alley was pried open, splinter-

ing away.

"Officer, what's happening?" Daniel said in full voice.

The answer hissed through the crack between the chest and the house, misting the crawlspace.

"Pepper spray!" Daniel recoiled, scrambling back, the others reflexively imitating him.

They scrambled to the other side of the foundation and watched the chest, holding their shirt collars over their noses. A scraping sound came from the chest as it rocked in the hatch, and Graham envisioned the stone jars being pulled out the open end.

A car door slam, gunned engine, and a spray of gravel signaled the departure of the van. Daniel took a big breath, shot across the space and rammed the empty chest the rest of the way through the hole. By the time Graham and Nagi followed, Daniel was bent over the prone form of the female officer, pulling a tranquilizer dart from her collar. The guard from the gate was nearby, also unconscious.

"They'll be okay," Daniel said, springing to his feet. "What do you have on the fence jumper?" he barked into the mic.

"He's just a kid," the officer responded. "He said a man gave him a roll of money to climb over a certain part of the fence when he texted a signal. He's shaking he's so scared. No way he's your guy."

"Has to be the other guy," Daniel said. "If we hurry, we might still be able to catch up to him!"

"How?" Graham asked. "He could be anywhere in this maze."

"GPS tracker," Daniel said, breaking into a run toward the SUV. "Remember?"

THIRTY-SIX

"Yaniv, track the GPS!" Daniel barked into the phone as he threw the van into gear. "Karanlik's got the jars."

By the time he finished quickly briefing Yaniv, Daniel had careened through the neighborhood, and was turning on to Ma'alot Ir David Street toward the southern wall of the Temple. The adrenaline in the SUV crackled with energy as though they ought to race, but they were blocked by a tour bus slowly negotiating the narrow, congested street. A second bus followed them, trapping them in a train.

"I see him." Yaniv's speakerphone made him sound like he was in a tin can. "He is on Ma'alot Ir David."

Daniel craned his neck, trying to see around the traffic in front of them. "Can't see anything ahead of us."

Graham rolled down his window and started to lean out to look past the bus behind them.

"Don't do that," Daniel commanded. "If he sees you looking for him, he might take a shot. You're making yourself an easy target."

"Turn right at the intersection," Yaniv said. "Let us see if he follows you."

"Why would he follow us if he's trying to get away?" Daniel barked.

"Right now he has no choice," Graham said, pointing

to another bus on the left, blocking the road as it unloaded tourists.

Daniel turned right, following the bus ahead of them, reversing the route they had driven that morning. Thick silence filled the van as they waited for an update.

"He turned," Yaniv said. "He is following you."

"I don't see a van anywhere," Graham said, taking advantage of the turn to scan the cars behind the bus.

"Must've switched cars," Daniel said. "That's what I would've done."

Graham kept his eyes on the side mirror as the train of busses flowed past the archaeological park, then the cemetery.

"Here comes the next test," Yaniv said.

Graham looked away from the mirror to the approaching intersection.

"No way he'll turn left," Daniel said.

"Still there," Yaniv reported.

"I don't know which one it could be," Nagi said, studying the traffic as he pressed his forehead against the window behind Daniel.

"Let's see if we can pull him out of the crowd." Daniel punched the gas, shooting the SUV forward, accelerating quickly as he veered into the oncoming lane to pass the tour bus ahead of them. He whipped the truck back into their side of the road, slotting into a space behind another bus as they headed toward the junction with Sultan Suleiman.

"Anyone following?"

"I can't tell," Graham said. "The bus is in the way."

"He is still right with you!" Yaniv said.

"Impossible!" Nagi exclaimed. "Unless he's on the bus behind us."

Graham looked at Daniel. "Makes sense. Karanlik could've mixed in with a tour group."

"They would have known he was not part of the group,"

Yaniv said. "And what would he do with the jars? He couldn't take them on the bus with him."

"Keep an eye on the busses, just in case," Daniel said as they shot through the three-way intersection across from The Rockefeller Museum and into the lot behind the building.

"The one behind us went north," Nagi said. "The one behind that just turned along the Old City."

"He followed you," Yaniv said urgently.

All three men looked around, confused.

"He is there! He is there!" Yaniv repeated.

"No one's there, Chaim," Graham said.

"What do you mean?"

"I mean no one followed us in."

"But I watched him," Yaniv said, sounding vexed. "He followed you in. This does not make sense."

"Actually, it does." Daniel threw his door open and bolted out.

Graham watched as Daniel circled the SUV, closely examining it. After completing a circuit, he dropped to the ground and looked under the car. He crawled to the rear and ran his hand along the inside of the back bumper. He got to his feet holding a black rectangle the size of a car key fob.

"What is happening here?" Yaniv said as he burst onto the loading dock.

"You weren't tracking *him*. You were tracking *us*," Daniel said. "He found the GPS tracker and put it on our car."

"How did he know to look for a tracker?" Graham asked.

"He didn't," Daniel said. "We expected him to take the whole chest, not unload it. The box that holds the tracker is magnetic, and since the jars had metal washers, I attached it on the outside of one of the jars. He must have seen it when he pulled the jar out, then put it on our SUV as he left."

"But the GPS said he was behind us," Graham said.

"Because of latency." Daniel shook his head, apparently rebuking himself for not realizing what was happening. "There's a delay between the ping and when it registers on the map. Most of the time it's too short to notice. And we were moving slow because of traffic a lot of that time, so it would be harder to see the lag. Looks like we fooled ourselves."

Graham let out a sigh of disappointment and relief. "Chased by our own shadow."

THIRTY-SEVEN

"So, what do we do now?" Graham collapsed into what had become his usual chair in Yaniv's office, feeling like he would never move again. "This whole charade was supposed to get Karanlik out of the way. It's almost like he was expecting a trap."

Daniel's cheeks puffed as he made a deflating sound. "The real question is what he will do now that he knows we were trying to trick him."

"That is not the question." Yaniv snapped his fingers and pointed a finger at Daniel. "That is the answer!"

Graham glanced at Daniel to see if he was following Yaniv's train of thought, then turned back to Yaniv. "What do you mean?"

"We *know* what Karanlik is going to do because it is the final clue."

"The scroll says the treasure is in the great cistern at the end of the double gate," Graham said. "Cistern 8. Which helps us how?"

Daniel sat up straight as he grasped the implication. "So far Karanlik hasn't known where we would be looking. He depended on our interpretation of the clues. But this time the location is so specific that he does not need to watch us. Which means—"

"Which means we do not need GPS to find him. We

can be watching for him." Yaniv smiled. "He also has the same problem we do: How to get into the cistern. The only entrance is on the Temple Mount. Adjacent to the al-Aqsa Mosque."

"We'll have to send Nagi home," Daniel said, working out the logistics. "He'd consider it sacrilegious. And he'd probably say the Jews would use it as an excuse to find a new way to claim the Mount is theirs. Especially if the treasure is actually there."

Graham didn't like the thought of excluding Nagi from what was possibly a monumental discovery, but the memory of the debate in the car as they drove through Silwan convinced him Daniel was right.

"Nagi does not know the final location, does he?" Yaniv asked.

Daniel shook his head. "We never told him where we were going until we got in the car. He doesn't know about Cistern 8."

"Good, good. I also think you should change hotels. If Karanlik has been following you to the sites, then he must know where you are starting from. We should take advantage of him thinking he does not need to know where you are staying anymore."

"Good idea," Graham said, despite feeling they were betraying Nagi in some way.

"It is settled then. I will arrange rooms at the Notre Dame. It overlooks the northwest corner of the Old City, not far from the Church of the Holy Sepulcher."

"We need to see the entrance to the cistern," Daniel said. "We can't make plans until we know what we have to deal with."

"Let us save that for tomorrow." Yaniv folded his hands in front of him. "I will meet you in the morning at the hotel. Then we can go up to the Mount."

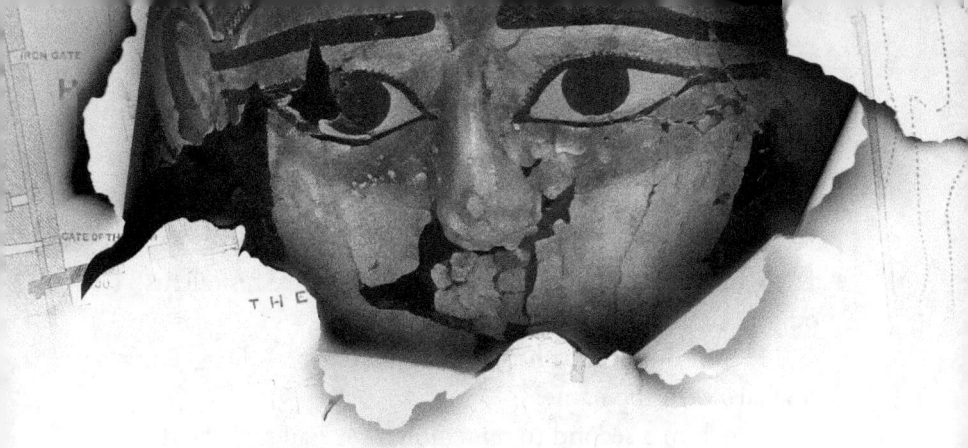

THIRTY-EIGHT

An hour after leaving the Rockefeller Museum, Graham and Daniel walked to the elevator in the lobby of the Pontifical Institute Notre Dame of Jerusalem Center, keycards in hand. Although it looked like an ancient castle made from stone that matched the Old City, it had been built for pilgrims in the late 1800s.

"Seen the Shroud exhibit?" Graham asked.

In addition to the guest house, the Notre Dame was home to an extensive permanent exhibition on the Shroud of Turin, the burial cloth of Christ, featuring a full-sized replica of the original housed in Turin, Italy.

Daniel knitted his brow incredulously.

"Dumb question," Graham said, chastising himself. "Sorry."

"I'll tell you the real reason people come here." Daniel pointed to the ceiling. "They've got a restaurant on the rooftop terrace with the best view of the Old City. Mount of Olives in the background, on the other side of the Temple Mount."

"Wish Nagi could see it," Graham said.

"We could use more like him. Hope he stays with the IAA for a while."

Graham could hear affection in the reply and was glad

that Daniel and Nagi's disagreement in the van didn't seem to have damaged their relationship.

"I wish there was a better way for him to use his talents, though," Graham said.

"Me too. But at least he's helping us." Daniel shrugged. "So what's with the name?"

It took him a second to remember they had registered under assumed names as an extra precaution.

"Peter Bravestrong?" Graham laughed. "I'm not used to this spy stuff like you. I couldn't think of anything, so I used the name Prince used when he checked into hotels."

"Prince?"

"It was just some trivia I read in an in-flight magazine on the way over. It was the first thing I could think of. How about yours?"

"Eli Pearl?" Daniel raised his brow. "First name of one grandfather, last name of the other. I get my impatience from Eli. In fact, it killed him."

"Really?"

"He got tired of waiting for an elevator. Decided to take the stairs down even though he was almost ninety. Fell down the flight and never recovered."

"I'm so sorry. That's awful." Graham looked at the floor, not knowing where else to look. "It's strange, though. Prince died in an elevator."

"Hmm. That is strange. Can't win either way you go."

The elevator doors opened, and they looked into it without moving, offering a choice between Eli or Prince. The perfect timing made them laugh as they stepped in.

Graham hit the button and smirked. "To quote the great philosopher Warren Zevon: 'Life'll kill ya.'"

THIRTY-NINE

The Western Wall Plaza looked almost empty, the light stonework peppered with black coats and hats of only a couple of dozen worshippers offering prayers before work and without tourists. It had opened at 7 a.m.—an hour earlier—and lacked the chaotic atmosphere Graham normally associated with the place, and as he walked across it, he thought this would be his favorite time to come if he were Jewish.

As he watched worshippers press themselves against the wall, he thought of the tradition that God stands on the other side, watching through the cracks while remaining unseen. A sign beneath the scalloped roof of the entrance pavilion—just outside the metal detectors—reminded visitors that they had come to the place "where the Divine Presence always rests," but the security measure itself was a tacit reminder that it was also a place where evil never rests.

They had arrived early enough for Graham to take a quick look at the progress of the excavations on the west side of the plaza, a hundred yards from the Temple Mount. A section of the pavement sixty feet wide and fifteen feet deep had been removed to reveal the street level from the time of Jesus. The Romans had constructed a market there when they rebuilt the city after AD 70, but it had been buried when the Muslims captured the city in the eighth century and built the plaza over it.

They joined the line of people queued at the entrance of a long, wooden ramp that began parallel to the southwest corner of the Mount, then curved toward the Mount as it rose, skirting the archaeological park. Graham thought it looked like an enormous, j-shaped wooden zipper.

"I can't believe this thing is still here," Graham said, shaking his head. "It's like a deck-builder bribed the city council to get the job."

Yaniv chuckled. "Just so. If they had known it would become permanent they probably would have done it differently. But every time they try to build the permanent entrance, the Muslims threaten a new intifada. They claim we are trying to weaken the Mount so that the mosque will collapse. Ridiculous, of course. But this is the only gate they allow non-Muslims to enter, so what are we to do?" He shrugged in futility.

The line began to move, threading through an airport-style metal detector and x-ray machine supervised by soldiers wearing machine guns and yarmulkes.

Graham looked over the wooden railing on his right, into the remains of the Second Temple that had been thrown from the platform when Jerusalem had been destroyed by the Romans in AD 70. He knew some of what he was seeing was found when the earthen ramp that had been the prior entrance to the Temple eroded, necessitating the permanently temporary bridge he now ascended.

At the far-right side of the park, near the southwest corner, he spotted the courses of stone barely jutting from halfway up the wall, thirty feet above the ground. The remnants of the colossal arched stairway had been one of the entrances to the Second Temple and was now known as Robinson's Arch, named for the man who identified it in 1838.

"Hard to believe that was at ground level in 1967," Yaniv said, following Graham's gaze. "Imagine the riots that would occur if we tried an excavation like that now."

Graham shook his head as he pictured it. "It'd be World War III."

The ramp turned to the right, giving them an aerial view of the Western Wall from the left side of the ramp.

"Even harder to believe this was still a neighborhood in 1967," Graham said, picturing the photographs he'd seen of the excavation that became the Western Wall Plaza. "And that bulldozers knocked it down less than a week after the war. And then lowered the street level. Talk about a recipe for riots."

"Just so," Yaniv said. "Many times my parents would tell me about the narrow alley along the wall where they used to pray. Men and women together, not separated."

Graham looked across the worshippers at the Western Wall as they shuffled to the end of the ramp, past four more soldiers sitting in white plastic chairs. The bridge deposited them on a stone landing lined with two dozen transparent Plexiglas riot shields leaning against the wall next to the opening.

Like so many features of the Old City, the pointed arch that led onto the Temple Mount had several names. The sign embedded in the wall identified it in Arabic and English as the Morocco Gate, though it was also called the Gate of Moors and the Mughrabi Gate. All referred to the neighborhood of emigrants from North Africa whose neighborhood had been destroyed. It had also been called the Prophet's Gate. And, like much of the Old City, it did not date to the time of Jesus. The gate Jesus used to enter this part of the Temple Mount had been buried underground over 1,000 years ago after being blocked up. In 1852 it was discovered by a missionary, whose name it now bore: the Barclay Gate.

A heavy wooden rectangular door stood open on the inside of the arch. Much of its green paint had worn away, making it look like reclaimed wood that had yet to be abandoned.

"Sure it's okay for you to go in?" Graham asked Yaniv as he followed him across the threshold.

"What do you mean?" Yaniv said over his shoulder.

"The warning sign over the metal detectors. It said, 'According to Torah Law, entering the Temple Mount area is strictly forbidden due to the holiness of the site.'"

Yaniv glanced back. "You are serious. I was not sure. Yes, it is okay. Although that warning is from the Chief Rabbinate, there is debate about what it means exactly. But I think as long as we do not go there to worship there is no problem." He faced forward again, then spoke over his shoulder. "Actually, it is you who should be worried."

"Why do you say that?" Graham had no intention of worshipping any god, here or anywhere else.

"Remember the Temple Warning inscription?"

Graham laughed as he pictured the inscription uncovered on the Mount in 1871 by Charles Clermont-Ganneau. It came from the *soreg*, the small wall that marked the boundary on the Temple Mount platform beyond which non-Jews and non-converts were not allowed to go. "'No stranger is to enter within the balustrade round the Temple and enclosure.'"

"Just so," Yaniv said, then completed the quote. "'Whoever is caught will be responsible to himself for his death, which will ensue.'"

"Well, let's hope it doesn't come to that."

FORTY

Within the special fascination he had for Jerusalem, two places captured Graham's imagination in particular: The Church of the Holy Sepulchre and the Temple Mount. In Graham's theology, they were bookends—the Temple was the symbol that pointed to the work of Christ on the cross, which vouched for the Resurrection.

He stepped out of the shade of the gate and looked to his left, down the inside of the Western Wall, toward the magnificent dome rising above the trees, covered in gold. He tried to picture the Temple in its place, rising even higher, built on the spot where Abraham had brought Isaac to offer up to God. But the thing Graham always had a hard time picturing was how the enormous blocks of stone forming the Temple had been knocked down and thrown off the edge of the platform when Jerusalem fell in AD 70.

He couldn't view the Dome without seeing it through the layers of history, overlaying images of the buildings that had stood there before. After the Jews revolted again in AD 135, hoping to rebuild the Temple, Hadrian built a temple to Jupiter on the spot to erase the Jewish claim to the Mount. Graham took that as an act of spite more than a devotion to a Roman deity. Constantine seemed to agree and had razed the shrine, erecting an octagonal-shaped church in its place.

Fifty years after the Muslims laid siege to Jerusalem in 637, they constructed the Dome of the Rock on the foundations of the church. Crusaders converted the Dome back into a church, but the Muslims took control again, and it reverted to a mosque. And twice Jews had attempted to build a third Temple only to have it taken from them and destroyed.

"We need to go straight." Yaniv motioned to the open area in front of them.

Graham looked to his right as they passed the Islamic Museum, a thousand-year-old building that sat on the southern end of the platform. Several dozen capitals taken from pillars that had once stood on the Mount were displayed on pedestals, forming a grid of ruined columns. A cat lounged on top of one of the capitals, another rubbed its side on the base.

"I always forget about the cats."

Yaniv shrugged. "They are better than the rats that would be here without them."

Graham tried not to let the image distract him as he left the cats behind.

The al-Aqsa Mosque sat on the other side of the stand of pillars, built on the spot where Allah had transported Muhammad after taking him from al-Haram, the Great Mosque in Mecca. It was here Allah revealed surah 17, an event that gave the chapter its name—*al-Isra*, The Night Journey—and the mosque its name: *The Farthest Mosque*. The place was so important that Muslims faced it when praying until Muhammad received a revelation to face the Ka'aba in Mecca instead.

During the Crusades, the Templars used the building as their headquarters. A portico of pointed arches sheltered the entrance to the mosque. Two rows of arched windows covered with arabesque screens sat high on the wall. The trim—as well as every other entrance to a sacred place on the Mount—was painted the same green as the Morocco Gate, a color that symbolized paradise.

Graham fixed his eyes on the balustrade in front of the building. What looked like a New York subway entrance descended from the esplanade, leading to the original area of the mosque. The mosque had been constructed in the remnants of the foyer and ornate hallways of the Huldah Gates—the main entrance to the Temple when Jesus was alive. Two sets of gates—one double, the other triple—had originally stood at the foot of the southern wall and contained underground flights of steps that conducted worshippers to and from the platform. The entrances on the wall had been bricked in by the Crusaders, but the passage of the Double Gate was now the basement of the mosque, closed to all but Muslims. Graham still thought of the passage as the Huldah Gates. He looked deep into the stairwell wishing he could explore one of the few authentic features left of the Second Temple.

To his left, a large round fountain fenced with an ornate green grille stood between the mosque and the Dome of the Rock. Several worshippers were seated in the stone chairs surrounding *al-Kas*—the Cup—performing ablutions before entering the mosque.

"Amazing how much the Temple Mount has changed," Graham said.

"No more talk about the Temple Mount," Daniel said quietly. "We don't want to call attention to ourselves."

"It's gotten that bad?"

"The Waqf doesn't allow it at all," Yaniv said. "Since you were here last, things are more…tense—if that is possible. Despite the Status Quo. They've started reprimanding people for calling it the Temple Mount. It's either the Haram al-Sharif or Noble Sanctuary."

Graham scanned the Mount at the mention of the Waqf. They had overseen the Temple Mount since taking back the platform from the Templars, retaining administration despite several changes in the government. Since 1948 they had been

supported by Jordan, and though Jordan had lost the territory nineteen years later in the Six-Day War, Israel allowed the
Waqf to continue to administrate the Mount—an arrange-
ment known as the Status Quo. Unlike the Israeli soldiers
and police who patrolled the Mount, the Waqf were armed
only with walkie-talkies, ready to report anything profane or
suspicious.

"At least it's still open to visitors," Graham said, remem-
bering that non-Muslims had not been allowed on the Mount
for half of the twentieth century.

The other side of al-Aqsa opened into a sparse, unused
section of plaza that spanned the distance to the eastern wall.
A grid of nine column bases filled part of the space, completing the collection of pillar remnants. Graham looked past
them to the southeast corner, a spot that had always fascinated him.

"See something?" Daniel asked.

"That's where James was thrown from. Jesus's brother."

"That's in the New Testament?"

"No. Hegesippus. Second-century historian. It's also
where Jesus was tempted by Satan. That is in the New Testament." Graham motioned along the southern wall. "This
whole side was the Royal Stoa, the colonnaded market where
Jesus overturned the tables of merchants taking advantage of
the worshippers."

Graham could see Daniel imagining the structure.

"The columns were a hundred feet tall. The end of the
stoa on the southeast corner was the pinnacle. That's where
Satan tempted Jesus to throw himself down."

"And now the spot below where he stood is a mosque,"
Yaniv said contemptuously.

Graham followed Yaniv's gaze to a wide flight of stairs
descending below the surface of the platform—the entrance
to the al-Marwani Mosque. "It's still hard to believe the Waqf

would violate the Status Quo so blatantly."

Yaniv shook his head. "They did not even do us the courtesy of giving us most of the material they excavated. Four hundred truckloads of fill, and we were given only 60. And it took enormous pressure to get that."

"The amazing thing is that you've had it since the 90s and its still being sifted through. Imagine how long it would take to search all 9,000 tons."

"Imagine what was lost," Daniel said. "So far we've recovered—what—5,000 coins, a bulla dated before the Babylonian captivity, jewelry, arrowheads, mosaic fragments, and even the capital of a pillar."

"It is maddening to think what got thrown away," Graham said. "But what really baffles me is why they built it at all. That's the place the Templars called Solomon's Stables. They kept horses there. Why would a Muslim worship in a stable when the third most sacred mosque in Islam is literally feet away."

Yaniv led them across the plaza, and they sat on a retaining wall in the shade of several olive trees, facing al-Aqsa.

"This is it," Yaniv said softly. "Cistern 8."

FORTY-ONE

The pavement before them was studded with several well caps—thigh-high concrete stumps. Each was sealed with a square, tread-plate-patterned hatch painted sacred green and secured with a padlock.

"When I was a boy," Daniel said, "I heard that Jews threw themselves into one of these wells to commit suicide during one of the Muslim attacks. They say that on the anniversary of the destruction of the Temple you can still hear weeping coming from the well." He scrutinized the half a dozen hatches between them and the mosque. "So, which one is it?"

"Let me check the map," Graham said, fishing out his phone.

He opened the survey drawing made by Wilson and Warren. The perimeter of the Temple Mount was outlined, and the footprint of each structure was lightly shaded. Irregular shapes filled in with dark shading indicated underground cisterns. Each was numbered in the order of discovery. But one thing missing from the diagram was the location of the access points. In most cases, the cisterns were small enough that there was no question which cap opened to it. But a few of the reservoirs were large enough to have multiple manholes.

"From what I can tell, number 8 is directly below this big area we're looking at. The one in front of us on the far side, closest to the fountain"—Graham nodded—"is probably number 6. The one directly to our left has got to be 11. That leaves the three out in the open. Wilson and Warren said there were three mouths in use when they were here. Those must be them."

"Completely out in the open," Daniel said, turning to the other two. "All these trees and buildings with niches, all these little sheds, and the one place we have to find a way into is where we can be seen by everyone entering the mosque."

Graham guessed about a hundred people milled around the area between al-Aqsa and the Dome. Half of them were tourists clustered around guides. The other half were Muslim worshippers, the women in burkas and hijabs, the men a mix of western dress and those wearing *taqiyah* skullcaps. Israeli soldiers and police were sprinkled throughout the platform. All of them maintained a respectful silence.

"Just so," Yaniv said. "Too many witnesses. But it is also a crowd that can make us anonymous. And the hiding places you see can still be useful to us."

"What about security cameras?" Graham searched the flood lights and loudspeakers artlessly mounted to the buildings.

"There are cameras on the Mount," Yaniv said, nodding toward each location. "I know they are over the entrances to the mosques and the Dome, but there are none *inside* the mosques."

"We'll be watched the whole time. Even now," Daniel said.

"We must assume that, yes."

Graham returned to the notes on his phone. "Here's what Wilson and Warren say about Cistern 8. It's known as the *Great Sea*, but is also called *Bir el Aswad*, which means *Black Well*. Starts five feet below the surface of the platform and is forty-three feet deep." Graham looked at the center of the plaza and tried to imagine the space below before returning to his phone. "Okay, listen to this: Wilson says, 'The entrance to this is by a flight of steps leading down from a hole on the northern side of the workshops east of al-Aqsa.'"

Graham had always been shocked at how dilapidated the Temple Mount was. Piles of building debris and drifts of garbage marred areas across the platform—including the entrance of the newly built al-Marwani Mosque. Rickety outbuildings, sheds, and lean-tos imposed a shantytown quality on the holy precincts where the House of God once stood, now the third most holy site in Islam. And the ugliest building on the Mount was suddenly the most interesting to them.

When they had entered the platform, Graham thought the long, narrow structure looked like an abandoned trailer someone had attempted to reroof with scrap panels of corrugated tin. As they walked past it, he thought the bottom half of the walls looked like they had been scavenged from the fuselage of a wrecked plane. It was an inexplicably ramshackle building that would have been at home in a slum. And it stood—barely, by appearances—as a shelter over a flight of stairs descending into the platform.

"He must mean the old entrance to Solomon's Stables," Yaniv said. "Now it goes to al-Marwani."

"Think there's still a way in from there?" asked Daniel.

"Even if there were, we'd never get access to it," Graham said. "Muslims only."

"There is even a guard at the top of the steps." Yaniv bobbed his head toward a green shack, the size of a small elevator car, standing to the side of the landing.

"What did they find in the cistern?" Daniel asked as he kept his eyes on the shelter.

Graham skimmed his notes. "The roof is held up with stone pillars made when the rock was hollowed out. Most of the roof is rock. The rest either has flat stones or is vaulted."

"Was it full of water?" Daniel studied the green hatch, as if trying to see through it.

"Not at all. There was some dry floor, but mostly it was covered in shallow water. Of course, you have to remember they only examined it from the bottom of the steps and from the hatches on the platform. Who knows how much water is in there now?"

"That could make things very difficult," Yaniv said.

"Think how difficult it was for Warren and Wilson," Graham said. "Wilson records that they dropped their light into the water as they were investigating it. They lost their measurements and had to make some of the map from memory. Apparently, there is a circular chamber in one of the corners." Graham switched pages and found it on the map, then went back to the notes. "Warren estimates it holds two million gallons. But again, they weren't able to make a proper survey of the cavern. They even saw a conduit cut into the rock that they couldn't reach."

"So we'd be going into a network of caverns without a complete map," Daniel said.

"Do not sound so hopeless, my friend," Yaniv said philosophically. "That is what life is."

FORTY-TWO

The Arabic words of *Dhuhr*—the noon prayer—floated above the Old City, into the rooftop restaurant of the Notre Dame Hotel. The Temple Mount had closed to non-Muslims for the ritual, and the three men used the time to compare notes. Graham's iPad formed the centerpiece on the table as they ate, studying Warren and Wilson's survey map displayed on the screen. After an hour of brainstorming how to enter Cistern 8, they were no closer to a solution.

"Still hard to believe a 150-year-old map is the best information we have to work with." Daniel's heavy sigh pushed him back from the table.

"Graham is right, though." Yaniv steepled his fingers and rested his chin on his thumbs. "Even if time were not an issue, we could never build up enough good will to receive permission to explore as Wilson and Warren did."

"I still think we should do what Montagu Parker did," Daniel said.

"And dress as Arabs?" Graham chuckled incredulously. "Do I look like Richard Burton?"

"Depends on the movie."

"Hilarious," Graham deadpanned. "No. The British explorer. Searched for the source of the Nile. Traveled Saudi Arabia in disguise so he wouldn't be killed. Translated *The*

Arabian Nights into English. Spoke twenty-nine languages. Perhaps you've heard of him?"

Daniel smiled. "Good to hear you know something other than music trivia."

"Actually, it is not a terrible plan," Yaniv said.

Graham studied Yaniv to see if he was serious.

"But it wouldn't necessarily have to be as Arabs. There are people from all over the world who visit the Mount."

"We could get some Israeli Army uniforms." Daniel leaned forward. "Or police. Hide in plain sight dressed as the kind of people the Waqf wants to avoid."

"We can already walk around the Mount anonymously," Graham said, looking intently at the iPad. "We'd still need to find a way into the cistern. And it definitely doesn't get us into the mosque since we'd be dressed in official Israeli clothes."

"Just so. Whatever we choose to do, we must take care not to create an incident like Parker did."

Daniel chuckled. "Especially since we have no yacht to run to."

"We have a bigger problem than that," Graham said. "It's not just getting in we have to worry about. It's getting out. Especially if we find fourteen talents of silver down there."

"That is more than 150 kilos," Yaniv said. "About 350 pounds."

"Without anyone seeing us," Daniel said.

Graham's phone began to vibrate on the table as Gideon Ravid's name appeared on the screen.

"Gideon. Shalom." Graham put the call on speaker and held the phone between them.

Ravid's voice was caught in mid-sentence. "...with IAA identification came into the shop asking if I had seen you."

"That's strange," Graham said, trading looks with Daniel and Yaniv. "What did you say?"

"I told the truth: that you had come a few days ago, but it was near closing time, so you promised to return soon. He wanted to know where you were staying. You never mentioned it. But even if you did, I would not have told him. I got the feeling he was not actually IAA. He had identification, and he wore the blue shirt, but something about him did not seem legitimate."

"Like what?" Graham asked.

"It was mostly a feeling, but there were two odd things. He had an accent. Very slight. Maybe Turkish. And, as he was leaving, he commented on one of the large oil lamps by the door. Said it was a nice piece. But it was—how should I say it?—not as old as it appears to be."

"Did he leave a phone number or any way for you to contact him?" Graham asked.

"No. But the identification said his name was Bezalel."

Yaniv and Daniel both shook their heads.

"There is no one at the IAA with that name," Yaniv whispered.

"Can you tell me what he looked like?" Graham asked.

"Not quite as tall as you. More full, but not a big man. Black hair, short. He kept his sunglasses on—that was another odd thing—so I could not see his eyes. His nose had a hook to it. And he had quite a large overbite."

Graham imposed the features on the man he had seen in the background of the photo from the conference and on the security videos from Dallas and Maalik's break-in. The details all seemed to fit. He made a note to himself to let Bremmer at the FBI know.

"This is very helpful, Gideon. Thank you so much for calling."

"My pleasure, Dr. Eliot. Shalom."

"Bezalel?" Yaniv raised his brow.

"Ironic, I know." Graham nodded in agreement.

"What do you mean?" Yaniv asked, confused.

Graham hesitated as he realized they weren't on the same page. "Bezalel. He was the artisan God gifted to create The Tabernacle and everything that went in it. Exodus thirty-something? But *this* Bezalel can't tell the real thing from a fake. It's ironic."

"Yes, I remember," Yaniv said. "But you miss the most important meaning. *Bezalel* means *in the shadow of God.*"

"Karanlik," Graham said. "He's figured out we moved. Must've changed the name he's using. But he doesn't know where we are." He nudged Daniel. "Your plan worked."

"Yes," Daniel said. "For the first time we are one step ahead of *him*. We need to go back and watch the area some more before we try to make any final decisions. Maybe something will occur to us if we get a fresh look."

"The Temple Mount is about to reopen," Yaniv said. "But it is only open for an hour in the afternoon. And we do not want to make two appearances in one day. Let us meet here in the morning like we did today."

"I feel like a Levite, going up to the Temple each day," Daniel said.

Graham thought of the daily sacrifice that had been done there for hundreds of years. "Better to be the Levite than the lamb."

FORTY-THREE

Graham exploded to the surface, gasped violently, bobbed once, then sank back into the blackness, pulled under by a weight whose grip he couldn't feel. He kicked powerfully and climbed again, gasping when he reached the pocket of air.

I'm drowning, he thought, part of him detachedly cataloging features of his struggle. I'm drowning, but I don't feel wet.

Again, some unknown force yanked him beneath the air. Not underwater. Just under. Like shadows that wouldn't let him breathe, trying to keep him from shadows that would.

Push! he told himself and kicked again.

He gulped for air in the breathing shadow. Then he saw them. Olivia and Alyson. Their hands reaching for him, trying to pull him up. He whipped his legs, scissoring them twice to avoid being swallowed by the drowning shadow.

He thrust his arm toward them, immediately pulled it back, not recognizing the black smear, the fringe of fingers. He reached again, thinking there had been some kind of mistake. Again black.

It's not pulling me under. It's becoming me. I am becoming shadow.

The thought was like a spell, the words tugging the thread of details until it had been removed, only the hole remaining.

Graham awoke to a room almost as black as his nightmare.

He looked to the door just as a pool of blackness—fluid but dry—expanded, erasing all it touched like a living veil drawing itself across the room. He piled himself in the middle of the bed, making a castaway of himself, stranded by a rational response to what was irrational.

He watched as it crawled over the edge of the mattress, moving in slowly, malignantly. He screamed but never heard the sound.

Graham awoke from the dream-within-a-dream in a sweat and fixed his eyes on the door even before they could adjust. There was no darkness seeping in, but he knew better. The blackest darkness is invisible. And it was already here.

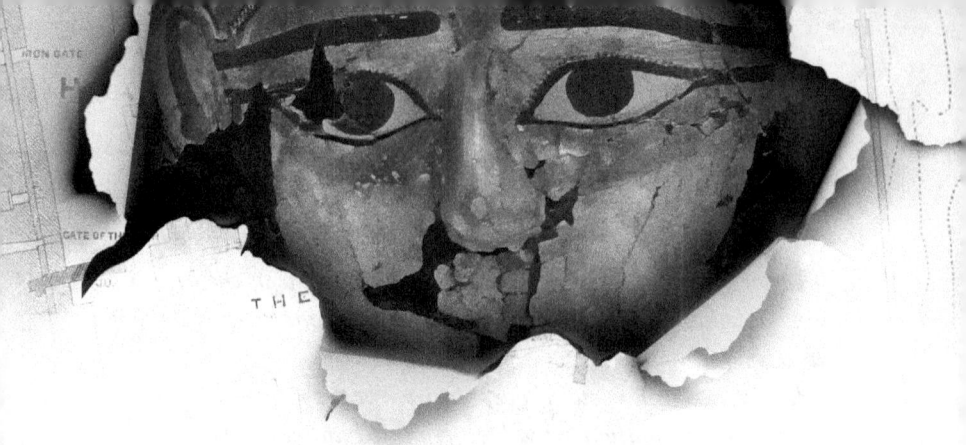

FORTY-FOUR

The octagonal pyramid skylights of the al-Marwani Mosque had been installed on the newly repaved platform, capturing light the way the cisterns captured water. Their location between the tumbledown shed over the small entrance to the mosque and the southern wall enabled Graham to feign interest in them while facing the three caps of Cistern 8 and keeping Daniel and Yaniv in sight. They had joined the line to the Temple separately to make it less obvious they were returning. By 9 a.m., they were each on different parts of the platform after taking separate, meandering routes, watching to see if they were being watched.

As they crossed paths, they murmured notes and observations, then moved on. On the other side of the esplanade, Yaniv sat in the shade of the trees between al-Kas and the stairs leading to the Dome of the Rock. Daniel sat on one of the column pedestals displayed on the east side of al-Aqsa, his chin propped up on his palm as his elbow rested on one of his thighs.

Graham couldn't resist sending him a text. "You look like Rodin's *Thinker*."

He watched Daniel break the pose to read the message, then smile as he started to respond. Daniel glanced up as he typed, distracted, and abandoned the reply.

Graham traced Daniel's line of sight to a man standing outside the al-Marwani shed. He wore a black baseball cap, dark sunglasses, black quarter-zip pullover, olive cargo pants, and black work boots. The effect was enough like the police, a soldier, and a Waqf guard that each could confuse him for one of the others from a distance. But what made him stand out was the large black backpack he wore in addition to the duffel slung around his neck. His left hand was lowering a walkie-talkie. He stowed it and extracted a cell phone. After pressing a sequence of buttons, he held it to his ear as he stared at the ground in front of him.

The explosion shattered the air to Graham's left, loud enough to feel, but not close enough to be endangered by the blast. A trail of smoke blossomed into a blemish on the sky. Judging from the distance of the sound and the location of the smoke, Graham put the detonation somewhere near the entry to the Western Wall Plaza.

Daniel remained within his field of vision, and Graham was surprised to see him still staring in the same direction, undistracted by the explosion behind him. Confused, Graham again looked to the man by the shed. A chill spread across him as he comprehended what Daniel was seeing. The man hadn't moved. He hadn't been surprised by the explosion. And he was dialing another number.

The realization of what was happening hit Graham as a second explosion yanked him from behind and to his left. This time the column of smoke rose outside the Dung Gate, the access to the Western Wall Plaza. He spun back to Daniel and found him still concentrating on the man with the backpack.

The peaceful atmosphere on the Mount turned instantly chaotic as worshippers, tourists, and guards ran toward the Western Wall in a torrent of panic. Screams raked the air, colliding with shouts of angry voices in Hebrew, Arabic, English.

Emergency sirens added a mournful wail to the havoc as they made their way to the blast sites.

As Graham watched the effect of the devastation, the bomber stepped into his eyeline, walking with purposeful haste directly toward one of the Cistern 8 caps. Dozens of people cut across his path, running in a panic for the gates, ignoring him in a frenzy of self-preservation. The man reciprocated by being oblivious to them.

Graham started toward Daniel, but Daniel waved him back. They watched as the bomber walked to the most exposed of the three well caps and set his bags down. A metal trash can stood next to the well, mounted in the pavement. He knelt on one knee, unzipped the backpack, and pulled out a rope Graham thought looked like the kind used by rock climbers. After feeding the end of the rope through the handles of the duffel, he threaded it through the top handle of the backpack, then clamped the rope to the base of the trash can with a carabiner.

Without looking up to see if he was being watched, the man pulled a small bolt cutter from the backpack, slid the open jaw between the prongs of the lock, and cut it open with little effort. He dropped the cutters back into the pack. As he zipped it up, he raised his head and looked toward the entrance to al-Aqsa and the Morocco Gate as if noticing the hysteria on the Mount for the first time.

The glance put the man's face in profile, and Graham could make out a pronounced overbite. Karanlik. Bezalel. The Shadow.

Apparently satisfied, Karanlik lifted the green cap, took a quick look inside, then lowered the bags through the opening. He threw in the remainder of the rope, then climbed into the hole. He pulled the lid down onto his head and let gravity close it the rest of the way as he descended.

Daniel sprung from the pillar and ran to the cistern, Graham close behind him.

"We have to follow him," Daniel said, bending down to assure himself the rope would hold.

"I can't climb down there. I don't know how to free rappel."

Daniel spoke in a rapid, harsh whisper despite having no one near to overhear them. "We'll never get this chance again. He just did in a minute what we've been trying to figure out for days—what people have been trying to do for years. It's not just about the treasure anymore. It's about stopping him. Now let's go! I'll help you. But we have to move."

Without waiting for a response, Daniel lifted the hatch, then sat on the edge with his legs dangling into the hold. He pulled up a couple feet of rope, draped it over the top of his left foot, then ran it under his right, pulling it tight. "Wrap your feet around the rope like this. It'll give you some leverage and act as a brake so you can control how fast you go. But don't slide your hands. If you want to slow down, just pull up on your right leg. It's easy. Follow me. And do it *now*, before the guards see us."

Daniel slid off the side and into the well. Graham sat himself on the ledge and watched the rope twitch with weight. When it stopped, he pulled up some slack, wrapped his feet around it, and scooted, slipping gradually into the well. He was surprised by how secure the foothold was. He reached for the lid, and lowered it onto his head, just as Karanlik had done. As it closed, he glimpsed Yaniv protesting to Waqf guards as they shepherded visitors to the exit. Then he descended, swallowed by the square of black.

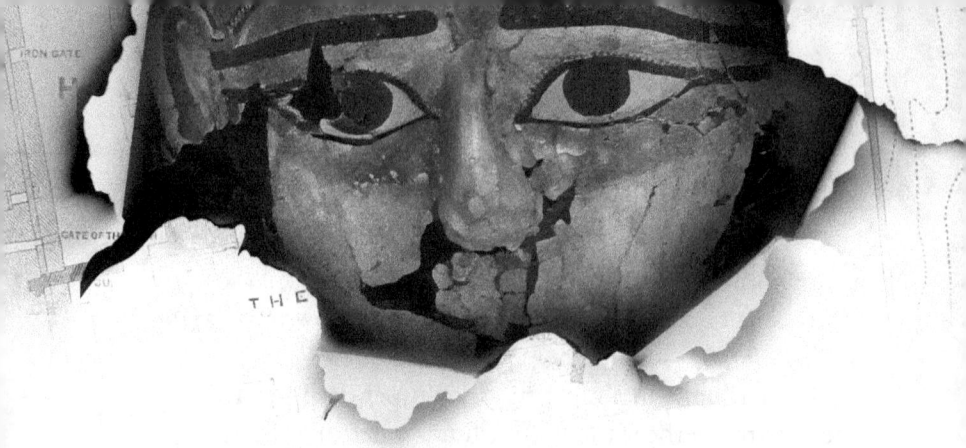

FORTY-FIVE

The last light from the surface remained burned into Graham's eyes, dissolving in the darkness as he sank into Cistern 8. He had expected to see *something* below—a few feet of stone or water with a lantern at its center, or a flashlight beam angling around the walls—but there was nothing. The only light came from luminous needles that speared through two or three small drain holes on the surface that collected rain. The pandemonium of sirens, screams, and panic disappeared with the light, as hidden from the cistern as the surface.

Graham clung to the rope—the only tangible part of the world left to him—and descended without any sense of movement except gravity's pull. He reminded himself it was only forty-three feet, but it seemed to him that he had dropped at least twice that far.

"Almost there."

Daniel's whispered words were closer than he expected, both startling and comforting him. A few seconds later, he felt a hand on his boot guide him the rest of the way down.

Although the rock floor provided instant security, it wasn't what Graham had expected.

"Where's the water?" he whispered.

The reply came in the form of a series of splashes across the cave, someone walking through water. The splashes stopped as abruptly as they started.

"There is no need to whisper." A tenor voice shaped by a Middle Eastern accent sounded from the direction of the splashes, awash in reverb. "I can hear and see you clearly."

The voice carried a malevolent calm that unnerved Graham far more than the panicked shouts he left on the surface.

"You can't do anything from over there." Daniel's voice mirrored the threatening control. Graham wasn't sure if Daniel was trying to pinpoint his location or simply distract him. "You wouldn't risk firing a gun in here. The ricochet's too dangerous."

"Only if I miss."

Graham tensed at the logic.

"But maybe you are right," Karanlik continued. "Maybe I will use a rock."

"Like you did with Dr. Singer?"

Graham crouched down instinctively at Daniel's accusation and felt around him for anything he could use to defend himself. He expected to touch stone and was surprised when he touched canvas.

"Found the tool bag," Graham whispered.

Daniel knocked into Graham as he blindly scrambled for the gear. The sound of a zipper being yanked open released a new mood into the cave.

"Stand up!" Karanlik barked.

Graham climbed to his feet, but from the clattering sounds in the bag, he knew Daniel was still feeling for something he could use as a weapon. Watery steps erupted as Karanlik tried to reach them before they could become armed.

A stream of light shot to the roof of the cave, wobbling like a powerful jet of water coming from a hose not quite under control. Daniel aimed the heavy-duty flashlight in the direction of the splashes.

Karanlik grunted as the light struck him, saturating his night vision goggles, rendering him technologically blind. He swatted the mask from his face, letting it dangle from a strap around his neck as he jumped behind a rude stone column.

Graham took advantage of the moment to look for a flashlight of his own and found a survival lantern near the top of the pile, half embedded in equipment. He pulled it out, extended the collapsed telescopic housing that protected it and powered it on.

The vast space—unseen for 150 years—inflated with light, its far wall barely within reach of the lantern. The irregular boundary reminded Graham of a puzzle piece, as if one were missing from the Mount. Four pillars, roughly cut from bedrock, held the roof in place, their shadows jittering on the uneven walls. Black water blanketed the floor except on the rise beneath Graham's feet. Narrow, uneven steps extruded from the wall on his left. They led from the de facto landing where he stood to a walled-up passageway. Twenty feet above him, Graham saw a niche in the rock and wondered if it was the passage left unexplored by Wilson and Warren.

"Look out!"

Daniel's warning came at the same time as a slosh of water spilled from behind a pillar. Half a second later, a rock clacked as it skidded past his feet, barely missing the lantern.

Graham dropped to the floor, making himself as small a target as he could. He lay on his stomach and watched Karanlik step out from behind one of the pair of columns nearest them and throw another stone. He tracked the trajectory of the rock and realized he was not the target a split-second before darkness returned with the sound of splintering plastic.

"See if there's another lantern."

Daniel pointed the flashlight at the column, pinning Karanlik behind it. Graham kept his eyes on the spotlight as he bent his knees, groped for the duffel bag, and dragged it in front of him.

Enough glow from the flashlight bled onto the bags that Graham could see the shapes inside, though the light was dim enough that he had to lift some items closer to the beam to identify them.

"Pry bar. Folding shovel. Pick hammer. Looks like a… rope ladder. Couple climbing pulleys. A few spikes. Some carabiners. Trowel." Graham touched what he thought was the bottom, then felt it slide loose. "There's several empty backpacks on the bottom." He rotated the bag to change his angle. "Weird. Got some clothes in here, too. Feels like they're packed around something."

"Check it."

He tugged the bundle free, stripping off the outer layer of khaki pants, then unwrapped a balled-up Oxford shirt. Inside were two socks, one nested in the other as they stretched around the cargo they protected.

"That's probably what he wore onto the platform," Daniel said. Graham assumed that he had stolen a glance toward the bag. "Changed out of it somewhere in the mosque."

"Yeah, but there's something inside the socks." Graham started to peel back the cloth. He froze when he revealed the keypad of a disposable phone with bands of electrical tape wrapped around it.

"Give that to me. Very. Carefully." Daniel emphasized his words with a pause between them.

Graham tensed, terrified he would drop the bomb or accidentally trigger it. His forearms jittered in contradiction, not wanting to move while wanting to hand the device off as quickly as possible. As Daniel gently took it from him, Graham distanced himself slowly as if it were a coiled snake. "Why does he need another?"

"I don't know. But he's not going to set it off in here and trap himself. Hold this on the pillar," Daniel said, handing

Graham the flashlight.

Graham stole repeated glances, monitoring Daniel's progress as he cautiously walked away from the water, set the explosive down against the wall at the shallow end of the cave, below the stairs.

A single splash rippled from behind the pillar, and Daniel scrambled back to Graham and plunged his hands into the duffel.

"What are you doing?" Graham asked, watching Daniel wrap Karanlik's shirt around the claw of a hammer.

"Keep your eyes on the pillar," Daniel rasped.

Graham felt a sudden heat and saw that Daniel had ignited the shirt with his butane lighter, improvising a torch. Daniel held it away from his body as he clamped the metal end of the lighter in his teeth and pried it off the plastic reservoir, careful not to spill the fluid. He pressed a thumb onto the open top of the tank to seal it. Without warning, Daniel charged into the water.

He was halfway to the column by the time Graham understood what was happening. Karanlik's masked face popped out from behind the rock, then he tore away the goggles and tried to shrug off the backpack as he emerged. The left strap came free, but the right swayed under the free weight and twisted, keeping it from sliding off. Graham saw the gun in Karanlik's right hand and watched panic flood into his face as the delay gave Daniel an opening.

Daniel high-stepped into deepening water, holding the torch in his left hand at arm's length until he had almost covered the distance. He simultaneously flicked his right hand and released his thumb. Graham watched the lighter fluid travel through the air—almost in slow-motion—landing on Karanlik's shirt and face, but mainly his hands, which he had raised instinctively, dropping the gun. Daniel capitalized on the confusion and thrust his torch onto Karanlik's shirt long enough for the butane to bloom into flame.

Karanlik slapped at the fire, then realized his mistake. He held his blazing hands in front of him and screamed, plunging into the water. Daniel anticipated the reaction, wrapped his right arm around Karanlik's neck, and grabbed his left bicep. As Daniel squeezed his right arm, his left hand pushed forward on Karanlik's head. Nine seconds later, The Shadow stopped moving.

FORTY-SIX

Graham kept the light trained on Karanlik as Daniel dragged his limp body to dry ground.

"Is he dead?"

"No. Choked out," Daniel said between jagged breaths. "Get the rope. We have about twenty seconds."

Graham grabbed the slack tangled at the bottom of the line they had descended, more than ten feet of surplus. He handed it to Daniel as the body thudded to the floor in a final heave. Daniel formed two loops, overlapped them, and pulled one through the other, fashioning makeshift handcuffs. Graham helped him slip the loops over Karanlik's wrists and cinch them tight. By the time they finished, Karanlik began to show drowsy signs of consciousness. Daniel sat back, draped his arms across his knees and put his head down to catch his breath.

Graham kneeled next to him, putting a hand on his shoulder. "That was incredible. I think your smoking habit saved our lives."

Daniel responded with a smileless puff of laughter. "Be sure to tell that to Yaniv."

"Wish he was down here with us. We could use him. I saw him arguing with the Waqf as I shut the hatch."

"I was wondering what happened," Daniel said. "Maybe

he ran interference and distracted them from seeing us go down."

Daniel got to his feet, then seemed to remember Karanlik. He looked around him, reached into the duffel bag, and grabbed a sock that had covered one of the cell phone bombs. He shoved it into Karanlik's mouth and looked up at Graham. "Let's go see if there is anything we can use in the backpack."

Daniel picked up the duffel bag, and they plowed through the knee-deep water until they stood between the columns where Daniel had knocked out Karanlik. Daniel reached into the water, recovering the pack, the goggles, and a pick hammer, which he added to the duffel. Graham pointed the flashlight into the bag and found three more LED lanterns. Daniel pulled one out and turned it on, revealing the gun under the water. After inspecting it, he pressed the safety, then dropped it into the bag.

"Right. Where does the clue say to go?"

Graham had almost forgotten what had brought them there. It seemed like years since he had last thought about the Master Scroll. He dug for his phone, opened his notes, and read aloud.

"In the great cistern which is in the Court of Gentiles at the end of the double gate, in the middle of the farthest pillar on its northern side: fourteen talents."

Daniel repeated the landmark in a distant voice as his eyes searched the well. "In the middle of the farthest pillar on its northern side..."

"That's north," Graham pointed, comparing the contours of the cistern to its shape on the survey map. "And I assume 'farthest side' means farthest from the entrance, which would be the bottom of the steps. Let's go see if x marks the spot."

As they passed the second set of pillars, a wide mouth opened on the right side of what they had thought was the back wall. They rounded the stone partition, their progress combining with the edge of the wall to create a shadow that retracted across the space like an opening curtain. Behind the veil they stopped in the water, looking into a smaller chamber than the first room, though it was still large enough to warrant a pillar at its center.

"That has to be it." Graham's voice bounced off the walls, sounding like he was in a racquetball court. "The farthest pillar on the northern side."

They waded closer to the column, Daniel walking around one side while Graham walked around the other, meeting on the side hidden from the opening. A pile of rocks was stacked around the base of the pillar, tapering in as it emerged from the water.

Daniel lifted his lantern and looked up to the ceiling. "Think that's from the column? Partial collapse?"

"Too deliberate." Graham glanced up, double checking. "And this is the only place with rocks like this. I think we found our spot."

"We'll need to set our lanterns down somehow..." Daniel scanned the wall, then looked toward Graham. "You said the duffel had spikes, right?"

Graham ran through the inventory he had found. "Uh... yes. Four or five."

"Hold this." Daniel handed Graham his light, then slung the canvas bag open. "Those are pitons. Climbers use them." As he spoke, he stirred the gear, searching. "We can hammer a couple into the wall and hang the lanterns."

He pulled one out, positioned it head-high on the pillar above the rocks, and tapped several times with the hammer. He looped the handle of the lantern over the piton, then repeated the process on the wall behind them, illuminating their work area. Daniel found two more of the spikes at the bottom of the duffel, pounded them into the wall, and hung the bags from them.

As Daniel worked, Graham took photos of the site, shifting his position to document several angles. "It's like Christmas morning."

"Mmm…you mean Hanukkah?" Daniel said sarcastically.

"Well, you are setting up the lights." Graham gave a pained smile, then reached for a rock. He tossed the stone backward without turning, releasing a swirl of sediment, clouding the water.

"We're going to kick up too much stuff if we do it like that," Graham said, criticizing his own work. "We'll have to set each rock down."

They fell into a rhythm, unstacking and restacking, and the pile soon dwindled below the waterline. The repetitive motion put them into a mechanical rhythm until a glint of silver sparkled under the water, making statues of them as they waited for the surface to calm.

Graham reached into the water, pulled up a silver shekel, and turned it in the light. "Just like in B'nei Hezir." He handed it to Daniel. "Absolutely amazing."

"It's really here. After all this time." Daniel handed the shekel back to Graham. "Just think what we might find if we had the entire Master Scroll."

"Let's see how much there is here before we get too excited."

They dismantled the remainder of the hiding place, exposing a cache around the column that was entirely silver, as if they had performed some work of alchemy. Five stone jars—each standing almost as tall as Graham's shins—were filled with silver shekels and half-shekels. The fragments of at least two more jars littered the floor, buried under the coins they once held. A half-dozen silver bowls were stacked alongside the jars.

Graham and Daniel stepped back to better appreciate the scope of the discovery. Out of all the reactions Graham thought he might have, it was the one he least expected that overcame him: tears welled in his eyes. He didn't know if they were from relief, the magnitude of the find, or the stress of the last two weeks. Maybe all three.

"I don't know what to say."

"Congratulations, Dr. Eliot," Daniel said, putting a hand on Graham's shoulder. "And now we know what the empty backpacks were for." Daniel was already pulling them from the bottom of the duffel by the time Graham finished taking photos of the site.

"I'll hold, you fill."

Daniel peeled one of the bags open as wide as he could above the surface of the water. Graham cupped the edges of his palms together and scooped up a pile of coins. They glistened—looking newly minted—as water dripped from them before he shoveled them into the bag. As Graham filled the bag, Daniel had to adjust his grip to accommodate the weight, finally slipping the backpack on.

"Take a break," Daniel said as Graham pulled the zipper of the first bag closed. "I'll go put this by the rope."

He plucked a lantern from its perch and headed for the dry ground. He disappeared around the corner, and Graham watched the light slide across the wall, growing fainter as it moved. Daniel grunted with effort, and Graham heard the rattle of metal as the backpack landed on the floor. Almost in answer, a muffled groan protested.

"Shut up," Daniel said, coldly.

Graham listened to Daniel splash his way back.

"Trouble?" Graham asked as Daniel appeared around the corner.

"Not really. He's a shadow of his former self."

FORTY-SEVEN

Graham closed the zipper on the fourth backpack and looked down at the shekels left in the water. "We barely got half of it."

"There's still two more bags."

"No, this is the last one."

"Not if we take out the gear we don't need," Daniel said. "Then we can use the duffel and other backpack."

"Good idea."

"I'll go dump them out at the front of the cave."

Daniel started lumbering through the water as Graham stowed the night vision goggles, a flashlight, and the pistol in the duffel. He slipped his right arm through the canvas handles until they hugged his shoulder, then rotated the bag to his back and took a lantern from a piton.

By the time he turned the corner, Daniel was stepping out of the water on the other side of the cave. The three loaded backpacks sat in a row at the foot of the rope, and Graham could see Karanlik's legs sticking out from one side of the wall of bags. Daniel shuffled to the space at the opposite end, pivoted to face Graham, and crouched down until he sat, placing the bottom of the backpack in line with the others.

"Did you get everythi—"

Daniel's head flew backward, his neck bending over the

top of the packs. The lantern rolled away, kicked over in a spasm, whipping shadows around the walls. In the confusion of light and dark, Graham saw Karanlik crouched behind the bags. One hand held a fistful of hair and was pulling it back, pinning Daniel down. The other hand was a blur of motion as it swept across Daniel's exposed neck. It wasn't until the hand stopped moving that Graham saw the knife. And the red streak that traced its path.

The attack was over before Daniel's hands could reach behind his head to defend himself. Instead, they changed course and tried to cover the wound. Karanlik batted the hands away, stabbing at them with the knife, as he continued to pull back on Daniel's neck. Blood sprayed from the gash in a pulsing fountain as the heart continued its pressure on the carotid arteries.

Daniel writhed—pushing up on his feet, twisting, bucking—but the only thing he accomplished was to change the direction of the blood. He gasped for breath, pulling air through the wound in futile, grotesque wheezes, exhaling in sickening gurgles.

By the time Daniel stopped moving, twenty seconds had passed. It took another ten for the spurts to stop. And for Graham to find his voice.

"No!"

Karanlik looked up—his face a mask of blood—locking eyes with Graham as he stepped over the backpack wall. He bent down and turned the lantern off, throwing the southern half of the cave into a formless void. Graham lifted the lantern in his hand as if it would increase its reach, then realized the only thing it lit was himself. He was completely exposed while Karanlik once again became The Shadow.

The gun!

The words screamed into Graham's head, but he couldn't tell if he'd said them aloud or not. He ducked behind the pillar on his right—the farthest from Karanlik—and swung the duffel to his front. After ripping open the zipper, he pawed the tangle of equipment for the pistol. His fingertips brushed across the grip, and he clamped his hand around it. As he tugged the gun free, he let the bag fall. It wasn't until the light suddenly disappeared that he realized he had let go of the lantern, the duffel smothering it as both sank.

Graham craned around the column and peered futilely into the well of shadow, toward where he'd last seen Karanlik, then looked at the gun. He held it pointed upward, trying to catch the dim ambient light from the final lantern, hanging over the silver behind him. It was the first gun he'd ever actually held, and he was surprised by its weight. He'd seen Daniel chamber a round, then press a small button on the side that he assumed was the safety before stowing it in the bag when he recovered it. Graham found the switch just above the trigger and pressed.

"You will never shoot that gun in here." Karanlik's taunt slithered from the darkness, hinting his location. "You do not even look like you know how to use it."

"Stay where you are!" Graham extended the gun with both hands, pointed it in the general direction of the sound, then randomly adjusted the aim in jerks.

Two splashes came from in front of him and to the left, and he swiveled to face them. Two more came from the right, and he spun himself again before guessing Karanlik was trying to confuse him by throwing rocks.

"You are never going to leave this place." Again the whisper—everywhere and nowhere. "You are going to become one of the artifacts that is discovered down here a thousand years from now."

Graham thought the sound might have come from behind him and turned, talking to cover his movement, hoping Karanlik's reply would expose his position.

"It's you who won't win. The Jews will never give up the Temple Mount or the country."

"Do you really think I did all this to bring down Israel? They do not need my help. They are doing it themselves by making enemies of the Arab world." Karanlik's voice grew stronger as he spoke.

Graham looked down at the glow seeping from beneath the submerged bag and remembered the night vision goggles. He crouched to feel for them, keeping the gun aimed at nothing, as Karanlik continued to speak.

"The Palestinians are no different. Their god and the god of the Jews will kill each other."

The voice was closer now, and Graham could tell he was running out of time. "And whose side will you choose?"

"The side of money. It was here before Moses and Muhammad, and it will be here long after you and I are dead."

Karanlik had dropped his voice down to a whisper again, but it was enough for Graham. He impulsively grabbed the handle of the lantern, wrenching it free. He sprung up as he swung his arm, pounding the spot where the voice had been, then kept hacking in different directions. Frenzied shadows stretched, shrank, and slid across the cistern walls. Water erupted with turbulence as Karanlik dodged the blows.

But Graham could see him. That's all he needed.

Karanlik's back was turned to Graham, hunching to shield himself as he took small, backward lunges to close the gap. Graham stopped flailing the light, lowering it in his left arm while raising the gun in his right. The dropping light threw a shadow that rose behind Karanlik as he turned toward Graham.

Graham tried to step away reflexively, but his foot caught an outcrop of rock at the base of the pillar, sending him backward. He held his right arm in front of him, trying to keep the gun above water, more focused on protecting it than his body. The shock of water burying his head muffled the sound of the shot. He wasn't sure he'd pulled the trigger, and sat up quickly, expecting to continue the fight.

Karanlik looked at a palmful of blood in his left hand, then pressed it against the dark stain spreading across his abdomen. He tilted his face—a mixture of disbelief and malice—to glare at Graham.

Graham realized he had dropped the pistol in the fall and scrambled backward, feeling wildly for the gun as he went. He touched a handle and grabbed it, not comprehending that it was the pick hammer until he lifted it from the water. He cocked his arm, threatening to throw it as Karanlik staggered toward him. Karanlik's face suddenly transformed with confusion as he tripped on the same rock as Graham and fell forward. Graham raised his arms for protection just before Karanlik collapsed onto him.

Karanlik's body pinned Graham under the water, sending him into a panic. Graham flailed as Karanlik's weight settled on him, tearing at his clothes, looking for advantage, then realized Karanlik was not wrestling back. He wasn't moving at all. Karanlik's chest pressed against Graham's, and his head draped over Graham's right shoulder. Graham pushed Karanlik's torso hard on one side, rolling him onto his back.

For the first time, Graham looked clearly into the face of the man who had called himself The Shadow. Terror had frozen Karanlik's expression, held in place by the claw of the pick hammer embedded in his left eye, penetrating his brain.

FORTY-EIGHT

A film of vomit undulated on the water's surface like a grave marker floating above the man's body. Graham sat on one of the packs of silver, staring across the cave at the spot, waiting for Karanlik to spring up. Tremors shook his body in the traumatic wake of the last few minutes. Daniel's final moments.

Graham had needed to see Daniel, needed to keep him company even though he knew there was no life left to share. Tears coated his face before he stepped out of the water, carrying the lantern, and kneeled by the body. But the butchery was too gruesome, and he had instantly vomited again, this time in dry heaves.

He had crawled to the far side of the row of packs—where he couldn't see the body—and cried. For Daniel. For Andrew. Soon the compartments of grief dissolved, and he cried for Olivia and Alyson as well, conflating them all. When he had cried himself out, he was left with a treasure that was worthless compared to his friends who had died for it.

A squeak of metal sounded high above Graham, and a square of light unfolded on the floor before him. He looked at it without comprehension until the voice floated into the chamber.

"*Burakgazi…*"

The voice sounded timid, not wanting to be heard except

in the cistern.

Graham looked up to see the hatch standing open, the outline of a man leaning into the aperture. He assumed it was Yaniv and was about to call up when the voice sounded again.

"*Burakgazi…*"

The word was meaningless to him, but something in the timbre of the voice seemed familiar, though Graham couldn't place it. He stood, moving to a better angle to see who was speaking.

The man pulled his head back and raised it to look around the area near the well cap, allowing light to land on him. A white *keffiyeh* headscarf was wrapped around his face, hiding his features. Graham felt dread flood back into him as he registered that he was looking at an accomplice, not a rescuer.

The man peered into the hole again. "*Burakgazi…*"

This time the word died before he finished.

"*Min 'ant?*" Graham called in Arabic, asking W*ho are you? "Madha turid?"* What do you want?

The question was met with dense silence, and Graham wondered if his fear had mangled the words in mispronunciation.

"If you want to get out of there, you will have to send up those bags first."

Again, the Arabic words were spoken by the voice Graham thought he had heard before.

"You can't do anything with these," Graham said. "The Waqf guards will see you."

"I *am* Waqf." The man paused, letting the words settle. "Now, you will tie a backpack to the rope. Once I have pulled it up, you will send the next one. When I have them all, I will pull you out."

"You're not Waqf," Graham yelled.

"One bomb remains."

The calm words unnerved Graham, and he glanced impulsively at the phone still sitting against the far wall where Daniel had laid it.

"I see you have found it already. Good. Listen to me." The man held a phone next to his head. "I have the number. And I will dial it if you do not do as I say. I will dial if you even go near it."

"You wouldn't risk damaging the Noble Sanctuary." Graham stabbed the air, spearing each word.

"Move!" The man's bellow reverberated in the cave as he made a show of lifting the phone, preparing to enter the number.

Graham knew the buffer of time between him and whatever was about to happen had almost dwindled away. He sagged in resignation, then bent over to grab the straps of the closest backpack. As he lifted it, he glimpsed Daniel's hand. Instantly, the bag's weight was not made of shekels. It was Daniel. It was Andrew. It was the metal grate of the Gihon Spring. It was the bullets piercing the tarp. As always, it was Olivia and Alyson. And it was the loss of meaning, the hole left by a God who wasn't there. Failure and fear were smothered in a self-destructive, intense anger. He lifted the heavy bag with no effort, rotated once like a shot-putter, and flung the bag deeper into the cistern, into the water.

"No!"

Graham ignored the man's protest, picked up another bag and threw it at the first. When he looked up, he could see the man's finger poking the phone with rage. *How many numbers has he dialed?* Graham thought abstractly. *How many does it take?* He knew the answer was unimportant.

Instinct kicked in, and he bolted into the water—not wasting time to grab the lantern—and plowed toward the back of the cave. The glow from the lantern that still hung on the pillar over the silver grew brighter as he forced himself forward through water that suddenly felt like syrup. A faint hope washed over him as he turned the corner of the partition.

He felt his body lift, thrust forward as if pulled by the treasure.

Then there was nothing.

FORTY-NINE

A faint glow of light slowly dawned, staining the utter blackness as it flickered from the other side of the rock partition. Listless smoke wafted through the cave, molded into a dark cloud by the boundaries that trapped it.

Graham twisted and found himself looking down at a lifeless face, barely lit by the exhausted glimmer. The eyes were closed, pressed together with the rest of the face in an expression braced for catastrophe. It took him a moment to recognize the man he had seen only in photographs and mirrors. He was staring at himself.

The comprehension arrived without alarm, freeing his detached perspective. His face appeared to sink as he began to rise, floating higher above the scene. His body was splayed across the remainder of the silver, which had kept his head above water. He reached out as his body drifted away, but no hand and no arm appeared before him.

As Graham rose higher, the smell of smoke traveled through him, communicating its unnerving stench without choking him. The thickening billows enveloped him, sponging up the light until no illumination was left. A cold hardness entered him—or he entered it—somehow penetrating what Graham knew was solid. But almost as soon as it filled him, a plane of white, stone pavement opened beneath him.

For a moment, Graham could smell the gritty limestone and feel the heat of the sun trapped within it.

The pavement dropped beneath him and the entrance to Cistern 8 slid into his field of vision. The green hatch was bent outward, hanging from the cap by one hinge as a thin trail of smoke snaked into the sky. He continued to ascend until he was about twenty feet above the Temple Mount, and around the same distance north of the well.

Waqf guards were running to the cistern. They were halfway across the plaza when Graham noticed them. He dispassionately counted six of them, four coming from the direction of the Morocco Gate and al-Aqsa, and two from the shed covering the al-Marwani stairs.

The first man inserted his head into the opening in defiance of the smoke, but quickly pulled away. He called into the tunnel to see if anyone was there, if anyone needed help. He seemed unaware of the three men who crowded around him, making wild gestures as they traded barbs of Arabic Graham couldn't pick up. A fifth man hurled himself to a stop, tore off his fleece jacket to reveal a red polo shirt, then flung his arms wide as he kneeled, wailing a lament. He looked directly at Graham without showing any sign of seeing him. The sixth guard stood apart from the others, almost directly below, talking on the phone.

"Hunak! Alrajul!" The man on the phone speared his arm toward the near corner of al-Aqsa. *There! The man!*

The others at the cistern spun around, following the pointing finger. A six-foot-tall stone wall ran the length of the eastern side of al-Aqsa, creating an alley about ten feet wide. Two gray water tanks—modern replacements for the cisterns—stood near the entrance to the alley. Next to them was a square well cap and green lid Graham knew from his research was Cistern 9. The other side of the alley held a basin where water could still be drawn.

Graham watched as the man in the alley emerged from hiding behind the water tanks and started running deeper into the passage, though it was obvious he was trapped. As the men at the cistern funneled into the alley, more Waqf guards appeared in the plaza.

Graham hovered across the expanse until he was above the knot of shouting men who kept pointing at Cistern 8 as they battered the man with accusations. He couldn't hear the man's replies, but several men suddenly bolted away from the interrogation, one back to the well, the others into nearby outbuildings.

As the mob began to drag the man toward the cistern, Graham felt himself rise once more. The roof of al-Aqsa appeared to his side, and something on the surface pulled his attention away from the man. He had to stare at the object for a moment before he recognized it as a pair of sandals, one sitting perpendicularly on top of the other, forming a cross. He wondered how they had gotten there, who was missing them.

"Daddy."

Alyson's whisper came from behind him, and he spun toward the sound.

And then it was gone. The mosque, the Waqf, the Mount—all of it. Replaced by blackness. He was once again in the bowels of Cistern 8. The Black Well.

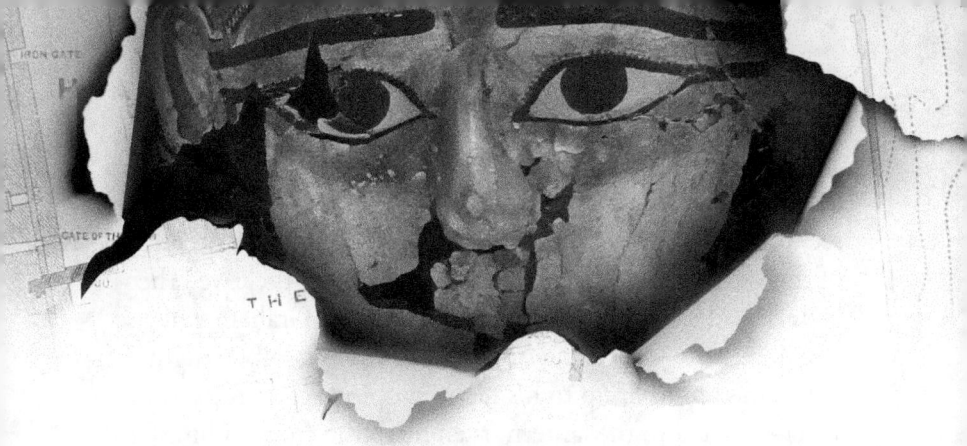

FIFTY

Graham reeled from the instantaneous inversion of his world. He had been above the Temple Mount, but now he was below it. He had been able to see, but now was blind except for a weak glow tainting the darkness. He had been able to hear, but now was deaf except for a single, high-pitched ringing, like the last thread from an unraveled sound. He had been able to breathe, but now gagged on air turned partially solid with smoke and dust. He had been able to understand what was happening with hyper-clarity despite how surreal the experience was, but now shuddered in confusion.

He was alive. That much was clear. But what had he just been? It wasn't a dream—the weight of reality had always been present, holding everything in place. In fact, what he had just experienced seemed more real than anything he had felt in his life. So what did that make this?

He tried to prop his arm underneath his back to sit up and felt an unexpected drag of water. He realized he was wet, lying half-submerged on a pile of debris. He scooted into a sitting position, felt metal beneath his hands, and pulled a handful of shekels out of the water. The sight of the silver coins triggered an epiphany, restoring his senses, making him fully present.

His eyes adjusted to the dark, allowing details to come

into existence like a developing photograph. What he couldn't see, he filled in with memory. Weak light skimmed the surface of the water like black glass near the corner of the cave. The lantern had survived the impact of the blast. Graham whispered, "*Thank you*," not daring to take his eyes off the light. He pushed himself up to his feet—slipping across the settling silver—waded to the lantern, then held it in front of himself as he started for the other side of the cistern.

The two pillars farthest from the bomb still stood, rising to the ceiling with no apparent damage. Graham hunched over and swept the lantern slowly above the waterline behind the columns until he found the duffel he had dropped in the fight. He felt the presence of Karanlik's body and carefully avoided looking in its direction, refusing to allow it to have any power over him.

After slinging the bag onto his shoulder, he walked past the remains of the other pair of columns. The detonation had shredded rock from their trunks, reducing them to irregular, emaciated spindles. Stone that had held the Temple Mount aloft for 2,000 years lay disintegrated and pulverized. Silver coins were scattered across the floor, speckling the rubble. It could still be recovered. He was the one lost now.

The sight of Daniel's boots at the edge of the water paralyzed Graham. The two backpacks of silver he hadn't thrown provided a shield from the explosion that had kept the body from being destroyed. He was thankful the boot didn't seem disembodied, but at the same time, he did not want to see what damage the bomb had added.

Graham skirted around the corpse and stepped onto the shore, giving himself a small sense of safety. He knew he had to escape, and the solid footing gave him one less thing to worry about. It felt like progress.

The pall of smoke dissipated slowly as it discovered the open hatch in the ceiling. From below, the hole was an amorphous light gray patch in the cloud. The rope they had descended lay tangled across the rock floor, stranding him inside.

The Waqf would investigate the blast soon, and he would be discovered. Although it meant rescue, it would almost certainly also mean being accused of trying to destroy the Dome of the Rock or al-Aqsa Mosque. He feared what would happen to him before the IAA could be notified and explain who he was. He had to find another way out.

He set the duffel down, then coiled the rope on top of the bag. Holding the lantern over his head, he revolved in place, searching the cistern walls, and found the other entrance.

Only the upper half of the ancient flight of steps remained on the wall where Daniel had placed the bomb, clinging pointlessly to the threshold of the walled-up entry. The steps triggered a memory from what seemed a lifetime ago, and he looked up at the wall to an opening twenty feet above the water's edge.

Wilson.

Graham patted his pants for his phone, then worked it out of the wet pocket hoping the case's waterproof guarantee was founded. He pressed the Home key and the screen lit up. No cell signal, but he downloaded the notes of the only people ever to have surveyed the well. More progress. He opened the digital copy of Charles Wilson's *Ordnance Survey of Jerusalem* and skipped to the section describing each cistern from his exploration in December 1864. All of what was known about the hole in the rock was contained in one sentence:

> *A conduit cut in the rock was seen coming in from the east, but it could not be reached.*

He did a text search for "Great Sea" and found one other hit, a passage where Wilson introduces the cisterns.

> *Access was obtained to the water conduits*
> *through a hole in one of them in front of al-Aq-*
> *sa, and they were traced as far as possible, but the*
> *rubbish has fallen in in many places, and with*
> *the exception of two or three, the branch ducts*
> *are too small to admit the passage of a man.*
> *From the number of openings seen, there must be*
> *a perfect network of small subterranean channels*
> *in this part of the area, but without excavation*
> *they could not be traced. It is very difficult to*
> *judge of the age of these conduits, but where cut*
> *in the rock they have been probably made at*
> *the same period as the cisterns, as the one which*
> *enters the large cistern east of the "Great Sea,"*
> *and this was found to be in connexion with*
> *another conduit leading down to the "Well of the*
> *Leaf" and one running up in the direction of the*
> *Fountain al-Kas.*

Again, Graham wished Wilson or Warren would have been allowed to explore the network of channels. But the pasha of Jerusalem had given them limited amounts of time and even less latitude, forcing them to focus on documenting the wells as quickly as they could. Now the job of exploration had fallen to him as an act of survival.

He opened an image of the map that compiled the findings of Wilson and Warren, zooming in on the area around Cistern 8. Dashed lines formed a fragmented grid connecting Cisterns 6 through 11 with presumed passages. Other clusters of cisterns were also joined by suspected passages. A branch from Cistern 7 almost reached Cistern 5, but stopped short, at the edge of the highest tier of the platform, a dead end pointing at the Dome of the Rock.

Graham opened Warren's *The Survey of Western Palestine*

and repeated the search. He hit on a section where Warren described the passages that ran underneath the Triple Gate, now the smaller entrance to al-Marwani.

> *The passages were blocked up to the north by walls of hard old masonry. On removing these, they were found to communicate with Tanks 10 and 11, and probably with the Great Sea.*

Again, Graham was left with nothing more than the 150-year-old assurance of *probably*. But the hole in the wall was the only *probably* he had.

He tapped the surface, intending to close the notes, but swiped the screen just enough to shuttle it to the next document. A watercolor painting of Cistern 8 filled the display, created by William Simpson after being invited by Warren to accompany him on some of his excavations. Simpson primarily documented wars before photography assumed the task, and Warren thought he could put him to use creating a visual record to accompany the survey. Graham had studied Simpson's rendering of the Great Sea when he had done his initial research but hadn't given it much thought since then.

The image showed a man from behind, standing near the water in Arabic dress, holding a staff in his left hand as he gestured up to the ceiling with the other. The square manhole at the surface was open, and a bucket was suspended on a rope. Two pairs of columns rose from the middle of the pool. Two more Arabs looked on as they rested against the wall on the left. Above them—about the height of four men—a hole opened in the wall. Graham stood approximately where the man with the staff stood in the painting and looked up and to the left. It was the same opening. What he needed now was a way in.

Graham's first thought was of the rope. It was long

enough, but he had no way to secure it to the mouth of the opening. He remembered how difficult it had been to heave the backpacks into the water, and he knew he'd never be able to throw one into the passage to anchor the rope. There weren't enough large rocks to pile against the wall to give him something to climb. And even if there were, they were probably too heavy to move. The rope ladder was still in the duffel, but it had to be anchored just like the rope. What he needed were spikes he could—

The pitons!

There had been four before the explosion, at the cache of silver on the far side of the partition. He immediately splashed his way to the other end of the well. Graham almost laughed when he found all four still embedded in the rock. He was able to pull three of them out by hand; Daniel hadn't sunk them very deep since they only needed to hold the lanterns. The fourth held the equipment bags and had been buried into the wall for strength. Graham realized he needed the hammer, then remembered where it was: in Karanlik's eye.

He trudged back around the wall trying to work out how to locate the pick hammer without looking at the grisly face of the corpse. When he reached the pillars, he walked backward. He found Karanlik's feet, then followed the legs to the chest. Karanlik's belt had come undone, revealing a blade concealed in the buckle. Graham assumed it had been how he had cut himself loose. He felt behind him, searching the space where he guessed the pick's handle would be but touched only air. He snapped his head around and looked back, glimpsing the wooden handle sticking out of the water.

This time when his fingers reached out, they contacted wood. He closed his eyes and turned around to give himself leverage, then pulled. The weight of the body tugged passively against the force, clinging to the claw. Graham tried not to picture the scene as he pulled again, bouncing Karanlik's head repeatedly until the hammer came free. It wasn't until he was turning the corner of the wall that he realized he hadn't been breathing, shocking himself with a sudden intake of dank air.

He tapped the final piton loose, then waded across the pool, stepping out at the wall below the conduit. He set the lantern at the base of the wall, pulled out his phone, and took several photos of the scene, recording the aftermath of the explosion.

He set the first piton two feet off the ground, pounding it into a crack, then spaced the three remaining spikes the same distance apart, creating a ladder up the wall. After tapping in the top piton and seeing that it only marked the halfway point to the passage, Graham realized that even if he could balance on the top spike, he still couldn't reach the edge of the tunnel. He climbed down to look through the duffel, hoping he could adapt his plan to his tools.

He grabbed the rope from the top of the bag, tied it to the loop on the end of the bottom spike, then threaded the rope through the loops of the other pitons. He tied the other end of the rope to the handles on the duffel. Then—as an afterthought—he added as many silver coins to the bag as he could.

Graham climbed to the second step, grabbed the third step, and hung from it with one hand as he held the hammer in the other and knocked the bottom piton loose. He hoisted it up, climbed up a rung, and hammered it above the fourth spike. After repeating the process three more times, he pulled himself into the mouth of the passageway, then hauled up the bag on the other end of the rope.

He lay back in relief, feeling a sense of achievement. Progress. And yet, the goal still hovered above him, on the other side of an impenetrable layer of rock. For all the accomplishment he felt, he had merely found his way to the start of a forbidden maze that people had died to protect, and—as far as he knew—no one had ever solved.

FIFTY-ONE

Graham held the lantern out in front of him, creating a bubble of light sliding through a stone tube. The broad mouth that gaped on the wall had constricted to a narrow, irregular artery slightly wider than his shoulders, and the low ceiling forced him into a walking crouch. It looked to him like it may have been an ancient storm sewer that fed overflow into the Black Well.

He kept the map displayed on his phone and referred to it repeatedly, gambling that its informed guess was better than his ignorance. But the map almost immediately showed signs of unreliability. He didn't doubt the location and shapes of the cisterns, but some of the passages didn't seem to be where Warren and Wilson had plotted them. They had described a conduit coming from the east, but the one in Simpson's painting—the one he was in now—opened on the west.

There was no opening on the wall to the east; not that he could see. The image of the watercolor hadn't been transposed because the stairs were in the correct place. And there were other problems with the map. The grid-like network that connected Cisterns 6 and 7 also communicated with Cistern 8 in the room behind the rock wall at three different spots, but he hadn't seen any tunnel entrances.

Graham juggled three explanations: the passages had been

walled-up or filled with debris, the passages were at a different depth than Cistern 8 and ran below it, or there were no passages at all—at least not as described on the map. He suspected the answer was a combination of the first and last options, which made him wonder how useful the map would be.

What most surprised Graham was that the conduit was almost as straight as it was depicted on the map. He had expected wandering, jagged tunnels like the ones from the Gihon Spring, but this was much more like the few water channels that *had* been explored on the Temple Mount, such as the conduit that fed the al-Kas fountain.

His confidence in the map grew as an intersection appeared just as marked. According to the map, the left branch would take him to the area under the al-Aqsa Mosque—the ancient foyer of the Huldah Gates. He had no plan for what to do once he got to the mosque but decided to worry about that if he actually made it that far. One escape at a time.

He started to crawl forward, then rocked back, thinking that he needed to mark the spot so that he'd recognize the route if he got lost. After contorting himself to reach the duffel on his back and extract the pick hammer, he used the claw to scratch the floor. The shape was intended to be an arrow bent at a right angle, indicating where he'd come from and the direction he had turned, but the rough floor distorted the inscription so much that Graham judged it wasn't worth the effort. He decided the best way to keep himself from becoming lost was to make only left turns—left being the direction of al-Aqsa, according to the map. Assuming the tunnels didn't form any loops, the method would lead him back here if nowhere else.

The stones used to block the left branch of the tunnel appeared after only fifty feet. Graham had never suffered from claustrophobia, but the dead end made the passage seem tighter, constricting him.

He looked at the map and saw the passage marked as continuing under the mosque. Given that they had not entered the Cistern 8 conduit, he assumed Warren and Wilson had found the tunnel from within al-Aqsa, saw it was blocked, and postulated how the passageway continued to connect to Cistern 8.

Graham awkwardly pivoted around and crawled back to the intersection, turning left again. After about the same distance as the first turn, he found himself blocked again, this time by fill. The compacted dirt and debris clotted the diameter. Even if he could wield the tools in the bag, he had nowhere to put the displaced material.

Again, he reversed himself, returned to the first intersection and turned left without much hope. Warren and Wilson showed this branch as a dead end, but when Graham reached the end of the tunnel on the map, the rock corridor continued on. According to the map, he was headed for al-Kas, probably underneath it. He checked his phone's compass and confirmed he was headed north, and a few degrees west—directly toward the Dome of the Rock.

The tunnel curved to the right, and Graham's sense of navigation positioned him near the grid that connected Cisterns 6 and 7 on the map. After a meandering route he assumed followed the contours of the bedrock or original mountain, Graham found himself at a literal crossroads, as well as a figurative one.

Neither the shaft he had just passed through nor the intersection he was at were indicated on the map. His internal compass plotted him at a point where the right turn would lead to Cistern 7, which connected to Cistern 11, and then to al-Marwani. That's if the map was accurate and he was correct about where he was. But if it—or he—was wrong then he'd be lost. Instinct told him to turn right. Logic told him to turn left.

Graham turned left, adding to his worries a gnawing sense

that safety was growing farther away behind him.

The passage ran in a long straightaway, then angled to the left, curved right, and devolved into a serpentine route. Each time Graham checked the compass it pointed in an unexpected direction, confounding his instinct. Every turn added to the conviction that he should have followed his intuition to the right, and yet he had gone too far to turn around. The tunnel had to go *somewhere*.

As he shuffled forward, his hearing returned by degrees, transforming the friction he felt from the walls into sounds. The noise of the tunnel seemed unusually vivid after the unnatural silence.

The acoustics became deeper, more hollow, with more echo, and he assumed the change in nuance was due to the widening spectrum his ears could discern as they healed. But as he rounded a bend, the change became pronounced as Graham understood the real cause.

A cavern expanded before him, not as large as the main room of Cistern 8, but equally tall. He crawled to the edge and looked down but couldn't see any sign of the bottom. He dropped a small stone into the void, and listened expectantly until it clattered against the floor, followed by a small splash. Graham guessed he was at least as high up as he had climbed to enter the tunnel.

The walls naturally arched as they rose, giving the space a rough egg shape. As he raised his head, he saw the opening of another tunnel on the other side, approximately twenty feet away and a few feet higher. The lantern struggled to penetrate the shaft, but it revealed enough for Graham to see that something was sitting in the mouth on the other side.

A coil of thick fabric—like a roll of carpet—flattened under its own weight, deflated as it blanketed the width of the floor. Graham couldn't see how far the roll extended into the tunnel, but he could see the end was frayed with rot. What looked like two staffs or spear shafts were nestled into one of the curves of the roll and the wall of the passage, their tips catching the light. Deeper in the passage, at the very edge of the lantern's reach, a patch of dark gold smeared across the shadows. He squinted, straining for more detail, and he thought he could just make out the edge of a corner, an angle in the smudge.

The bizarre storage space made Graham wonder where the other side of the tunnel led. There had to be another access than the passage he had taken. It was too impractical, and the chasm couldn't be crossed. He looked up, trying to understand the context of the cache, and fixed on a shape floating about thirty feet above him. A perfect plane of flat stone, like a large tile of marble, sealed a square opening—six feet across—hewn into the stone ceiling. A second slab, half the size of the first, capped another square hole.

"What is this place?" Graham's whisper slipped into the cave, imbuing it with an unexpected reverence.

He pulled out his phone and looked at the screen, wanting to mark the spot with GPS coordinates, but still had no reception. He switched back to the map of the Temple Mount that identified all the buildings and looked for ones he might be under.

Although he hadn't been able to track his route, he was certain the tunnel didn't lead to the eastern side of the Mount, especially since there were no buildings on that side of the complex. On the western side, a chain of buildings ran the length of the platform. He could be underneath one of the gates, the administrative offices, the minaret over the Chain Gate, the Dome of Moses, the prayer room where Muhammad kept his horse Baraq, or the *Madrasa al-Ashrafiya*—one of the Islamic schools on the Mount. Another possibility was that the tiles were the underside of the platform itself.

But if what he was looking at across the cavern was what

he suspected—if it was furniture from the First or Second Temple, hidden away—then he was under the Dome of the Rock. And not just under it, but under the prayer room beneath the rock.

He was in the Well of Souls.

The conversation in Yaniv's office about Montagu Parker replayed in his mind. Was this place really what the rabbis in Jesus's time claimed, the center of the world, where its very foundations were anchored? Was it where Muslim souls of the dead gathered every Friday to worship Allah? Was this the chamber that answered taps on the prayer floor with a mysterious resonance? Was the slab above him the one Sir Richard Burton had wanted to pry open? Was it the place Pierotti claimed to see? Did it close the hole that Parker had entered?

"Incredible…" Graham's voice quavered, falling into the sacred space.

He drank in the scene, consciously trying to retain every detail, catalog every feature. The lantern didn't give the camera much light to work with, and the iPhone's lens didn't have an optical zoom, but Graham wanted some kind of record of what he was looking at and hoped however the images came out, they would be better than nothing. He took several dozen additional pictures, changing the exposure to catch each of the items in the best light, and got multiple shots of each to protect against bad focus. He tilted his face up toward the slabbed holes and added more images to his camera roll, as well as a video showing the whole cave.

He stowed the phone and sat, absorbed in an ambience that—against all his efforts at apostasy—felt holy. In the course of finding what had been lost, Graham himself had become lost. And in the course of trying to escape, he had found a place he didn't want to leave.

He could hear Yaniv's voice respond to Graham's observation: "Just so. Such is life."

FIFTY-TWO

Graham reluctantly pushed himself back into the tunnel, away from the Well of Souls, hoping the pictures showed enough to warrant an investigation by Yaniv. He followed the channel blindly, processing the discovery as he backtracked to the intersection. He felt he had covered the distance to the junction long before he reached it. When it finally came into view, he knew something was wrong.

The intersection that fed him into the tunnel leading to the Well of Souls had been a T-bone where—in keeping with his method—he had chosen left instead of right. He expected to return to the spot and find two choices: straight, and a branch on the right. Instead, he was confronted with three options: left, straight, and right.

Panic overpowered all thoughts about the Well of Souls. He was certain he hadn't missed any turns, and the only four-way intersection he had navigated was the one that connected Cisterns 8 and 9.

He turned left, despite the erosion of confidence in the method. But without a map the only other choice was randomly picking directions, which he had no confidence in at all.

A T-bone appeared, but it wasn't the one he expected. The combination of intersections made him think about the gridded network he saw on the map. He opened his phone to see if he could locate himself, but there was no four-way junction followed by a three-way on the survey. Again, he turned left.

Twenty feet later, the acoustics began to change, signaling another cistern. At first, he thought he had made his way back to Cistern 8. It was roughly the same height, and he was about the same distance to the water below. But as his eyes adjusted, he saw a single pillar in the middle.

He opened Wilson's descriptions of each cistern, comparing what he read with what he could see. After skimming the first seven, he skipped number 8, then found a match.

> *Cistern No. 9, under al-Aqsa, known as the "Well of the Leaf," 42 feet deep, 3 feet 6 inches water at northern end; at southern, deeper; on the north side there is a curious branch or arm, and near the centre a pillar has been left to assist in sustaining the roof. Whilst proceeding toward the south, a sudden fall into deep water extinguished the light, not however before the southern boundary was seen; the measurements were lost, but the plan was made from memory immediately after ascending; the conduit seen in the "double passage" was noticed entering the shaft.*

"The double passage." The phrase opened the image in Graham's mind of the stairs descending into the platform in front of al-Aqsa. If he could reach the conduit Wilson saw then he might have a way out.

He scrolled to Warren's descriptions, saw that it agreed, and was reminded of the legend associated with it.

> *No. 9. Called Bir el Warakah, or "Well of the Leaf," is under the Aqsa Mosque, south of the last. This tank is 42 feet deep. There is a branch on the north and a central pillar supports the roof, which is of rock. The*

name is due to a legend related by Mejred Din, according to which, in the time of Omar, Sheikh Ibn Habashah, of the Beni Temim, let his bucket fall, and descended to recover it. He found in the well an entrance to Paradise and brought back a leaf of the "tree of life" with him. An aqueduct leads from the Well of the Leaf through the passage of the Double Gate under the Aqsa. Various ducts conveying surface drainage into the Well of the Leaf were also found about 5 feet below the present surface of the Sanctuary.

"The door to Paradise would be incredible. But I'd settle for the door to al-Aqsa." Graham mumbled it aloud, but the joke reminded him of Daniel, and he had to work to staunch his grief and keep moving.

He stuck the lantern into the cavern and searched each side of the mouth, looking for a passage. An odd, curved arm cut a large branch into the wall on his left. To his right, he could almost touch the corner of the cavern. On the other side of the corner, rising out of the water below him, he saw the tunnel he assumed would lead to the Double Passage—the entry hall of the Huldah Gates, now the basement of al-Aqsa Mosque.

Graham opened the duffel and rummaged through it for the pick hammer and a piton. He pounded the spike near the edge of the tunnel, then tied the rope ladder to the loop and dropped it over the side. Carrying the equipment had made navigating the channel arduous, and he was glad the effort was justified.

The water was deeper than in Cistern 8, and he was surprised to find it above his waist. He lifted the bag over his head, feeling the water grow deeper as he waded to the conduit. The floor of the tunnel was higher than the cave's and he moved through the stone hallway in knee-deep water. The lantern reflected off the surface, making the space shimmer around him. Wilson and Warren's map showed the conduit as a straight channel, and Graham was glad it was accurate. No surprises this time. Progress.

Stone steps climbed from the water at the end of the tunnel, leading to an arched wooden door, held together with corroded metal straps. The threshold, lintel, and jambs were tiled, a sign that this had been a public passage at some point. He pulled the handle toward him and discovered that the door was locked from the outside. He looked on the opposite edge of the door and found two sets of hinges. Again, he offered an aimless prayer of thanks for the tools and pulled out the pick hammer.

As he tapped out the pins fastening the hinges, he began to feel time pulse again. How long had it been since he entered Cistern 8? How much time did he have to find a way out? And what—or more importantly, who—was on the other side of the door? The sound of the second pin bouncing off the stone steps into the water made him wonder if he was unhinging more than a door.

FIFTY-THREE

Time, neglect, and the elements conspired to hold the door in place even without the pins. Graham wedged the claw of the pick hammer into the joint, pressed his weight against the handle, and rocked against it several times before he felt it give. It took two more tries before the heavy panel fell inward.

He stepped into a room the size of a closet. The back wall of the narrow chamber opened to a tunnel of worn stairs ascending through the rock. Corroded grilles were mounted over openings at the bottom of each side wall for ventilation. Graham walked up the steps as silently as he could, listening for any sound from outside the stairwell that might give him a clue where it was leading.

When he reached the top, he found himself on an awkward, irregular landing, just wide enough for a door to swing open. The problem was that there was no door. The tiled arch had been walled up, blocking the passage to what he guessed was the basement of al-Aqsa. He released a sigh as he remembered the mosque had changed since Warren and Wilson had recorded their findings.

In 1927—sixty years after the creation of the map he was using—al-Aqsa was almost completely destroyed by an earthquake. A whole wing on the east side of the mosque appeared on the survey map but had not been rebuilt during the reconstruction. It never occurred to him that the change in architecture above the cisterns had also changed access to them.

Graham plodded back down the stairs. His only options were the grilles. Warren had mentioned ducts, and Graham assumed they were what lay behind the vents.

He stood in the middle of the room and opened the survey map. He wasn't far from the front of al-Aqsa, but he couldn't think of anywhere the northern duct could lead that included a hidden exit. If anything, it would open into either the sanctuary of the mosque or the platform in front of it—both too risky. The southern duct had a better chance of leading to an unnoticed outlet, either in al-Marwani or the basement library of al-Aqsa.

He knelt down, laced his fingers through the square openings in the antique mesh of metal and yanked hard. When it didn't give, he fished the pry bar from the bag. The grille gave surprisingly little resistance, and after two forceful pushes, Graham peered into a muddy shaft, four feet high, two feet wide. He picked up the equipment bag and the lantern, then he grudgingly slipped into the passage.

Graham crouched while he walked with his left shoulder twisted forward so the duffel would fit in the confined space. It scraped against the walls, the drag adding to the feeling that the building was resisting him. Five minutes later, he saw a faint glow suspended from a point in the low ceiling.

A small spot of light pooled on the floor, fallen from a four-foot-long shaft of stone beneath another ancient grate. The bottom six inches of the conduit was rough stone, but the rest of the way was smooth masonry. The transition between the two surfaces left a lip that gave Graham an idea.

He rose to his full height, guiding his shoulders up through the opening, then pressed his hands down on the ledge to boost himself into the shaft. He tucked his legs until he was able to get a foothold on the ledge as he pressed his back against the opposite side of the duct. Once he trusted his leverage, he pushed up, sliding the rest of his body closer to the grille.

Unlike the grille he had entered, this one had a layer of metal mesh on its underside. Graham ripped it away and let it fall below him. He grabbed the lattice, rattled it hard, and discovered it was closed with a keyed padlock like the cistern hatches. He reached back and extracted the pry bar from the bag by feel. Once again, the grille gave way without much effort, popping loose with a clatter.

Graham froze, listening for movement or voice. But there was no alarm, no shouts, no sound of any kind in response. He let another moment pass, then forced himself to wait one more.

The grille protested with a harsh screech he thought he could control by opening it slowly. When it was clear he was only sustaining the sound he was trying to prevent, he thrust it the rest of the way. He stilled himself again and listened, but the silence he had broken healed itself.

He checked his relief. He was no longer trapped, but he was not yet free. Progress.

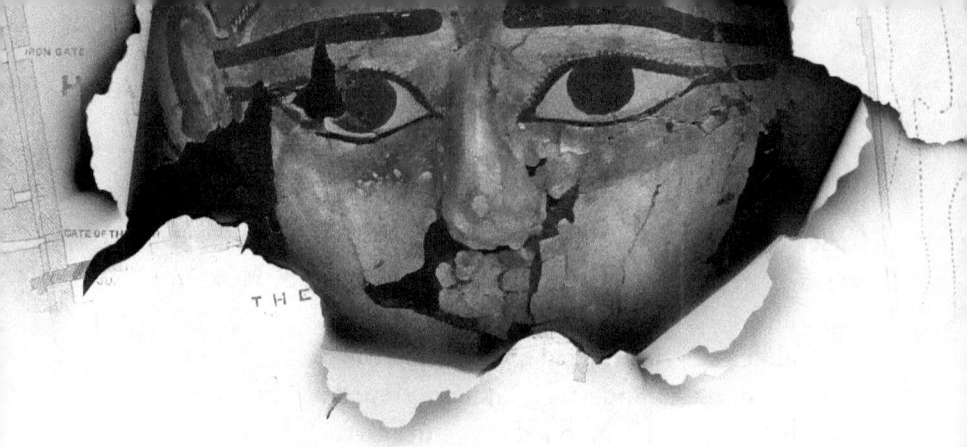

FIFTY-FOUR

Graham peered cautiously over the top of the shaft, restraining himself from leaping into the bright, open space after so long underground. The room was empty of people and furnished with a single chair in the corner. Three smooth walls coated in fatigued white paint stood in contrast to a wall of the familiar stones of the Temple Mount, the inside of the southern wall. A fan encased in a protective grille, was bolted onto the masonry, its wiring exposed on the outside of the wall. A thick stone pillar stood in the middle of the room holding four fluorescent lights vertically mounted on one of its four sides. Red pile carpet patterned with large yellow arches comprised the sole design feature of the room.

He hoisted himself up onto the ledge of the manhole, which extruded from the floor like the surface entrance to the cisterns, covered in solid red carpet. His legs were halfway out of the opening when he remembered where he was: the basement of the al-Aqsa Mosque. Not only would his muddy shoes leave tracks across the carpet, but all shoes were forbidden in the mosque. He peeled them off his feet, and added them to the duffel bag, then winced as the grille screeched close.

He padded to the doorless threshold and stepped through, down three broad steps into a larger empty space with the same tired walls and patterned carpet. The middle of the room was divided by a pair of ancient pillars that had been reinforced by a modern exoskeleton of concrete piers. Fluorescent lights had been mounted vertically on these pillars as well, even though gaudy electric chandeliers hung on each side of them. To his left, the southern wall, an arch had been walled in. He looked up and found the last vestiges of ornamentation on concave domes hovering at least twenty feet above—two on each side of the columns. He knew exactly where he was: the vestibule of the Double Gate. Jesus and the Apostles had walked through this very space as they entered the Temple.

Graham walked quickly to the middle of the room, between the pillars, and looked to his left again. This arch—the twin of the blocked entrance—was walled only with a partition of wooden dowels with a matching gate. During the Crusades, a tower had been built off the southern wall of the Temple, blocking one arch and enclosing the other to prevent easy access to the platform. Now the Tower Room was part of the library run by the museum.

The door stood open, but there was no sign of any activity. He resisted the impulse to go inside since there was no possible exit from the library except this gate. That left only the long hallway that led to this spot.

Graham turned opposite the library to face two sets of stairs that connected the vestibule to a landing ten feet higher. Halfway up the stairs, he realized this side of the Double Gate's passage had been walled up behind a low platform. Most of the arches of the arcade that had divided the tunnel of the Double Gate had been walled-in as well, leaving only the ones at either end open. The other side of the hall led to the stairs to the surface of the Mount. Unless there were side rooms or niches in the corridor, he would be exposed as soon as he stepped into it.

Two small bookcases stood along the walls, providing Qur'ans to those who came to pray. In front of them he found several pieces of clothing scattered on the floor, abandoned as if their owners had suddenly vanished. He picked up one of the keffiyeh headscarves, assuming it had been forgotten in the chaos of the explosions. It occurred to him that he could use it to hide his face and fitted it on his head, leaving a slit for his eyes. He looked at the rest of his clothes and saw how filthy he was, like he'd just performed a stunt where he escaped after being buried alive. He knew he needed to cover himself but found nothing useful among the rest of the garments.

He crossed into the eastern hall, saw that it was empty, and jogged the thirty yards between him and the exit. He hopped up the small landing at the bottom of the final flight of steps. One was fitted with a grid of small compartments for the shoes of visitors. The other wall opened in a low arch filled with a wooden lattice that screened a room on the other side. Graham assumed it was a small office for the administrators of the basement.

Through the slats, he saw a black fleece jacket draped over a molded plastic chair. The door looked flimsy enough to force open, but Graham tried the knob first and was surprised to find it unlocked. He slipped on the fleece, zipped it over his grime-covered shirt, then grabbed his shoes from the duffel and put them on. He picked up a walkie-talkie from the seat of the chair, hopefully approximating the look of a Waqf guard. As he turned to leave he saw an arch in the back wall blocked with stones and mortar and wondered if that was the arch at the top of the steps leading to the Well of the Leaf.

He started up the stairs to the platform and heard the sound of arguing before he saw it. He pictured the opening to the steps that looked like a subway entrance from the surface, and guessed the angry voices were coming from the cistern cap he had entered forever ago. Before reaching the top, he stopped to prepare himself.

Act like you belong here. Don't draw attention to yourself.

It took all Graham's self-control not to run as he stepped onto the Temple Mount. He glanced to his right as he walked forward toward al-Kas, trying to show the proper amount of interest without appearing suspicious by not joining the crowd at the well. The trees on either side of the fountain gave him some cover as well as a place to plot the best route back to the Rockefeller Museum.

Most of the gates were to his left, along the Western Wall, giving him the most options for escape. But because of that, it was where most of the soldiers would be. It was also where the Waqf headquarters was. Too much risk. Ahead of him was the upper tier, the massive platform for the Dome of the Rock. Far too open and empty to remain inconspicuous. To his right, between the upper tier and the eastern wall, was a grove of trees that ran all the way to the northern wall. But to get there, he had to cross the plaza with the Cistern 8 entrances—and the furious guards standing in it.

Graham slipped into a copse of trees on the middle tier to his right that shielded him half the distance he needed to go. The rest of the way was open ground.

Act like you belong here. Don't draw attention to yourself.

The argument at Cistern 8 was so animated that it absorbed everyone near it, making them oblivious to the rest of the platform. At least that's what Graham was betting on, especially since it had been evacuated.

Walk normal. But as soon as he thought it, he felt unnatural, and his gait stiffened with self-consciousness. Was it too fast? Too slow? Where should he look? How long should his stride be?

By the time he reached the other side, he was sure every person in the plaza was staring at him. But in the cover of the grove, he stole a glimpse and discovered no one was paying attention. He was the invisible man.

A paved walkway ran through the trees parallel with the upper platform, then angled right to the northeast corner of the Mount. The progress instilled Graham with enough confidence to carry him out the Gate of Tribes unchallenged, its guards assuming he was Waqf. Progress.

He lost himself in the Old City, weaving anonymously through the neighborhoods of the Muslim Quarter until he arrived at Herod's Gate. Again, he passed through easily, onto Sultan Suleiman, almost directly across the street from IAA headquarters.

Thank you! It was not the first time that day he had offered a prayer of thanks to the God who wasn't there, but this time he had a vague impression that someone was listening.

FIFTY-FIVE

"Graham!"

Yaniv shot to his feet and shoved past the desk as Graham burst into his office.

The safety of the room deactivated Graham's survival mode, and he collapsed onto the floor in a paroxysm of sobs. He tried to speak through the tears, but the words broke apart in meaningless fragments of sound.

"Are you hurt?" Yaniv kneeled next to Graham and put a hand on his shoulder.

Graham shook his head, keeping it bent toward the floor.

"You are in quite a state, my friend," Yaniv said, scanning the mud-caked pants and shoes. "I have been trying to contact the Waqf to explain what was happening. But from your clothes, I see they already—"

"Gone!" Graham looked up, the keffiyeh dangling from his neck, unraveled.

"It makes no difference," Yaniv said. "We knew the treasure probably was not there. It may never have been there. Even if it was, it may have been found hundreds of years ago. Perhaps more."

Graham shook his head again, but before he could speak, Yaniv continued.

"You have done a brilliant job following the clues and

getting as far as you did. You achieved more than anyone else who has tried. You even made some important finds. It really is quite a remarkable accomp—"

"No!" Graham stared fiercely into Yaniv's eyes. "You don't understand. The treasure is there! *All* of it! And *more*."

Yaniv rocked back—as if pushed by the news—and shifted himself to a seated position on the floor. "You are telling me—"

Graham raised his hand as he sat up opposite Yaniv. "Daniel…" He closed his eyes as if he were afraid to see the words. "Daniel is dead."

"No." Yaniv shrunk, his face contorting. "How can that be?"

"Karanlik killed him. He jumped up behind Daniel and…cut him. Across the throat." He wiped his eyes with the heels of his hands. "We didn't notice Karanlik had gotten free. Daniel had knocked him out and tied him up, but we got distracted moving backpacks of silver from the other side of the cistern. It happened so fast. I didn't do anything…I couldn't…"

"If only I had entered the cistern with you. Maybe Daniel would still…" Yaniv left the sentence unfinished as he looked away.

"What happened? You watched us go down. I saw you." Graham hadn't intended the hint of accusation he heard in his voice and felt instant shame.

"The Waqf were nearer to me than you," Yaniv said, patting his palm to his chest. "When they started to evacuate the Mount, I was too close to escape them. I did not even try. Instead, I tried to tell them who I was and what we were doing there. But they would not listen. They only wanted to clear the platform as quickly as possible. By the time they started escorting me away, you were inside the cistern. They must not have seen you in the turmoil."

Graham nodded and closed his eyes. "That's what Daniel said probably happened."

"Just so," Yaniv said. "But how is it you are alive?"

"Karanlik attacked me, too. I was holding a pick hammer and we both fell. He landed on it just right. It was an accident."

"But there was a third explosion."

"There was someone else," Graham said. "Someone on the platform. He knew Karanlik had another bomb. He said if I didn't send up the silver then he would call the cell phone that triggered it."

"And you did not do it?"

"I don't know what happened." Graham sighed. "Maybe I was in shock over Daniel or Karanlik. There was rage that came over me. And I just threw the silver into the water. When I looked up, I could see him tapping his phone. I ran behind a wall separating part of the well. That's when the bomb went off."

"Extraordinary." Yaniv steepled his fingers. "How did you get out? I have not heard anything about someone being rescued."

"Escaped. Through the tunnels."

"They exist?" Yaniv's brow raised as he leaned forward.

"They are real. A whole network. I tried to use a compass and Wilson and Warren's survey map as much as I could, but I got completely lost. And then..." Graham hesitated, wondering how his own words would sound.

"What happened?"

"The tunnel led to another cave, but the opening was high up, in the side of the wall, and I couldn't climb up or down. I could only look into it using the lantern. Part of the ceiling looked like it had a hole that had been covered with square slabs of stone. Looked like marble."

Yaniv's eyes narrowed. "How big?"

"The big one was maybe six feet across. The other one was half that size."

"Was there a pattern? Like a mosaic?"

"No. Why?"

Yaniv reached over his head and grabbed the laptop from the desk. He opened a file, then angled the computer so they could both see the image on the screen. Two Arabic men stood inside a cave holding back a strip of carpet, exposing the marble floor underneath. Part of the floor was comprised of a ten-foot-square mosaic of black and brown marble inlaid in a white slab edged with black. What looked like a compass rose was surrounded by a circle of inlaid triangular and diamond shapes.

"This is the cave beneath the Dome of the Rock," Yaniv said. "Someone took these with a cell phone camera when new carpet was installed."

He advanced to another picture. This one showed the entire mosaic from the perspective of one of the corners. The next image showed a smaller mosaic with an octagon framed by a square and bordered by a pattern of black, white, and amber tiles.

"Incredible. I didn't know there were photos of the floor. Just the Simpson painting," Graham said, recalling the same man who had painted Cistern 8 also recorded the cave under the Dome of the Rock, including part of the mosaic on the floor.

"Do you think this is what you saw? The underside of these?"

"I can't say for sure. The pattern would only be on the top, of course. But yes, they look like they'd be the same size as what I saw."

Yaniv pivoted the computer back to face him, then spoke as he tapped the keys. "Remember Pierotti, the Italian architect who said he found a way to the Well of Souls? Here is what he said he saw.

> *"The form of the lower chamber is an irregular sphere, about 22 or 23 feet in diameter, its floor is covered deep with dry mud with a few stones. On a careful examination I saw, at a height of 12 feet, the mouth of the hole leading to the upper chamber, about 6½ feet in diameter and 4 feet long, and the marble slab, which we have already mentioned as covering it. This it was that the Santon struck with his foot or stick to prove the existence of the Well of the Souls below!"*

Graham's eyes widened as he recognized his own memory described in the 150-year-old words. "That's what I saw. He was there, too."

"Did you see anything else?"

"Actually, yes," Graham said. "On the other side of the cave, there was an alcove. Possibly a tunnel. Something was there. It looked like a roll of carpet. And there was something behind it that I couldn't make out. It was metallic and looked gold."

"Surely, you do not mean to suggest it was the Ark." Yaniv smiled doubtfully.

"I don't know. I could barely see it. It seemed like it could be some kind of chest to me. But I was so exhausted and so upset by everything that had happened that I don't really trust myself to…Wait! I took some pictures."

Graham pulled out his phone and transferred them to Yaniv's computer. Yaniv spun the screen back around and scrolled through the images. The pictures were speckled with digital noise, the result of too little light. But *something* was there. The coil of material swirled from the darkness, and splinters of light slid down the side of the two poles. Behind them, the gold smudge marred the blackness around it, offering no more clues to its identity.

"Astonishing...I am speechless." Yaniv stared at Graham in wonder. "The Well of Souls. You have found what Montagu Parker was looking for."

"I don't know," Graham said. "Maybe. Yes, I thought so."

"This coil you said looked like carpet—it is possibly the veil that separated the Holy of Holies."

"That is the only thing I could think of. Except that Titus used the veil to carry away the Temple treasures. Maybe it was an older veil. Or maybe it was left from the Tabernacle."

Yaniv shook his head in disbelief as he scrolled through the photos again. "But you said you were lost. How did you get out?"

Graham told him how he'd tried to retrace the route but wound up in the Well of the Leaf. He explained how he'd found his way into, then out of, al-Aqsa, and finally made his way to the museum.

Yaniv bobbed his head in thought. "I will alert the police and the Yaman to be on the lookout for this man you saw at the top of the cistern."

"The Waqf already found him." Graham said the words before he realized he would have to explain them.

"And you know this how?"

Graham's eyes grew unfocused as his gaze drifted to the floor. "I watched it happen." He looked back up to gauge Yaniv's reaction.

"I do not understand."

"I'm not sure I do either," Graham said. He stammered several false starts before finding the right words. "After the explosion, I could see myself, lying in the cave. Then I sort of drifted up until I was above the Temple Mount. I was looking down at the hatch where we had entered. Smoke was coming out. Some men started running to the cistern."

"How many?"

The unexpected question made Graham think for a moment. "Six. Two from the al-Marwani stairs and four from al-Aqsa."

"Go on," Yaniv said flatly.

"You think I was hallucinating, don't you? But this was real. I could smell the smoke. I could hear them. One of the men tore off his black jacket and he had a red shirt underneath. One kept yelling into the hatch. Three of them argued. The other one was on the phone. He was the one who saw the bomber and started pointing. The man was hiding in the alley next to al-Aqsa. They started to drag him to the cistern, but I floated upward again and got distracted by something on the roof of the mosque."

"What was that?"

"A pair of sandals." Graham stared at the floor as if looking down on them. "But one of them was on top of the other, turned at a right angle, like a cross. It was so strange that I focused on it. The next thing I knew, I was in the cave again."

"I think you may have a severe concussion, my friend. You are in shock. There is no shame in that. It is a miracle you are still alive."

"I know what I saw," Graham said. "And I know it was real. There was too much detail. Nothing about it was like a dream except my perspective."

"Then how would you explain it?" Yaniv turned his palms up, showing them empty. "Are you saying you had…What is it called? A near death experience?"

"I don't know. I've wondered the same thing. But I'm certain that if you went on the roof right now, you'd find those sandals."

"That would be a good test. But for now, it is not important. You know, there is one good thing about the explosion in the cistern: It gives us a reason to enter it to assess the structural integrity of the platform. And while we are down there, we might be able to recover some of the silver. Maybe even explore your tunnel. Most importantly, we need to recover Daniel."

"I still can't believe what happened." Graham closed his eyes, as if blinding himself to the memory.

"But we will have to act quickly." Yaniv emphasized the last word with a snap, forcing Graham's eyes open. "We may have an opportunity here to work with the Waqf. They will be glad to hear this was about money, not ideology, or religion, or politics. I will brief the IAA chief, and hopefully he will be more effective in reaching the appropriate authorities. They need this information as soon as possible to keep it from getting out of control."

Graham pulled himself onto the chair behind him. "Sounds good."

"What you need right now is rest," Yaniv said. "But do not fall asleep. Not with a chance of concussion." He lifted Graham's feet and scooted the other chair under them.

Graham barely noticed Yaniv leaving. Recalling all that happened had overloaded his senses, leaving him in a kind of trance. Against Yaniv's orders, Graham quickly fell asleep.

FIFTY-SIX

The entire world had become a plane of white without seams or corners, no edges to delineate it. There were no shadows cast, and no objects to cast them. Just featureless white. Light came from everywhere equally, as if the air itself were glowing. It was an atmosphere of purity—empty, yet full.

Graham swiveled around, and although he felt his body move, his perspective didn't appear to change. There was no shift in what he saw to measure his motion.

Until the leaf drifted into view. It looked like it was being blown by a wind, though Graham felt no current. The leaf stopped, tumbling to a fixed point, suddenly immovable, instantly substantial.

It was hard to calculate the distance because it was so small in his field of view. He leaned forward and started to walk toward it, then noticed he could feel the soft jog of each step, but he couldn't hear it. He didn't sense that he was deaf, simply that his steps made no sound.

The leaf grew so slowly that at first, he wasn't sure he was making progress. By the time it became discernibly bigger, he realized it wasn't a leaf at all, but the hatch of a cistern. He could see the elongated diamond shapes of the tread plate pattern embossed in the metal. The coat of grass green paint seemed both fresh and timeless, impervious to the environment it stood against. A golden keyed padlock was threaded through the hasp, but hung open, unlocked. Graham slid it out and dropped it onto the ethereal plane, apparently floating next to his feet.

He raised the manhole easily, rotating it without any objection from the hinges. When it reached the halfway point, a column of blackness shot from the opening, like a beam of light in reverse. Graham jumped back to avoid it, and looked up, tracing it as it disappeared into infinity, too far for his eyes to follow. He looked back down to the opening and wondered what had made him recoil. The pillar had no substance, like a tear in the world. He reached his hand forward, pushing it into the void, feeling nothing. And yet his hand was completely enveloped by it, disappearing as if it were eclipsed by a wall. He pulled his arm back, and his hand reappeared, unaffected.

"Graahhaamm."

His name floated out of the opening, sounding familiar, inviting.

"Graahhaamm."

He leaned his head into the black pier. The opaque column had made him assume he'd be blinded when he tried to see inside of it. Instead he saw with perfect clarity.

A black sheet of water coated the floor of the cistern, glistening, catching the light outside despite the pier of blackness. And standing in the center of it—illuminated as if they emitted their own light—were Olivia and Alyson. They looked up expectantly, waiting for him. Their faces were the most beautiful things Graham had ever seen. But it wasn't their features that made them beautiful, it was their expressions of profound peace.

I found it! I found the treasure.

He heard his voice, recognizing it though he hadn't spoken, then reached into the well, stretching his arm as far as it could extend. As he looked at the impossible span between his hand and their faces, it occurred to him that he didn't know if he was trying to pull them up or be pulled down. Should he join the treasure, or *should the treasure join him?*

As if in answer, the hatch slammed shut, removing the choice, the force blowing Graham from the opening as it descended. He was thrown onto his back, stunned by the expulsion. Grief began to splinter out from his chest like ice spreading through freezing water. He pushed himself into a sitting position and looked again at an empty field of white. The cistern was gone.

Something lightly touched his right hand, and he turned his head to see a vivid green leaf. He held it in his hand, transfixed by a mystical ordinariness. It was a symbol of the way things should be—the product of feeding on light. He knew there was only one place like that. It had come from paradise.

FIFTY-SEVEN

Graham awoke in the aftermath of the office door banging to a close and knew it had been the sound the cistern hatch made in his dream. Yaniv had flung it behind him, forgetting in his excitement that Graham had been resting. He grabbed the laptop, inserted a thumb drive, and dropped into the chair that had been holding Graham's feet.

"We have security footage from the camera above the entrance of al-Aqsa."

"What did you find?" The parts of Graham struggling to retain the imagined presence of his family instantly released their hold.

"I have not had a chance to watch it yet."

As he answered, the video player opened to show the general area between the mosque and the al-Kas fountain. Graham could see the entrance to Cistern 8 in the upper right quadrant of the shot. People moved across the platform in jerks, strobed by the low frame rate that enabled more storage. Yaniv shuttled the video forward until he saw the camera shake and panic erupt across the Temple Mount. As people started to run from right to left, toward the Western Wall, he let it play at normal speed. A man entered the frame from the right, walking quickly to the cistern, impervious to the commotion around him.

"That's him," Graham said, pointing at the screen. "Karanlik."

Yaniv paused, captured a screenshot of the frame, then resumed play. Karanlik kneeled to cut the padlock, glanced back, and gave a quick nod offscreen.

"Did you see that?" Yaniv scrubbed the playhead back and watched the gesture again.

"Not when it was happening," Graham said. "It was too chaotic. I didn't know there was another man until much later."

Karanlik dropped through the manhole with expertise, and his descent seemed to pull Daniel and Graham into the picture.

"Daniel." Graham sighed, part plea, part prayer. He cupped his hand over his mouth, though it was his eyes he wanted to shield. It wasn't the sight of Daniel that was unexpected to Graham, it was seeing him alive and in motion—stilted, though it was.

Graham was watching Daniel make the decision that would cost him his life. He wondered what Daniel would have chosen if he could have seen this video, if he could have compared it to a video showing what would happen if he didn't enter the well. But Graham knew better than to pull that thread of what-ifs. He had been caught in its web for more than a year and had only just started to escape its snare. The truth was that any Daniel that didn't enter the cistern would not have been the Daniel that he had grown attached to so quickly.

Yaniv shuttled forward again, skipping through the footage of the empty plaza until the man with the keffiyeh masking his face appeared. As the man lifted the hatch and leaned into the opening, Graham recalled the same moment looking up from the bottom of the cistern, creating a split screen in his mind. The man didn't move except to nervously glance around the Mount.

Graham stared as the man removed his phone and held it like a threat over the entrance, unable to look away from what he didn't want to see. The stuttering image showed the man drilling the phone with his finger. Then the man pulled the hatch shut and ran to the alley next to al-Aqsa.

The green hatch blew open so fast that it looked like a bad edit in the video or a special effect in a silent movie. Smoke billowed from the hole as if a subterranean factory were manufacturing black clouds.

As people ran into the scene, Graham felt a sense of déjà vu.

Yaniv paused the footage again. "Six people. Just as you said." He pointed to the screen. "Two from al-Marwani and four from al-Aqsa."

He hit Play and they watched one of the men drop to his knees and throw off his jacket, revealing a red shirt.

"The red shirt," Yaniv whispered.

One of the men was crouched as close as he could to the hatch, and another was on the phone. The man on the phone raised his hand and pointed in the direction the bomber had run. The others looked in the same direction, then poured off the bottom right corner of the screen.

Yaniv froze the video. "Everything is just as you said. Graham, I do not know what is happening..."

"I'm not sure I do either," Graham said. "But it wasn't a hallucination. I've heard stories about this kind of thing, but I never believed it. What do you think it means?"

"I wish I could tell you. Actually, I wish you could tell me."

Yaniv started the video again and shuttled forward until the mob reappeared, dragging the bomber to the cistern. Several of the men were shouting at him, jabbing their fingers, alternating aiming them at the opening and the bomber's face, connecting them. Then they were on the move again, shoving him toward al-Aqsa. His keffiyeh had been torn from his face, but it wasn't until he was almost under the camera that his features could be clearly seen.

Yaniv froze the image to take a screenshot of the man as he looked up into the lens.

Graham turned as still as the frame, frozen with shock.

"What is wrong?" Yaniv studied Graham and saw the answer. "You know this man."

Graham's face transformed in a sequence of emotions, melting from one to the next before he heard his own incredulous whisper. "It's Nigel. Nigel Horne."

FIFTY-EIGHT

"I can't believe it." Graham shook his head, trying to reconcile the explosion with the gentle, academic man he knew. "This has to be a mistake."

"He was the man hiding in the alley. He even had the keffiyeh around his face."

"I don't know…"

"You said the bomber spoke with an accent."

Graham recalled the strange diction that made the man difficult to understand, then tried to hear it in Horne's voice.

"When did you last see him?"

Graham searched the previous few days, shocked so little time had passed given how distant it seemed. "Three days ago, I think. Here. At the museum. He said he was doing some consulting for the IAA."

"Consulting? Did he say what it was about?"

Graham stared at the face on the laptop. "I don't remember. Where is he now?"

"I have no idea," Yaniv said with a futile wave.

"But you have the security video," Graham said. "Didn't the Waqf say what happened when they gave you the file?"

"There has been no contact with the Waqf. The IAA chief was still trying to reach them when I came back. The police and the Waqf share the video feed from the cameras on the

278

Mount."

"And they can arrest people without telling you?"

"No," Yaniv said. "But it does not mean they would not try. And obviously they have. There has never been a situation like this. They will claim to have the authority over it. However, the Waqf is a religious trust, and this is not a religious issue. It is for the police."

"So what do we do?"

"Now that we have proof the bomber was neither Palestinian *nor* Jewish, and that he was using the tensions between the two as a distraction, we should be able to find a way to cooperate. They will want information about this Horne."

As he spoke, Yaniv moved to his chair behind his desk, reached for the office phone, and punched a single button.

"Dr. Eliot recognized the man in the security camera footage...Nigel Horne. Horne said he was consulting for us...I do not know..." Yaniv fixed his eyes on Graham's face as he listened to the voice on the other end. "Yes. That is excellent news. Will they be with us?...That is fine...We have to do it...I agree." Yaniv put the receiver back on the cradle. "How do you feel?"

"Why?" Graham squinted. "What's happening?"

"We are going to need you. We are going back."

"Onto the Temple Mount?"

"No. Under it."

FIFTY-NINE

"It's like Montagu Parker all over again," Graham said, adrenaline animating him as he changed into the blue IAA shirt Yaniv provided.

"Just so," Yaniv said. "It is already more like Parker's situation than you probably know. Palestinians have gathered in protest between the Western Wall and Silwan. Some are already throwing rocks at the police and soldiers."

"How many people were hurt in the explosions?" Graham asked.

"Thankfully, none."

"Amazing."

"The bombs were apparently used for distraction," Yaniv said. "If Karanlik had wanted to injure people he could have selected better places. One was in the tree planters between the Dung Gate and the entrance to the plaza. The other was by the entrance to the Givati Parking Lot dig. Destroyed the office shed, but that was all."

Graham tucked his shirt into a clean pair of pants, also courtesy of Yaniv. "All set."

Yaniv quickly led Graham through the doors, into the exhibition hall of the museum, away from the loading dock.

"Where's the van?" Graham asked as they exited the main entrance to an empty parking lot.

"We will walk. Far too crowded at the Dung Gate. We would never make it through the mob."

They entered the Old City through Herod's Gate, then took the left branch until it terminated in the cross street parallel to the north wall of the Temple Mount one block away. They turned left and passed the street to the Gate of Darkness, stopping at the next gate.

"The Waqf will meet us here," Yaniv said.

Graham remained silent as he read the tiled sign set into the wall next to the entrance. He had never been a superstitious man but passing through this particular arch triggered his emotions. He blamed himself for Daniel's death and felt guilty that Daniel had given his life for something as trivial as a treasure hunt. He felt guilty for taking the life of Karanlik, even if it had been passive and in self-defense. He felt guilty that his thoughts of recovering what might well be the Ark of the Covenant—and the rest of the treasure—had kept him from properly grieving Daniel.

He entered the gate numb but exited the other side feeling ashamed of himself. And yet, he didn't feel hopeless. Graham told himself that exhaustion had put him in a susceptible state of mind, that there was nothing special about it because of its name. And yet, he couldn't help feeling that there was something symbolic about the Gate of Remission.

The Waqf guard escorted them around the east side of the Dome of the Rock, then south through the grove that had given Graham cover earlier. They arrived in the plaza and joined two dozen people already carrying out different recovery tasks. Waqf guards and administrators mingled with Israeli soldiers and police in a scene of cooperation that was the mirror opposite of the confrontation threatening to ignite 200 yards away at the entrance to the Western Wall Plaza. The paving stones within a ten-foot radius around the cap to Cistern 8 had dislodged in the upward thrust of the blast.

Graham was surprised to see the varying thicknesses of the tiles—some up to six inches—given the remarkable smoothness of the platform.

The green hatch had been removed and lay on the ground near the well. Graham could see it had bent backward, warped by the force that had wrapped it partway over the base of the cistern.

Yaniv parted the knot of people around the entrance and Graham followed him to its center. Two metal supports clamped to the outside of the wall, hooked over the top, and disappeared into the hole like a claw. He watched Yaniv steady himself as he turned backward and guided his feet onto the first steps of the escape ladder that clung to the surface, then descend.

Graham stepped to the hole and saw Yaniv lower himself into a warm glow very different from the well Graham had entered that morning. The inky blackness had been dispelled by a collection of work lights, some mounted on stands, some set on the floor, all wired to portable generators. Once Yaniv reached the bottom, Graham followed him down the ladder. The descent that seemed to last forever in the dark took a matter of seconds in the light, the dangling rope replaced by chains bridged with aluminum rungs.

Although it was still huge, the cavern seemed diminished by the light, revealing what had been a mystery for so long. The front two of the four piers had withered in the explosion, and Graham wondered if new supports would be added to shore them up. The rock partition was closer than he had pictured it now that it was exposed, and the chamber behind it was radiant with additional work lights. Fragments of black material from the shredded backpacks polluted the rock rise and the water.

Behind him, the top half of the ancient steps still clung to the wall, leading now to the rubble at the epicenter of the blast. Next to the wall, two long black vinyl bags shaped themselves to the corpses they contained. Graham hated one and loved the other but couldn't tell which was which.

"Graham, I want you to meet some people."

Graham shook their hands, barely hearing the introductions and too distracted to remember their names. One was the Grand Mufti, the leading Muslim cleric at the Haram. One was the director of the Waqf. And the last man was the director of Islamic archaeology at the Haram. Given how contentious the situation was, as well as the history of the opposing authorities, Graham was impressed by the civility the men showed Yaniv and extended to him as well.

"We are very happy to find you were not hurt, Dr. Eliot." The director of the Waqf gave him a concerned smile. "What an extraordinary thing to have survived."

"Unfortunately, to survive I had to enter al-Aqsa." Graham hoped the confession would give them a reason to trust him. "I am deeply sorry to have entered the holy place so unworthily. I meant no disrespect."

"It is quite the contrary." The Grand Mufti almost looked like a model in William Simpson's watercolor, still wearing his traditional robes. "The Noble Qur'an teaches, 'Allah guides whom he wills.' It is he who provided you shelter. It is he to whom you owe your survival. He is the one who gives life."

"Thank you." Graham nodded.

"We heard about your remarkable discovery, Doctor." The archaeologist motioned to the debris. "Unfortunately—as you can see—much of it did not survive the bomb. We did recover what was left of the coins in the rear of the well, however."

Graham followed the man's gesture and saw a five-gallon bucket of silver shekels, three-quarters full. "There was so much more…Doesn't seem worth two lives, does it."

"No amount would be worth even one life." The Grand Mufti gave Graham a look of compassion.

"Just so," Yaniv said. "Excuse us, please, while Dr. Eliot shows me what he found."

Graham kept silent until they had waded around the corner and into the back chamber. "This isn't how I left it," he whispered.

"But they admitted as much. They recovered what they could."

"No. There was more. A lot more. Even in the dark I saw shekels all over the floor in the water after the bomb went off. Now there aren't any. There were way more than what could fit in the bucket."

"What are you saying, Graham?"

"I'm saying I'm not sure they are telling the truth. Not the whole truth. How long were they down here before anyone from the IAA or the police arrived?"

"I do not know." Yaniv's face darkened at the thought. "Do not say anything. We will never get the chance to be in here again, and we can have this conversation with them later."

"But you'll never get the shekels back from them," Graham said.

"If we do it now, then I fear we will be locked out." Yaniv made his hands into scales, weighing the factors. "Now, I have not told them about what you saw. Let me speak to them and see if they will agree to exploring the tunnel you took. They are so paranoid that the Jews are always digging under the Mount, we can show them exactly what is there, that we are not tunneling below the Dome. I think we could build on the full disclosure of your actions that you offered them earlier. And if you accidentally-on-purpose find a way back to the Well of Souls and pretend it is your first time seeing it..."

"Then a Jew, a Christian, and a Muslim will—together—make one of the greatest archaeological discoveries in history."

SIXTY

Graham climbed the extension ladder leaning against the wall of the cave, into the mouth of the tunnel. The desperation that had driven him into the tunnel that morning had been replaced with the anticipation of discovery. He felt for the button on his headlamp, switched it on, and tilted his head, experimenting with different angles as he got used to it. As an added measure, he also switched on the tactical flashlight one of the soldiers had given him, flinching as the light geysered into the black hole. He waited for Yaniv and the director of archaeology to climb in behind him and get situated.

Yaniv turned on his headlamp and gave a thumbs-up. "Lead the way."

Graham held out his phone, displaying Wilson and Warren's map, and pointed to a spot on the screen. "Here's where we are. I tried to use the map, but some of it wasn't accurate. And much of what I found is not marked at all. To keep from getting lost, I made only left turns."

"Good thinking, Doctor," the archaeologist said.

"Please. It's Graham."

"Very good. You may call me Nabil."

Graham got up into a stoop and started moving deeper into the passage, surprised how much faster he could move without the duffel bag encumbering him. They reached the first intersection sooner than he expected, and he found the malformed arrow pointing to the left. He took the turn knowing it would dead-end, wanting them to see all he had seen. When the wall closing the tunnel came within range of the lights, he stopped.

"It's closed off. The map shows this tunnel continuing under the mosque, but there is no way through."

"According to the map, it leads to the western arcade of the al-Aqsa basement," Nabil said, looking at Graham's screen.

"It did at one time, anyway," Graham said.

"Fascinating." Yaniv turned in place, then followed Nabil back to the intersection.

"What did you find down this way?" Rather than turning left, Nabil peered into the tunnel.

"It's blocked with fill," Graham said. "It would be worth coming back to clean it out to find out where it goes."

Nabil went far enough to verify the clogged artery, then turned around. Graham led them into the remaining branch, where the passage became uncharted. For the second time that day, the twisting path confounded his internal compass, though this time the disorientation did not induce fear.

The fear came as the next intersection appeared. He had expected a T-bone, the choice he had made between logic to the left and intuition to the right. Instead, the choice was to turn right or continue straight. The left-turn method dictated the straight option, but Graham paused, unsure what had happened.

"Something wrong?" Yaniv asked.

"I just don't remember this…"

"Perhaps you passed it in the dark the first time," Nabil offered.

"Maybe." Graham forced himself forward, though without conviction.

A short distance later the light dispersed into a cistern.

All three of them crowded on the edge, showering the space with light. It was deeper than the Great Sea, with an irregular shape that made it hard to guess how much it held.

"Look over here!"

Graham and Yaniv traced Nabil's finger across the well to the bottom of the wall on the other side. More than a dozen white hands created a ritual design on the surface of the rock.

"Abyd a'eta." Nabil was suddenly agitated, as if one of the hands had slapped him from across the cave. "The White Hand."

"What is that?" Graham looked at Yaniv and saw that he was equally baffled.

"The sign of Musa. Surah 27." Nabil removed his phone and opened the Qur'an. "Verse 12. 'Put your hand into your bosom, it will come forth white without hurt. These are among the nine signs you will take to Fir'aun—that is the Pharaoh—and his people'…Then in surah…7, verse 108. 'And he drew out his hand, and behold! It was white with radiance for the beholders.'"

"But why is it here?" Yaniv asked.

"Let's see what Wilson says." Graham skimmed Wilson's notes. "This must be Cistern 7. He says there are two entrances…says there is a conduit communicating to the general system in this part of the area. That is probably what this is… two mouths to the tunnel…He saw the hands, too. Thought they were probably a charm against evil spirits."

"We should not be here," Nabil said gravely. "We must leave."

Graham started to turn. "We can't go forward anyway."

"No," Nabil said. "You do not understand. We must leave all the tunnels."

"Why?" asked Graham.

"There is a reason those hands are here. They are a sign from Allah."

"But it sounds like they were for protection," Yaniv said. "Allah will protect us, won't he?"

"There are no white hands *here*, only *there*," Nabil said. "The evil spirits would have escaped into the tunnels."

"You're serious, aren't you?" The words escaped Graham before he could filter them.

Nabil's dour face was answer enough, and Graham started back down the conduit in silence. At the T-bone, Graham angled himself around the corner to the left.

"No!" Nabil called from the rear. "We must go back. There is no time left."

"It's a left turn. This is the way we keep from getting lost," Graham said, truly not wanting to become lost, but also still hoping to find the passage to the Well of Souls.

"This is where we went straight," Nabil said, "so we must go straight across it."

"Nabil, it's easy enough to get lost down here as it is. I'm trying to take the safest route. And the safest way back is to turn."

Graham didn't wait for a response and rounded the corner. Almost immediately they were at the mouth of another cavern.

"Think this is the same one?" Graham asked. "Just a different arm?"

"No way of knowing without doing a full exploration," Yaniv said.

"No!" Nabil barked. "It does not make sense. You said this tunnel took you under al-Aqsa, but at this point we must be in front of al-Marwani. How can that be?"

"I don't know," Graham said. "I'm as baffled as you."

"I am not baffled. I am finished. *We* are finished." Nabil spun around and went back up the channel, turning left.

Yaniv looked in resignation at Graham, then followed, keeping some distance between them and Nabil. Less than ten minutes later, they saw Nabil's figure silhouetted by the lights in Cistern 8 as they turned into the branch of the tunnel they had started from.

By the time they stepped onto the cave floor, Nabil was speaking in a torrent of Arabic to the Grand Mufti and the director of the Waqf. The director broke away and hurried into the water between the shore and the first set of columns where two Israeli workers were combing through the rocks and silt.

"Stop what you are doing. There is nothing left to find here."

The Israelis looked at each other, apparently weighing whose orders to follow.

"Go!" The director then addressed the whole cave. "All of you. Out! This operation is over."

Graham started to walk over to the Grand Mufti, but felt Yaniv's hand take his arm, guiding him toward the escape ladder.

"The window has closed. There is nothing you can say to keep it open."

"But we were so close," Graham said in a harsh whisper. "We are right here."

"You have been in this place twice today," Yaniv said. "That is once more than any man alive, and twice more than most."

Graham's reluctant ascent to the surface was burdened with a sense of failure. He emerged from the hatch and found a spot against the low wall of one of the tree boxes. He bridged his forearms across his knees and rested his head. The sun neared the horizon, copying his posture on a cosmic scale.

"We did what we could, Graham," Yaniv said, taking a place next to him. "I believe what you told me. And we still have your photographs."

Graham remained unmoved, unconsoled. "I don't know what happened. All of a sudden everything just…changed. It was like Nabil used those hands as an excuse to leave."

"Just so," Yaniv said. "I have been thinking the same thing. I also reread Pierotti's account and something similar happened to him. The mood of his guide suddenly changed, and he was forced to leave. Maybe Nabil saw something that they plan to come back to later, after we are gone. He must have had a hidden purpose. Like us."

"What do you think it was?" Graham asked.

"I have no idea. But it may not be over quite yet. I had a message waiting for me. From Nagi. He said it is very important that he speaks to us. He says he has information about the bombings."

"Where is he?" Graham struggled to his feet, feeling leaden and rusted.

"He will be at a coffee shop in the Souk al-Qattanin. In the Cotton Market. After sunset. Which is happening now."

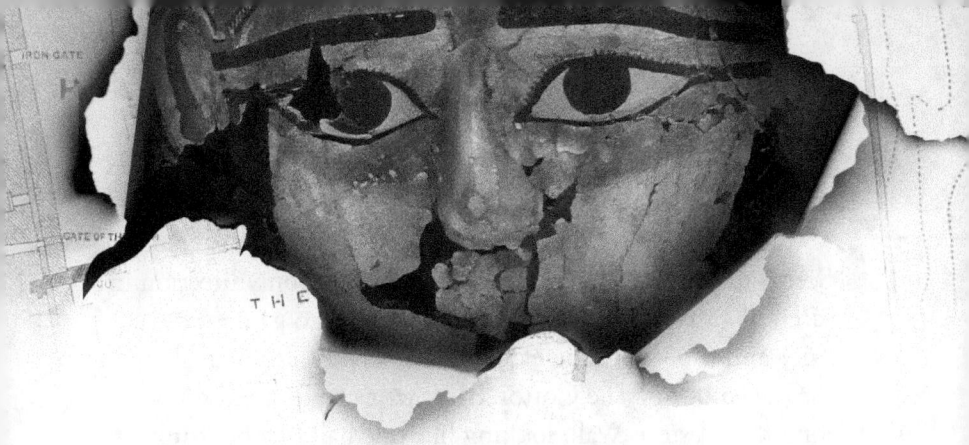

SIXTY-ONE

Bullhorn speakers strained the sound of the evening call to prayer, leaving a brittle hymn that reflected the tension in the air. Muslims on the rescue team stopped to pray—the only worshippers allowed on the evacuated Haram.

Out of respect, Graham and Yaniv avoided crossing the plaza containing the Dome of the Rock, the building protecting the place where Muhammad stepped off the earth to begin the Night Journey to heaven. As they circumvented the tier, Graham kept his eyes on the octagonal building, picturing caves beneath its prayer room.

"It's so close. Literally right under our feet."

"Just so." Yaniv sighed. "As it has been since Nebuchadnezzar captured Jerusalem 2,500 years ago. It has hidden beneath the ruins of two Jewish temples and a Roman one. Constantine, Crusaders, and Muslims have built on top of it without disturbing it. And earthquakes have not revealed it. It can wait a little while longer to be discovered. We are closer now than ever."

"*You* are closer than ever. *I* was there. And this is as close as I'm ever going to be again." Graham wondered if Yaniv was actually more discouraged than he sounded, if the measured words were meant to convince himself or console Graham. Whatever the answer, Graham appreciated being believed despite the failed attempt to return to the cave.

Yaniv put a hand on Graham's shoulder as they walked. "Seems to me like Muhammed went in the wrong direction in search of answers. Allah took him to heaven to gather evidence and proof, but the evidence was beneath him all along."

The edifice of The Cotton Merchant's Gate stood midway along the Western Wall, looking like one half of a building sliced in two. A half-dome was scooped out of the stone entryway, resembling part of a mold used to cast a small-scale model of the Dome of the Rock. The Ablaq style of alternating light and dark stones gave it a distinctly Islamic look, a feature that continued throughout the souk on the other side. The gate itself sat lower than the Mount, requiring the stairs that led to it to be sunken into the platform, forming a bowl. Two enormous wooden doors—paradise green—blocked the archway that had been cut into the Western Wall 800 years earlier.

They quietly stepped past two Waqf guards reciting the prayers of *Maghrib* and descended the stairs of the bowl. A pair of Israeli soldiers opened the left door of the gate and nodded to Yaniv and Graham as they slipped through.

They stood on a landing at the top of a dozen stairs that led into the Souk al-Qattanin. The market was inside a vaulted arcade a hundred yards long where cotton used to be sold. Now the clutter of the merchandise overflowing the stalls made the other end hard to see. Strings of colored lights zigzagged down the corridor like a multicolored stitch straining to hold together a rip in the market.

The buildings on either side of the hall contained two ancient bath houses and a *khan*—an inn for travelers. They also housed the offices of the Waqf and a campus of al-Quds University. Although daylight had stopped falling through the skylights in the vaults, the market was still crammed with people.

"Amazing to think the Jews used to come here to pray," Graham said.

"It is still the closest we can get to the Holy of Holies. But now…" Yaniv let the sentence die on his tongue as he looked at the table offering Qur'ans to those about to ascend to the Haram.

A coffee stand crammed into the next space, and they claimed three of the black plastic chairs. The vendor poured coffee from a chrome urn into two small clear glasses, set them on an ornate silver tray, and placed the tray in front of them on a knee-high plastic table.

"There is another stand at the other end of the market," Yaniv said, nodding at the entrance, "but when Nagi does not see us there he will check here. Hopefully."

Yaniv had finished his coffee and was asking for another when Nagi pushed through the shoppers. A smile lit his face when he saw Graham, and Graham stood to shake his hand.

"Where's Daniel?"

Graham looked away, grief stealing his thoughts.

"Sit, please," Yaniv said, not allowing an answer. "Daniel was not able to join us."

"I went to the Promised Land Hotel, but they said you had checked out."

"We had to after what happened at the Gihon Spring," Graham said.

"I can see why now."

"What do you mean?" Yaniv froze, his cup halfway to his mouth.

Nagi leaned in over the miniature table conspiratorially. "I heard that the man responsible for the bombings—this Karanlik guy—was involved with some very dangerous people."

"He set off bombs, Nagi," Graham said. "Seems to me *he* was the dangerous one."

"But the reason he did it was because he was trying to set himself up as a dealer on the black market." Nagi looked at Yaniv, buying his continued freedom with the information. "I heard that the Waqf found him. They forced him to say what was in the cistern. And then they went down and recovered what he was after. Turns out it was silver shekels, just like what we found at B'nei Hezir. Only more. A lot more. They got almost all of them out of there before you showed up."

Graham glanced at Yaniv who shook his head slightly, signaling Graham not to correct Nagi's misconception that there was only one bomber.

"We did find a few," Yaniv said. "What else did you hear?"

Nagi sat up and craned his neck toward the entrance suspiciously before continuing. "I heard they killed him. Karanlik."

"What!" Graham exclaimed, knowing Nagi was unknowing referring to Nigel Horne. He still couldn't reconcile the bomber who had been unmasked on the Temple Mount with the academic nebbish he knew. For the third time that day, death blotted out all other thought. He propped his elbows on his knees and put his head in his hands.

"Nagi, I have terrible news," Yaniv said, steering the conversation back to the explanation of Daniel's absence. He paused, emotions wrestling across his face. "Daniel was killed this morning."

"*Ya kazzab!*" Nagi spat the words violently. *You liar!*

"It's true, Nagi." Graham pulled his head upright and laced his fingers together. "I was there."

"But how?"

"I was in the cistern. Daniel and I went down after Karanlik. The first two explosions created the distraction he needed to get into the well. Daniel and I watched him do it and followed him in. Daniel surprised him and was able to tie him up. We found the silver—it was just as you said—and started moving it. But Karanlik cut himself loose. He waited until Daniel was facing away from him." Graham swallowed, not wanting to continue. "Karanlik slit his throat from behind."

"Ya hasrety." Nagi stared at Graham, tears moistening his eyes. *Oh, my heartbreak.* He glanced between Yaniv and Graham as if testing the words. Then his gaze settled on his coffee glass, and he stared at it as if wondering how it got there.

"I wish Karanlik wasn't dead already so I could kill him myself." Nagi slammed the coffee down.

Graham unwillingly replayed the accidental death, taking deep breaths to quell his nausea, and recognized a new dimension to his emotions. He felt no guilt about Karanlik—it was self-defense, after all. He had intended to use the gun even if he hadn't intended to pull the trigger at that moment. But the idea of taking a human life sickened him.

A heavy sigh rasped from Nagi as he stood. "I need to go." He offered Yaniv his hand, then turned to Graham. Graham took Nagi's hand and cupped his left hand over the top of it. Nagi did the same, signifying the bond that had formed between them.

"Stay out of trouble, Nagi. Go to school. Get some training to better yourself."

"In a perfect world, Dr. Eliot." Nagi nodded, shaking a tear loose from his eyes, then slipped into the mass of shoppers.

Graham lost sight of him within seconds, then noticed Yaniv staring at his phone. "What's the matter?"

"Horne has been found. His body was pulled from the construction hut destroyed at the Givati Parking Lot."

"But that bomb exploded before he died—"

"Just so. Apparently the Waqf has performed a miracle. But it is stranger than that. His throat had been cut."

SIXTY-TWO

Yaniv left Graham to his thoughts as they left the Rockefeller Museum the next day and looped south around the Old City, giving Graham a view of the bomb sites. Graham was shocked at how little damage had been done. The blackened ruins of the shed at the Givati Parking Lot excavation sadly did not seem out of place in the Silwan.

Crime scene tape wrapped the twisted metal, and Graham had tried not to picture Horne's planted body being recovered. The first detonation left a palm tree stump in the corner of a wall near the roundabout outside the Western Wall Plaza. Smoke stains marked the location as if the stone had been bruised, joining the other wounds that documented the Temple Mount's history.

They entered the highway, leaving the Dome of the Rock to sink below the hills. Although it was behind Graham, it still loomed over his thoughts, a symbol of all that had happened, a cap on a well that couldn't be entered.

"I made some calls this morning," Yaniv said, breaking the silence. "To dealers. I wanted to see if they had heard the same things Nagi had."

"Do you trust them to tell you the truth?"

"Some of them, yes. A couple of them did say they had heard rumors. But no one admitted any direct contact with

Horne."

"Sounds like Nagi earned his immunity."

Yaniv bowed his head. "Just so. I will make more calls to Tel Aviv and Alexandria."

"Why? There is no one to prosecute." The small part of Graham that still thought of Horne as a friend winced as he said it.

"Even so, we can learn how networks like this are set up. They are always changing, and that means we are always learning."

Graham shook his head. "It's still hard for me to believe it. Nigel Horne. He was a good scholar."

"Maybe that was the problem." Yaniv shrugged. "Maybe *good* did not seem so good when other scholars—people he knew personally—were making important contributions to the field. It could have made him jealous."

"I guess so. I can't think of any better explanation."

"I have been thinking of almost nothing else," Yaniv said, "trying to make sense of it. When Dr. Singer announced he was going to demonstrate his method for recovering papyri from cartonnage, I believe two things happened. One was that Horne wanted to be able to use the process himself to make his own discoveries. The other was that to fund the purchase of cartonnage he would need capital."

"I'm with you so far."

"Singer would have already locked up the money funding this kind of research, and Horne could not offer any innovation to the technique to be awarded a grant or attract investors."

"Horne was definitely not an innovator," Graham agreed.

"He knew Singer would use a piece of cartonnage that had a reasonable chance of containing something interesting, maybe even important. Horne wanted to be prepared to steal it. Then he could sell it to a collector—the kind who would not ask where the manuscript came from—and use the money to buy another mummy mask. But he could not personally do the stealing. He needed an agent he could direct if he saw something during the demonstration worth pursuing."

"Karanlik," Graham nodded.

"Just so. Except his name was Burakgazi."

The name transported Graham back to the floor of Cistern 8 as he looked up, unknowingly into the eyes of a man he thought was his friend. *Burakgazi*. That was what Horne had said into the manhole. He had been calling to The Shadow by name.

"Devrim Burakgazi. He was Turkish. From Demre."

Graham snorted.

"You have heard of it?"

"It used to be called Myra. It's where Saint Nicholas was from."

"And why would you know *that* useless trivia?" Yaniv said, making a comically sour face.

Graham pulled out the fact before he remembered the context it came from. He flashed back to Aly sitting on his lap during her last Christmas, asking if Santa was real. Graham had told her yes and no, then looked up some information about Nicholas, the bishop of Myra, and sorted fact from fiction. When they read how Nicholas had become so upset by the heresy of Arius at the Council of Nicea that Nicholas punched him in the face, they laughed trying to picture the modern, jolly fat man getting in a fight at church.

"It doesn't matter," Graham said, waving the distraction away.

"Well, like your Santa Claus, Karanlik sneaked into places. Only he would take things, not leave them."

"How do you know that?" Graham asked.

"When I updated Special Agent Bremmer, he did some checking. We are not the only law enforcement agency to turn someone we catch into an asset. Apparently, the Turkish government sometimes used him."

"Like Nagi," Graham said.

"Just so. But this man, Burakgazi, had far more ambition than Nagi. And more powerful contacts that took him around the Mediterranean."

"I do seem to remember Horne saying he had been in Istanbul, but I can't remember what he said he had been working on."

"Perhaps he met Burakgazi then," Yaniv said. "We will probably never know. But when I learned who this man was, I rewatched the video your FBI sent from the conference."

Graham pictured the scene in the conference center from the vantage of the security camera rather than his position in the room. "Did you find anything?"

"Let me ask you this: Did Nigel Horne wear glasses?"

An image of the last time he met Horne came to mind. Horne had been able to read Montagu Parker's name in the display case at the Rockefeller Museum when he stood at twice the distance that Graham had. He had not worn glasses. "No. Not that I ever saw."

"Interesting. Because he is wearing some very fashionable looking frames in the video."

"That's right. He did." Graham recalled thinking that Horne was a little vain for waiting until the room had been darkened before putting on his glasses.

"Even more interesting is that Burakgazi is wearing the same kind of frames in the back of the room. I did some quick research online, and I cannot be sure, but I believe they are both wearing sets of smart glasses. Google Glass or something like it. I think that is how Horne could communicate with Burakgazi during the presentation."

"I do remember zooming in to see Burakgazi blinking, like he had a twitch."

"Those glasses can be programmed to take photos when the person wearing them winks," Yaniv said. "Horne must have been using them to show Burakgazi what to steal. And as soon as Dr. Singer started to become excited about his find, Horne targeted it."

"But Andrew was murdered. I cannot believe Nigel Horne hired Burakgazi to kill him."

"I do not believe it either," Yaniv said, shaking his head. "But I do believe your friend hired a far more dangerous man than he realized."

"So what do you think happened?"

"When Dr. Singer cut the feed backstage, I think Burakgazi was already on the way to the pantry where the demonstration was and discovered that Singer had grabbed everything and left out the back door. Burakgazi followed the hallway to the nearest exit, then saw Singer in the parking lot and decided to follow him. Maybe Burakgazi could not reach Singer in time, or maybe he didn't want the confrontation to be caught on a security camera. That is how they ended up at Dr. Singer's office."

"But that still doesn't explain why he killed Andrew."

"It is possible that Horne's photograph was of a high enough quality to be able to read some of the text. If so, he could have used the database to identify it as the treasure map. Or maybe Burakgazi had the feeling that Dr. Singer's behavior was so unusual that what he found must be extremely valuable. And it is possible that he thought Dr. Singer would announce the discovery of the treasure map and that it had been stolen, which would put the authorities on guard and take away any chance to act on the map."

"I can start to see Horne wanting to steal it," Graham said. "But I just can't imagine him ordering Andrew to be killed."

"Maybe he did not order it," Yaniv allowed. "Maybe that

was something Burakgazi did on his own. But once Dr. Singer was killed, Horne was trapped. An accomplice to murder."

Graham mulled the idea over—Horne ensnared in his own trap. "Makes more sense than Horne being some homicidal mastermind."

Yaniv nodded. "I am sure Horne was smart enough to know that if he turned Burakgazi in to the authorities then The Shadow would disappear and he himself would be blamed for Burakgazi's crime. He also knew that the fragment he stole would be dangerous to sell. Maybe the collectors he knew were willing to acquire pieces of questionable provenance, but not loot from a murder. And he definitely could not claim to have discovered the manuscript, so it did not help him as a scholar. That would leave two options: do nothing or look for the treasure."

"And you think that he looked for the treasure as a way of acquiring items for a black-market antiquities operation," Graham said.

"It appears so, yes." Yaniv shot a sidelong glance to Graham. "That is my theory. He would not be able to claim to discover it legitimately because it would be a confession of complicity. He probably thought he could hide in plain sight, using his work as a reputable scholar while cultivating an outlet for whatever he recovered."

Graham released a long, resigned sigh, as if the weight of logic pressed out any remaining resistance.

"I have no proof yet," Yaniv continued, "but I think he was able to use his consulting work as an excuse to be around the IAA offices and keep track of our movements. That is how Burakgazi knew where you would be, as well as when. Horne knew he would not ever be able to take credit for his finds, but he would be able to use his specialized knowledge to make enough to be comfortable for the rest of his life."

"But he was the one who set off the bomb in the cistern,"

Graham said, still disbelieving his own words. "He tried to kill *me*."

"Yes, but he was desperate," Yaniv said. "He was not trying to kill you as much as save himself. The only thing between him and the success of his plan was forty-three feet of height. You can understand that part, at least."

Graham thought of the Ark of the Covenant, just out of reach across the Well of Souls. "I wouldn't have killed for it."

"Of that, I have no doubt. You do have to give Horne some credit though. According to the Dead Sea Scrolls team, the treasure of the Copper Scroll is a myth. What better thing to steal than a treasure that does not exist?"

Graham processed the theory in silence as he stared out his window, the Promised Land slipping by.

"Things could have come out much worse, my friend. The rabbis say all who descend into the Well of Souls perish immediately."

"Well, then it's a good thing I didn't descend," Graham said. "I entered it from the side."

Yaniv laughed. "Yes, you may have found the loophole in the curse."

He pulled the SUV to the curb of the drop-off area at the Ben Gurion Airport. Graham started to open the door but stopped when he felt Yaniv's hand on his arm.

"Graham, I have one more thing to tell you. Or show you, rather." Yaniv reached into the back seat, pulled out his laptop, and opened an aerial photograph of the southern end of the Temple Mount. Graham could see smoke trailing from the hatch of Cistern 8, indicating it had been taken while Graham was below the surface.

"What's this?"

"One of our helicopters took it," Yaniv said. "It was in the air when Horne set off the bomb, taking high resolution pictures of the first two bomb sites."

"Okay. Why are you showing me?"

Yaniv pointed to a tiny object on the roof of al-Aqsa, then zoomed in as he repositioned the object in the center of the screen.

"Oh my gosh," Graham pulled the computer closer and leaned toward the display. A pair of sandals sat on the roof, one on top of the other and turned ninety-degrees, forming a cross. "It's what I saw. Exactly."

"Just so."

SIXTY-THREE

The Souk al-Qattanin swarmed with tourists compressed between the stalls of merchandise as vendors cast enticements into the crowd, haggling with those who took the bait. Graham saw a small girl in a brilliant red dress slipping through the spaces between the shuffling adults, flitting from a stack of dolls to costume jewelry to stuffed animals.

"Alyson!"

He pushed his way through the crowd but couldn't close the gap between them. She darted deeper into the market, seemingly unaware of her father's desperation.

"Alyson!"

She stopped at a pastry stand and Graham saw a chance to catch up to her. But terror overcame him, turning him into a statue among the oblivious throng.

A shadow issued from the crush of people on the other side of her. It had the shape of a man and the substance and solidity of reality—a presence of darkness rather than the absence of light. As it moved, its featureless black form blurred slightly, temporarily smudging the space it passed through.

The shadow grabbed Alyson from behind, pulling her hair, bending her head back. Its free arm reached across her shoulders and rose, revealing a knife about to be drawn across her neck.

"NO!"

Graham heard his internal scream doubled by a woman behind him. He wrenched himself around to see Olivia at the landing on top of the stairs at the end of the souk. The Cotton Merchant's Gate stood open behind her, and Graham could see the Dome of the Rock reflect the sun off its golden roof. As Olivia's eyes locked on his, the ponderous gates started to close, their green paint darkening to black in the shadow of the souk. Graham pushed his way back to where he had started and slotted himself through the crack of light just before it disappeared.

At the top of the bowl of steps, he glanced to his right and saw the lid of a cistern falling shut. He ran to the well, threw back the hatch and discovered it wasn't a well at all, but a tunnel. He pulled out his phone and turned on the flashlight. Alyson's laugh reverberated off the stone walls behind him, spinning him around.

"Alyson!"

Graham scrambled toward the direction of the laugh, then froze again as Olivia's voice pulled the laugh deeper into the passage.

"Come on, Aly. Keep up."

"Olivia!"

Graham moved through the channel as quickly as he could, using his arms to both brace himself against the walls and push himself forward. The conduit twisted and wound, but it never forked.

He heard Alyson's laugh become more expansive—a slap-back echo doubling her voice—and he wasn't surprised when the next turn revealed a cave.

He looked up at the large and small openings in the ceiling closed by marble tile, then looked across at the tunnel on the other side, still containing the carpet roll and the gold smear. And standing with them—waiting for him—were Alyson and Olivia.

Behind them, deeper in the tunnel, a glow bloomed, growing more intense. Graham couldn't tell if it was getting closer or just brighter. As the light spilled into the cavern, Olivia and Alyson turned to face it and were enraptured, suddenly in a trance of peace and intense joy. Graham reached his hand out, irrationally, knowing he couldn't touch them. They turned their heads slowly, as if underwater.

"Come with us. Come."

Their words tugged him, but he couldn't move. The light continued to get brighter, flooding the well, and at his core he felt the peace he could see on the faces of his wife and daughter. The only place he wanted to be was the one place he couldn't go—across the chasm.

He looked down, expecting not to be able to see the bottom of the cavern. Instead, he saw a plane of inky water not far below him. A mummy mask floated face-up in the center of the pool, waiting for him just as Alyson and Olivia had. He watched as it began to sink into the water, its face becoming clouded by the liquid black.

Graham stared into the spot where it submerged even after he couldn't see it any longer. A flake of brown leaf inscribed with Greek letters floated to the surface. Graham realized it was a piece of papyrus that had come loose from the mask. Other shreds started joining it, drifting to the top like snow falling up instead of down. The fragments began to turn darker, as if they were charring without fire, and transformed into palm leaves like the ones they had found covering the vessels at B'nei Hezir. He kept his eyes fixed on the leaves as they broke apart, dissolving into the water, revealing jars of silver shekels beneath them. The jars started to warp, jittering under the lens of water, finally hiding the silver entirely beneath the turbulence.

Graham looked back to the tunnel on the other side, to Olivia and Alyson, but they were no longer there. A man in a radiant white robe waited for him, his arms bent in open invitation. Long white hair—incandescent—fell to his shoulders, framing a face of infinite compassion, somehow both ancient and eternally *present. Graham didn't need to ask who he was looking at. He knew intuitively.*

"Come."

The gentle voice pulled from across the Well of Souls with an irresistible force. Graham looked at the impossible distance between them. In another world, his logic would have argued against his intuition, holding him in place. But here—now—they were in agreement.

He stepped onto what he could not see and held on to what he could not touch.

SIXTY-FOUR

Graham jolted awake, tucked into the corner of a window seat on the back row of the first-class cabin. His head lolled against the pane separating him from the black Mediterranean night as the images from his dream lingered in his mind. The mundane sight of the back of the seat in front of him seemed almost profane compared to what he had just seen, and he closed his eyes again, coaxing the vision to stay.

Words began to form in his mind, words he had vowed never to say again but could no longer abstain from. His lips moved slightly, making the shapes of the words without giving them voice, sounding them out only as an imperceptible whisper. Graham found himself praying.

"Forgive me, Father. Forgive me."

He repeated the words internally as tears stung his eyes, then traced the curves of his face. Their taste made him feel ashamed of the bitterness he had held inside for so long. He tried to suppress his sobs, which only made him shake, dislodging his rage, upending it so that it pointed at himself.

He cupped his face in his hands and whispered into them. "Have mercy on me, Father. I need your mercy."

Graham sensed a glow hover over him and begin to bathe him, coating him in warmth. A grimace of intense passion kept his eyes crushed shut, but he knew if he opened them the cabin would still be dim. The light was only visible with his eyes closed, and yet he no longer doubted its reality.

Guilt melted from him as once fatal psychological wounds evaporated, leaving behind a profound and unexpected peace. The grief that had defined him—even as it had eaten him away—was transformed into a feeling he had forgotten so completely that it took him a moment to recognize it.

Hope.

For the first time, his sense of loss—which was no less present than before—was bearable. For the first time, he knew it wasn't meaningless even if he never learned what its purpose was. For the first time, he felt resolution—the natural evil of the deaths of Alyson and Olivia would not go unanswered but would be defeated.

Graham opened his eyes, seeing the world as if for the first time, reborn, feeling held rather than trying to hold on. He looked down the row, across the aisle to see who had been watching, but the other passengers showed no sign of noticing him despite the fact that his world had just been radically shaken apart. He thought about the phrase and decided it wasn't right. His world had not been shaken apart—it had already been fragmented. What had happened was that his world was shaken together, put right for the first time.

He slipped his phone from his coat pocket to check the time and see how much remained of the flight. But as soon as the screen displayed the information, he was struck still. Below the time—just after midnight—the date appeared, and he began to sob again. One year ago—to the day—Alyson had taken her last breath.

A day now shared with his own rebirth.

AFTERWORD

Biblical archaeology is full of stories that don't need any help from fiction to be interesting, and many of them are connected in fascinating ways. On the other hand, in doing research for my apologetics studies and writing, sometimes I would come across finds where connections suggested themselves though none actually existed. This book is a weave of both of these threads, real and imagined.

I didn't know it at the time, but the seed for this story was planted at a private conference I attended where I watched Dr. Scott Carroll demonstrate his method for deconstructing cartonnage in order to recover papyrus fragments containing ancient writings. For various reasons, he had kept his work secret for several years and this was one of the first times he had shown how it was done. The attendees at the conference then tried to identify and date the writings that were discovered. My sole contribution—besides geeking out—was to identify the word and in Greek. The rest was all...well, you know the joke. Six fragments from the New Testament and one from Jeremiah were recovered from a single mummy mask. A record of the conference can be found in the book God Breathed by Josh McDowell, who hosted the event and owned one of the two masks used that day.

The vast majority of texts recovered from the cartonnage

were not biblical, but all are important because they contribute to our understanding of the ancient world, and that often provides context for understanding the Bible. Although I appreciated this, I couldn't help but try to imagine what the most exciting and sensational text could have been hidden inside one of these masks. And that led me to The Copper Scroll.

The Copper Scroll is one of the most intriguing finds in biblical archaeology, and I am not the first novelist to take advantage of its mysterious list of treasure. John Marco Allegro—the controversial Dead Sea Scroll scholar charged with opening it—documented his expedition following its clues in The Treasure of the Copper Scroll. Like all those who came after him, he failed to find anything. The only item recovered so far by using the map is a small pot of oil or balm that is possibly from the First Temple Period. The discovery was made in the late 1980s by Vindyl Jones (who loved to point out what happens when the first and last letters of his first name are deleted).

The insertion of the Gihon Springs into the clue of item 18 is my invention. The Gihon Springs excavation is a vast project only recently completed that has changed how scholars reconstruct the ancient City of David.

The Tomb of Zadok—also known as B'nei Hezir—is the traditional tomb of James, Jesus's brother, the leader of the church in Jerusalem. Allegro gives a rather strange explanation for why he didn't conduct his search there, but rather in the unfinished tomb near it.

The "great cistern" mentioned in item 17 of the Copper Scroll never identifies it as part of the Temple Mount complex. Jerusalem was a dry city whose inhabitants stored water in cisterns in different parts of town, not just on the Mount. But after learning the Temple Mount has thirty-six cisterns—many of them connected by tunnels—I couldn't resist using them to solve the clue, especially since Cistern 8 is also called the "Great Sea." The only surveys ever done on the wells were by Charles Wilson in 1864-5, and Charles Warren in 1867. Their two examinations include a surprising amount of detail given the conditions in which they were made and how little time they had to visit. An excerpt from Wilson's Ordnance Survey of Jerusalem shows just how difficult the job was.

> "...the measurements were made with a rule when alone, with a tape when in company, and the bearings taken with a prismatic or pocket compass; neither can be considered very exact, as it is no easy matter to work with a candle in one hand and up to the knees in water; it was very difficult in some cases to determine the character of the roof, and be certain that no conduits existed, as candles gave but a poor light in such large chambers...the only trouble was in ascending, as the ladder, which often hung free in the air for 40 feet, swayed and twisted in a very disagreeable manner, and the wet clothes sticking to the legs prevented free climbing action."

That there are undiscovered conduits in forbidden caverns beneath a site sacred to three religions is tantalizing enough. Add to the mix that the most reliable map of this subterranean world was made by surveying it in candlelight—sometimes recorded by memory with estimates after returning to the surface—and you have a recipe for adventure. William Simpson's watercolor of Cistern 8 and the sketches he did of Warren exploring the shafts and tunnels look like storyboards of a movie waiting to be made. All citations of Wilson and Warren's writings are verbatim, though I did write Wilson's Roman numerals as English figures and used the more common spelling of al-Aqsa instead of their al-Aksa.

Tying together the Qur'anic verses with the white hands seen by Wilson on the walls of Cistern 7 was my own doing. The quotes from the Qur'an were taken from The Noble Qur'an in the English Language, translated by Muhammad Taqi al-Din al-Hilali and Muhammad Muhsin Khan.

The story of Montagu Parker trying to find a way into the undocumented conduits is true, as is his trust in Valter Juvelius, a Finnish theologian who claimed to have discovered a code in the book of Ezekiel that revealed the location of the Ark of the Covenant. Aside from the newspaper accounts of the riots, surprisingly little information exists about the expedition, and reports of what happened the night he dug under the Dome of the Rock are often contradictory. The paper trail of correspondence about the chests he left behind when he fled is quoted verbatim from documents at the Israel Antiquities Authority. And while the first memo mentions two chests, subsequence memos mention only one—a discrepancy I exploited, though I make no claim that the explanation in the book is what really happened.

Parker's attempt to enter the chamber that apparently lies below the cave under the Dome of the Rock—the Well of Souls—was not the first. Sir Richard Burton did indeed try to get permission to enter but was denied, though he was allowed into the prayer cave. Ermete Pierotti's account of following a conduit from Cistern 1 to the Well of Souls is the only record I could find of anyone describing it from below. Photos of the mosaic slabs do exist, apparently taken with a cell phone while the cave was re-carpeted.

The tunnel that connects Cistern 9 with al-Aqsa was dug by me, and is based on the speculations of others who believe a number of conduits may connect to it. The description of the interior of the mosque—including the grate opening into a cavity below—comes from photographs and videos. The room at the bottom of the entrance steps that is closed by a latticed screen does exist, although the walled-up passage was invented by me based on where the outlet from Cistern 9 would connect.

None of the legends referred to in the book were invented by me, and given that three different religions revere so many of the same places, there are often several legends for a single place. As for the Ark of the Covenant, there is no biblical account of what happened to it. The apocryphal 2 Maccabees says it was buried on Mount Nebo, the same mountain Moses was buried on. One Jewish legend puts it in Rome, while other traditions put it in Africa or Europe, stolen by Templars or hidden by various sects.

The work of traveling the world to different libraries and collections to digitize every known copy of the New Testament and make them available to scholars is being done by Daniel Wallace at the Center for the Study of New Testament Manuscripts. You can follow—and support!—his team's good work at csntm.org.

The FBI does indeed have an Art Crime Team for dealing with stolen antiquities. And the Israeli Antiquities Authority has a Robbery Division that is undermanned given the market for artifacts and the unauthorized digs that provide the supply demanded by unscrupulous collectors.

ACKNOWLEDGMENTS

For my limited understanding of GPR technology, I am thankful to Dr. Lawrence Conyers of Denver University who graciously took the time to explain it to me, helping me avoid a number of errors.

Austin P

owell (no relation) was kind enough to share his expertise as an in federal law enforcement with me. Our brainstorming phone call on how to rewrite the encounter with Bremmer was a highlight of my research.

Any inacurracies regarding GPS or the FBI are mine, not theirs.

Thanks to Frank Turek and Jorge Calderon, who took pictures of the well caps for me as I started the book. And thanks to Mike Licona and Sean McDowell for inviting me to tour the Holy Land with the Israel Collective, enabling me to visit some of the sites I was researching and to take my own photos of the Temple Mount.

I am deeply indebted to my parents, Richard and Gwen Powell, my brother Dave, Cyndy McRae, Jay Hollis, Mark Haggard, Eric Smith, Rick Altizer, and Jamie Brandenburg for being brave enough to read early drafts and offer many helpful suggestions.

Thank you Jamie Chavez for doing the initial editing on this pipe-dream, and giving far more time and insight than either of us could afford.

Ted Goldthorpe graciously shared his knowledge and connections within the world of music publishing.

David and Rosanna White at White Fire Publishing are models of graciousness, and I'm thankful for their encouragement and early support.

And I could not ask for a better champion than Dan Lynch, who became more than an agent, but became a co-conspirator—a Roy to my Walt, as it were.

Thank go most of all to my wife, Jennifer, who believed in the book before there were any words, and believed even more after they were finished.

PICTURE GUIDE

Mummy mask made of caronnage. (Photo: Doug Powell)

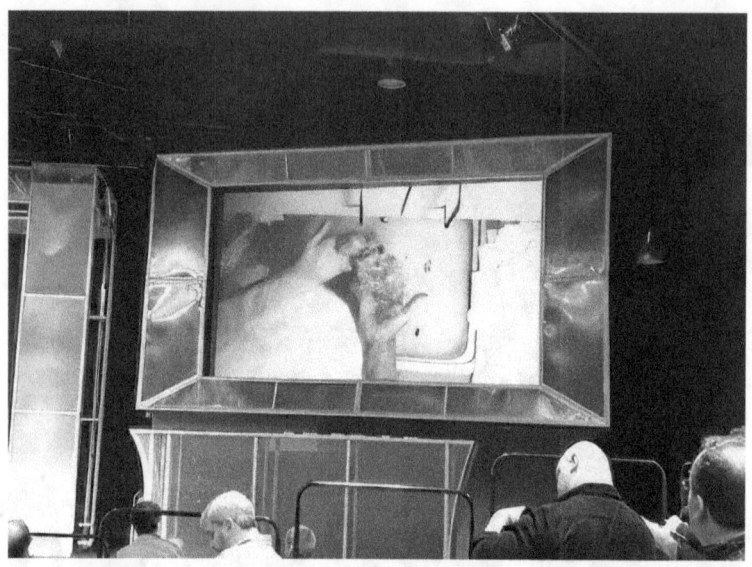

Demonstration of deconstructing cartonnage to recover papyrus
manuscript fragments (Photo: Doug Powell)

The Copper Scroll on display at the Jordan Museum in Amman.
(Photo: Copper Scrolls by Osama Shukir Muhammed Amin FRCP
CC-BY-SA 4.0)

Kidron Valley with the tomb of Absolom on the bottom left, the Silwan in the center, and the southeast corner of the Temple Mount on the right.
(Photo: Doug Powell)

Rockefeller Museum (Photo: Doug Powell)

B'nei Hezir, the traditional tomb of James, with the tomb of Absolom on the right.

The Gihon Spring (Photo: Assaf AvrahamCC-BY-SA 4.0)

Montagu Parker and Walter Juvelilus.

Silwan neighborhood (Photo: Doug Powell)

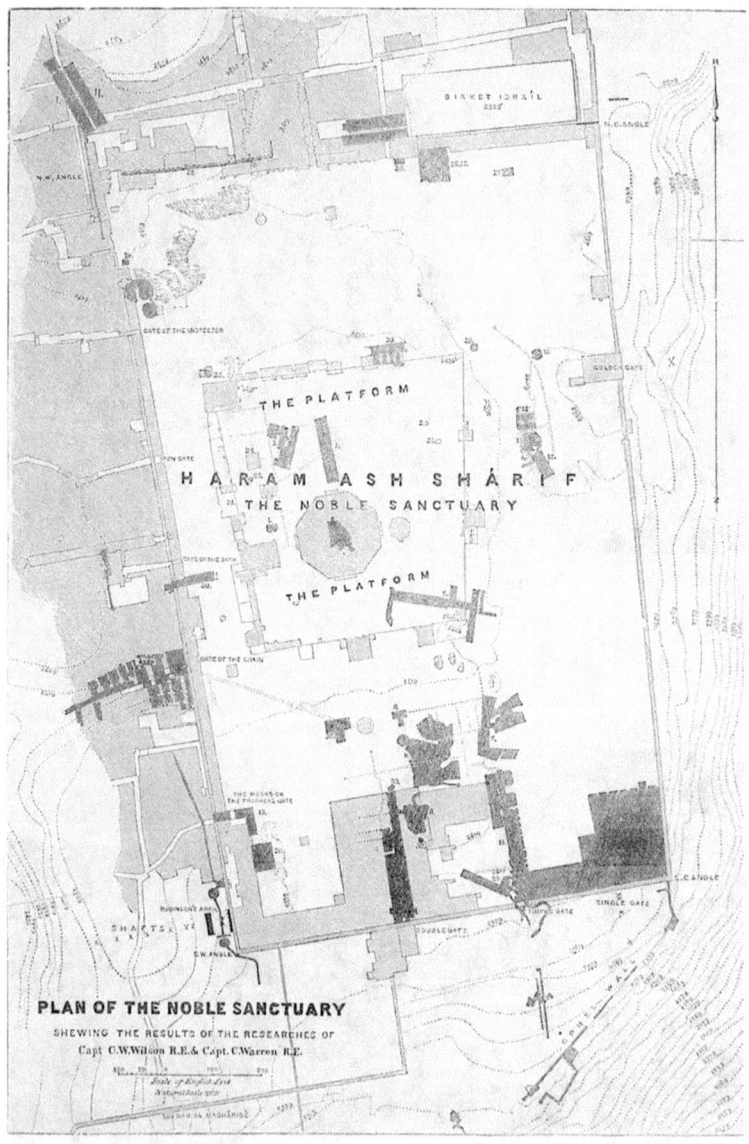

The Warren-Wilson survey showing the cisterns and other underground spaces beneath the Temple Mount.

Al-Aqsa Mosque with the well cap to Cistern 8 (Photo: Doug Powell).

William Simpson's sketch of cistern 8, the only known image of the inside.

See these and more images in the online photoguide at:

grahameliotseries.com

Follow the latest Doug Powell news at:

dougpowell.com

www.ingramcontent.com/pod-product-compliance
Lightning Source LLC
Chambersburg PA
CBHW051331020726
47501CB00007B/2024